BOOKER WINNERS AND OTHERS

glas

NEW
RUSSIAN
WRITING

7

Editors:
Natasha Perova (Moscow) & Dr. Arch Tait (UK)
Designed by Emma Ippolitova
Photographs: Y.Vladimirov
Typeset by Tatyana Shaposhnikova

GLAS Publishers
Moscow 119517, P.O.Box 47, Russia
Tel./Fax: (095) 441 9157
E-mail: Perova@Glas.msk.su
UK address
for enquiries, subscriptions and payments:
GLAS, c/o Dept. of Russian Literature,
University of Birmingham, B15 2TT
Tel.: 021-414 6044, Fax: 021-414 5966
North America
Sales and Editorial office, GLAS
c/o Zephyr Press, 13 Robinson Street, Somerville MA 02145
Tel: (617) 628-9726, Fax: (617) 776-8246

ISBN 5-7172-0015-3
US ISBN 0-939010-43-7
Printed in Moscow at the Novosti Printing Shop
© Translation copyright, 1994 by GLAS

A Note of Apology

Glas would like to apologise to the following translators whose work we used ostensibly without permission. This was due to a series of misunderstandings, lack of communication and inexperience in such matters.

Prof Michael Makin for using his translations of Yuri Miloslavsky's "Urban Sketches".
Prof Daniel Weissbort for printing Jim Kates's translation of Stratanovsky's Bible Notes without acknowledging its first publication in Modern poetry in Translation.
Prof Peter Henry whose translation of a poem by Olga Sedakova was first published in Scottish Slavonic Review No.15, 1991.

Contents

When the Booker Prize Committee decided to institute a special Booker Russian Novel Prize, there were no other literary prizes in the devastated post-perestroika Russia, the official Soviet prizes for literature having been abolished shortly after the collapse of communism, when most state-subsidised publishing also closed down. This left Russian authors with little choice but to flee abroad in search of employment and publishers, while most of those who stayed declared that the end of Russian literature had arrived, and set about dividing up the property of the Writers' Union among themselves. Authors, who earlier had not been published for political reasons, now were not published for economic reasons.

But Russian literature did not die. It went through a period of crisis — together with the rest of the country — and gradually began to recover, bringing forth a profusion of styles and a new freshness of vision. Into the atmosphere of confusion reigning in literary circles, and the overall public indifference to literary developments, the Booker Prize came like Santa Claus, offering not only a substantial money prize (which after all can only be awarded to one writer each year) but an exciting literary race which generated much needed publicity for everyone involved. In spite of mutterings from the nationalistically minded that Russian writers should be ashamed of themselves for accepting money from abroad, the excitement generated by the Booker Prize spread like wildfire, with heated debate breaking out in the press and among critics and readers alike. Passions ran high, and public interest in literature was markedly boosted. Perhaps, however, the greatest achievement of the Booker Prize to date is the fact that it has inspired a number of Russia's new rich to institute national prizes themselves. Let us hope that this process of revealing new talent and giving publicity to short-listed authors will ultimately lead to change in the publishing business in Russia. Russian publishers currently focus on translated literature, which the Russian public was starved of under the Bolsheviks and which, naturally, excites much interest today. They are not at present in any great hurry to publish new Russian authors. The time will come, however, when Russia's readers will want to know what has been happening in their own culture all this while, and at that moment they will be particularly appreciative of all the present efforts to preserve a Russian culture which, in the past, has given the world so many outstanding writers.

                                                        The Editors

W.Booker
Winners

VLADIMIR MAKANIN

Baize-covered Table with Decanter

The 1993 Russian Novel
Booker Prize

Chapter One

"Again and again, in memory and anticipation, the hero visits the Kafkaesque scene of his inquisition: the bare room, the table, and behind the table those recurring phantoms: "The Young Wolf", "The Beautiful Woman", "The Party Man", "The One Who Asks the Questions"...

"It's the table that gives power to the people behind it. Take it away and they are just ordinary folk, you and me, your best friends maybe.

"I've lived with these phantoms from childhood. Any Russian — it's an old Russian nightmare we're dealing with, not just a Soviet one — would recognise the situation. Having them rummage in your insides, being helpless, belittled. You needn't have done anything to realise your helplessness, your guilt."

Vladimir Makanin

He's a simple sort of chap. Out of all those sitting at the table, he's the one you notice first, perhaps because all along it's been you he was waiting for. "Aha! There you are..." his eyes seem to fire straight at you as you enter. He's lean, not tall, proletarian (no further up the scale than technician), and has a permanent feeling that life has played him false. An inner social consciousness, rudely awakened some time in the course of history, can still flare up and burst into flames in people like him, which is why in my mind I call him *The One with the Social Chip on His Shoulder.* He is a decent enough fellow in everyday life, ordinary, a bit dour. His stout wife goes to a resort every year and immediately finds herself a lover there who is the spitting image of her husband. It's not clear why she should need this, unless as a way of keeping old habits on the go. He guesses what's going on, but accepts it as inevitable. He threatens murder, falls into rages, but then tries to convince himself he's imagined it all and is just being over-jealous. His main grudge is that he has so few comforts in life. Everybody else has managed to grab something for themselves. Even the shop clerk, as uneducated as himself, are doing very nicely. The intelligentsia have been even better at it. Why is it being allowed? In our society everyone is supposed to have equal shares, aren't they? He grinds his teeth as he asks the question.

A simple sort of a chap, and a bit of a drunk. He smiles, a benevolent expression hovering uncertainly on his face. No, he isn't drunk now. He hasn't had a drop today; but yesterday, or the day before, he put away a fair bit. From time to time, above his smile or, as it seems, from inside his smile, there surfaces a glazed look from the day before yesterday, aggression like a sudden access of malice, because, although it was yesterday and the day before he was drinking, it is only today that he has managed to find an enemy... No, no, he knows how to behave. He isn't going to bristle at you or start shouting. He can control himself. He's not going to let anybody know about his little discovery. He just works the muscles on his face and slams a confrontational glance into you, and mutters in his mind, so no one can hear,

"You smug bastard!"

He's wearing a rather cheap but quite decent sweater. At his throat he displays the collar of a clean shirt. He hasn't turned up looking just any old how. This is serious business. There are things here to be sorted out, brought into the open, and everything has got to be done above board... And so he throws a sidelong glance to where, next to him, just to his left from his viewpoint, or just to his right from yours, sits the man who asks most of the questions.

The One Who Asks the Questions is sitting almost in the centre of the table, and he too is one you'd notice immediately. When he questions you he seems to be flipping you gently from side to side, not letting you get away, and setting you up for the others. He's like the beater in a hunt. When you're questioned you don't know yourself which way you'll run. Animals run in circles when they're being pursued, but when people are confused, who knows how or where they may run?

He doesn't probe deeply with his questions; that's not his job; that's everyone else's job; but he conducts the chase. The questions he suddenly comes out with, hurried and petty, seem to create both the feeling that you're being pursued, and also the feeling that you're trying to hide from your pursuers. "But why couldn't you have rung us yourself, even in the evening, to say you were ill? And anyway, what do you do in the evenings? Football? TV? Friends?..." There's no answer to all this because there's no question as such, but still, you have remained silent and failed to keep up. They haven't confused you, but you've somehow, inexplicably, lost your bearings, and your perfectly understandable dismay opens a gap for new questions. This is the territory in which he hunts. "So there really isn't anybody you can ring up in the evenings and have a heart-to-heart talk with?" "Have you always lived like this?" he asks with a smile of disbelief, and then pops in another tricky question to which there is no answer, and comes back at you again. What sort of man is this who's never found a mate he can have a heart-to-heart talk with in the evenings? Before you've time to answer you realise you've been knocked for six. The people sitting round the table have noticed it too. Only he, the person who asked the question and gave them their first scenting, seems not to notice anything and just carries on. Now he starts his run from a completely different angle, almost tripping over himself: "Well now, do you at least value a woman as an individual? You respect her, surely?" And again there's the implication, "What sort of a weirdo are we dealing with here, and how has he been living his life all this time?" It's all left hanging in the air unanswered, waiting to come back at you. A lack of human sensitivity always comes back at you.

The One Who Asks the Questions is an intellectual. He has smooth, dark hair and a firm, stern profile, emphasized by the way he turns his neck. His hands are on the table, long, beautiful fingers intertwined without any nervousness, or perhaps with a certain languid nervousness in no way indicative of temperament. He speaks fast, firing questions, but does not insist on a smile from you, although he smiles himself. He's probably an engineer on a middle salary in some research institute; probably sometimes checks over the final accounts himself, inclining his head with that same fine line emphasized by the way he turns his neck. He's usually taciturn, but here, sitting at the table of judgement, he's animated and thrusting, doing his bit not for himself, but for other people, for society. "What sort of a man are you?" A question without an answer, but a question asked and not withdrawn. It's the door he's always the first to push at.

Beside him is a *Secretarial Person*, a man who invariably seems younger than middle age, indefinably youngish. He sits at the exact centre of the table, directly opposite you. The decanter on the table separates the two of you, and it seems as though he will have to look out from behind it to the left or right in order to see you when he asks a question. And so he does, although he doesn't ask questions very often. Most of the time he writes, making little marks and notes on a sheet of paper, his fountain pen in his hand. If someone asks a question you weren't expecting (or he for that matter), while he waits for the answer he looks at you not round the decanter but straight over the top of it. It isn't very tall.

The glasses on the table are laid out lengthwise and give unity to all those seated and to the scene as a whole. Sometimes the glasses are complemented by bottles of mineral water, but the decanter is an obligatory feature of the composition. Whatever happens it will remain there, cementing the figures and objects around it. The presence of a geometric centre bestows a unity on the table and gives the words and questions of those seated around it the status of an inquisition. It is the accessories in the picture, elementary as they are, which give the questioners their status, forcing you to defer to them and to experience anxiety, and to feel you have to attune yourself before you come here, to get your courage up, for instance, or take tranquillisers (hard liquor isn't on).

Everything is interconnected. Their enquiries can elicit the fact that you were sacked again six months ago (So what!), or that your son has just got married and divorced for the third time (So what!), or they can bring to your attention that you tried to wangle a fake disability certificate for your misfit of a son, to get him a residence permit for a separate flat, and then to get it renewed... (So what!) The danger comes from the fact that this isn't a court of law, but just, you might say, a thorough-going enquiry with the express purpose of catching you out over something and, having once got you, nailing you to the wall. (And you'll fall silent, and hang your head in shame, and feel guilty just for being alive, for eating and drinking and evacuating your bowels in the lavatory.) Everyone has some private secret. Everyone has some grudge against life, and a few peccadillos stemming from it. More than that, we all have serious faults in our souls, and all the back-biting of our relationships with other people. There are the slippery slopes of one's inner development and all life's petty daily irritants. And finally there is the dirty linen of childhood, when you pee-ed yourself or dirtied your pants. Now do you see? Each one of us has those torn vests, those dirtied pants, the rubbish, the irritating gnat-bites and little snags of daily life. However strange it may seem, all these things are interconnected and are activated, as it were, in one fell swoop under the cross-fire of those apparently harmless questions. As though crushed by these interconnections and that hurried, interwoven quality of life, you yourself become hurried in your replies to their first, second, third, fifth, or tenth question. The odd thing is, you always respond with passion, with excessive sincerity, and a growing desire to answer each question ever more accurately and convincingly; more uprightly, even, than the compromised uprightness of the facts themselves which suddenly come leaping out at you from your life and your whole messy everyday existence for the sole purpose of impacting with your consciousness as it struggles to excuse them. It all seems intolerable, yet with incredible patience you tolerate it, and go on and on answering.

Of course it does happen that you go in to them with bravado, head held high. You snap back at them, right to the point and humorously to boot. Alas, your fine assertiveness doesn't last very long, and with every minute of their questioning your fighting spirit wanes, leaking like hot air from a balloon with a hole in it, a hole not made by their onslaughts, but one which was there all along, only now it's become obvious and the hot air is disappearing through it. The puncture was made from the inside. Your expression can only mask what is happening, not conceal it. All they have to do is drag out their trial which isn't a trial for as long as possible, minute by minute, word by word, while you grow emptier, become lighter, until you're just a shrivelled scrap of deflated rubber, shamefaced, nothing more to you than that. What's worse, now you're being sapped by further pangs of shame at your erstwhile boldness (or insolence) when you came in. After all, these are grown people who've come together, who are sitting here, giving you their time, and you come marching in with barely so much as a how do you do and start playing the fool.

"You're being asked a question, and you just sit there with one leg crossed over the other!" Or a variant: "You're being talked to and you just twirl that pencil around in your hand. Couldn't you have finished doing that at home!" Suddenly their voices are coming at you from all sides. They've got the measure of you. They didn't dare to talk like this when I marched in so boldly, but now their voices are coming from every angle. I don't get time to gather my thoughts about myself or the pencil. I just look from one to the other of them until finally I hear that shout. "Stand up!" or "Stand up when you're spoken to!" one of them will shout, beside himself. And the trouble is, you do get up. Without thinking, you get up. What else can you do? That tone and that shout are a kind of coded signal.

Once you've stood up, you may pull yourself together and answer back sharply. You might even shout at them, letting rip a shriek of rage, as though having hysterics. You might... but you have stood up. That's the nub of it. You got up and there you now stand, and that edgy shouting and those quivering lips are you.

"But surely, you must sit around with your pals and talk into the night? With some vodka, of course. Have a bit of a laugh with them?!" (My questioner wanted me to live a full-blooded life.)

"Rarely these days," I answered.

"You've a nice flat and surely you must sometimes want to get together with your friends, your mates. Tell us about it - we're interested. Everybody here wants to know you better."

He was smiling. They were all smiling. They wanted to know how I lived (if live I did) this full-blooded life of mine. This was their main reward for this inquisition. They got to find out, at no cost to themselves, about the ins and outs of an ordinary man. They got to live his life in imagination.

"You've got the kind of voice that says you might be a bit of a singer. When you're among friends. Am I right?"

"I don't sing."

They were disappointed.

"Come on. I bet you do. And I bet you do in front of loads of friends and relations."

I shook my head. Negative.

There followed a long, empty silence. At this point, for no reason, I allowed myself to lose face. Fading by the minute, I asked:

"Why, is that bad?"

They were nodding. Well yes, actually, it's not good the way you live. It's bad. (The guilt feelings were already taking hold of me.) I remember thinking, "Why am I kicking against this. They're right. We already know I'm guilty. I'd still be guilty even if I were a whole choir singing to all my relatives every evening in life."

Strictly speaking, only half of this is clear in advance, and that's the fact that they are right. That needn't necessarily mean that I'm guilty. Everyone is a living human being, and that puts you on your guard in case those times you really landed in it, beginning with the pants you dirtied in childhood and culminating in those drops of sweat on my brow when they are asking their questions ("What is it, by the way, that you're afraid of?"), in case those times should somehow come out and be made public, even though they're quite unconnected with the questions you're being asked. But, as we know, everything's connected. You're guilty, not in the sense of admitting guilt, but in the sense of feeling guilt.

"Everybody's busy," said the querulous voice (over the phone, in the evening). "You're not the only one. At the end of the day, you're the one who needs this, not us. You're the one who needs the reference, the certification of salary, and the note about the circumstances of your leaving the job. To say nothing of the fact that in five years time or so you'll need all these papers for your pension." (They know all about that!) "That's why we're expecting you."

"I see."

"We'll sit down together, have a chat. See what's what."

"All right, all right. I'll be there."

No sooner had I said it than I realized I should never have agreed. It could all have been ironed out some other way. With my nerves and heart murmur I really shouldn't sit in front of that table being questioned. I know what I'm like. (My blood pressure's nearly 200 already and the night is yet to come.)

"All right, all right. I'll be there." I even threw down the receiver as if to say, "I know what these guys are like. Makes you want to spit." What a hero! For as long as I can remember all I've ever got from sitting in front of their table has been humiliation. Just a feeling of being crushed (which of course is entirely my own fault).

"I don't want to go. I won't go," I tell myself, but of course I will go, if not at the first time of asking, then at the third or the fifth. There's no escaping them. The thing is, these people at the table are, as it were, already part of me. They know me as thoroughly as I know them. They get younger, changing the team from year to year, but I'm just me, so that our long relationship can only come to an end with my physical absence, my death. How else?

"Calm yourself, dear", says my wife.

"Uh-huh."

"Are you going to have some supper? We've got porridge. Yes, again. Yes, porridge is better in the morning, but the milk's going off and we ought to use it up."

We sit down to supper, calling our daughter through. I don't want (I'm ashamed) to admit that my nerves and my alarm are to do with tomorrow's summons, and so I think up some story and talk a lot of nonsense about complications at work.

"Don't worry then. Calm yourself, dear," my wife keeps saying.

But the conversation inevitably moves to tomorrow's summons, and without intending to I start talking about how tomorrow isn't going to be much fun for me, with those rubbishy people grubbing around inside me. I may be able to fend them off, but they still finger your soul. "Grit your teeth, dear," says my wife. We eat supper. The personnel department's commission will convene, just to have a chat and clear up a few matters. That's just it... to clear up whether you're a decent person, and while they're at it, whether you're a good family man, a good resident on your staircase. "What else are they going to enquire into," you wonder. You turn over all kinds of other possibilities but then, when you get there, you realize this is the same commission (what an idiotic word) you have known from time immemorial, from the tenderest years of your youth. One after the other, throughout your whole life, they've been trying to discover whether you are a good person, and they still haven't managed to make their minds up!

"Do stop moaning," my daughter begs.

I say no more. Neither do they. We rhythmically dip our spoons in the porridge.

In trying to hide my anxiety I seemed only to have made it worse. Such things happen. I should have taken a good dose of my tranquilliser. "Think ahead!" as the doctor who used to take care of me would say. I should have taken the medicine and relaxed, but I told the family I was tired and wanted to go to bed right away. It hadn't been an easy day. They were cooperative and we went to bed at eleven (or a bit before) and at twelve o'clock I had a seizure. I swallowed down some rather belated medicine, twice measured my blood pressure, and then we argued over whether we needed to call out the ambulance. "It's dangerous. You've no idea how dangerous it is," my daughter shouted, and even wagged a finger at me. I was shouting too and my wife was shaking all over, rushing from the telephone to me and back from me to the telephone. She evidently wanted to phone our son (who lives away from us). I continued to have pains in the heart, first pressure, then a treacherous easing. Before my eyes swam the faces of my wife and daughter, and beyond them the walls and a far away window with blinds. "I mustn't snuff it," I thought. Death appeared not frightening but so prosaically straightforward that I stopped arguing and became very quiet.

I just lay there with my eyes half closed and said to my nearest and dearest, "Go to bed. Let's get some sleep."

The straightforward way I said it persuaded them. They went back to bed and after a while first my daughter, then my wife fell asleep.

I lay prostrated. Now I particularly didn't wish to admit to myself (let alone my family) the reason for all these heart pains and my general anxiety and all this fuss in the middle of the night.

I even dozed off. When it was past one in the morning I again experienced an onset of agitation, and after two my heartbeat became irregular. I got up and sat for a bit on my couch, my bare legs dangling down. Was it time to think ahead?

Pushing my feet into my slippers, I went out into our small passage and noiselessly walked through into the kitchen. It was dark and quiet. I looked out the window. It was dark out there too, sleeping houses and roofs and dark, empty balconies. I ought to prepare another dose of valerian drops. Suddenly the realization came to me that my life was not that bad, and that I must have had a hundred, maybe two hundred, maybe more summonses to "conversations" like tomorrow's. Over the years there had been a long trail of petty inquisition: petty, certainly, but exactly as now, driving you into a state of anxiety, turmoil, and jangled nerves. Suddenly I could see the main point: for the questioners the specific reason for having you in was of no importance. It never had been. What mattered to them was something quite different. Having grasped this, you sit down in the kitchen in the middle of the night, already resigned and not angry with yourself, not swearing, and hold your head in your hands and ache from the inner pain creeping over you. A twinge. Another. And the night goes on.

When I pad along the passage at night-time, from my room to the kitchen and then back (sometimes sitting on a chair in the kitchen for a bit) I get the feeling that as I pad along my heart is growing stronger. My footfall is a rhythm of restfulness.

I don't want my wife to fuss over me again tonight. I don't want her anxiety. So I wander about quietly, wrapped in an old mack. I don't wear dressing-gowns. I don't possess one. I wrap myself up because I feel a chill. I don't feel fear as such, but that's because of a kind of mutual agreement: fear doesn't stare me in the face and I don't stare it in the face. It does, however, build up inside me, rising to the surface somewhere near the middle of my spine. I feel it as a chill. I walk about, honestly trying to keep myself occupied during the hours of darkness. I get a tablet ready in case my blood pressure shoots up suddenly; nitroglycerine as well, of course. Unhurriedly, I boil up the valerian root in the kitchen (there aren't any drops to be had. There's nothing in the chemists' these days.) On the whole, I'm fine on my own. Things are easier without sympathy. If my wife were to get up, what would she see in her half-sleep? A shambling creature in a mack with slippers over bare feet, a creature aged, bowed down from insomnia and a constant succession of alarming thoughts. A creature resembling a sick animal would suddenly flash

15

his eyes at her in the darkness of the corridor, and only then would she recognize and acknowledge me. Of course, she'd start to pity me and soothe me (I don't want this, it gets me down even more), but before the pitying and the comforting there would be that brief nocturnal moment of surprise, that instant of incomprehension when she would suddenly notice a hunched body walking along the passage from the kitchen wearing an old mack which hung awkwardly from its shoulders (the mack has long lost its buttons); and she would realize that this creature was her husband.

I am reminded of a very trivial incident I had almost forgotten. A year ago, when the food queues were enormous, a fight broke out in one of them. I was standing rather too close to people who first shouted at each other and then got physical. It came to blows, people being grabbed by the lapels. The police arrived, as always, just at the right moment and, as always, immediately got the wrong end of the stick. They rounded up all and sundry, about a dozen people, including myself. So there we are in the police station, hands behind backs. "All right, all right. We'll soon have it all sorted out! We'll release you right away, just as soon as we've had a look at your ID. How come you've no ID on you?" For some reason the police wouldn't resolve the matter themselves. They took the easy way out and booted their whole trawl over into the hands of the comrades' court. "Everyone into Room No. so-and-so (I think it was 27). Bugger off, all of you, into Room 27!"

When I walked into Room No. so-and-so, surrounded by much noise and shouting, I saw the oak table and the people sitting at it and, straight away, the familiar, non-police type of fellow, a simple sort of chap who looked a bit of a workhorse, *The One with the Social Chip on His Shoulder*, his face not as yet distorted by malice, but ready to be. Looking me over, he was saying, as yet quite calmly,

"Ah, come on in..." as though to an old friend.

After him, I saw the others. They'd already had time to constitute themselves. They dealt with the case within the half-hour, and I don't remember whether they even called themselves a commission.

One of them, needless to say, was a *Secretarial Person*.

"Sit down," he said.

Perhaps my memory is playing me false. It may be that the police themselves took down the details of the case and only afterwards said they hadn't the time to get involved in fights in queues and such like rubbish. "More than likely you'll get away with a fine, but... still we'd like you to have a word" (and promptly packed us off to another building, to the room with the oak table and the civilian people sitting behind it.)

So it was on another street and in another building that I saw that sturdy oak table and straight away noticed *The One with the Social Chip on His Shoulder*, and he also seemed to recognise me as he said, "Ah, come on in..."

I went in, and saw all the rest of them, and they were the same people.

Translated by Michael Falchikov

Znamya, No.1, 1993

Vladimir Makanin

Vladimir Makanin (b. 1937) is among the best known Russian writers of the last twenty years. In **Baize-covered Table** he pursues his main theme: the fate of the individual in Soviet mass society. In his inimitable cold and alienated style, Makanin has used a variety of genres and subjects to analyze this theme, from the parable **Fleeing Citizen** to the anti-utopia **Manhole** shortlisted for the first Booker Russian Novel Prize last year.

Makanin's **Baize-covered Table** penetrates to the very heart of the Soviet phenomenon, exposing the psychology of Soviet little man. The ritual of a "comrades court" evolves into an all-encompassing symbol of the nightmare of power in mass society.

See also Makanin's story **Klyucharev and Alimushkin** in Glas 6.

"One of the most serious, powerful, and intelligent writers of his generation whose work, for almost two decades, was ignored or later vilified by critics. Today his prolific work can be seen to form an integral whole, a painstakingly assembled study of the existential dynamics of life thrown into relief by the particular circumstances and psychology of communist (and post-communist) Russia. A central theme of all his work has been the relation of the individual to the collective: in this latest novella this theme is distilled to its abstract essence, presented as a play of archetypes.

"But for all its intellectual rigour—its dryness, its studied bareness—it has the mark of a deeply felt, introspective, intensely personal work. Its atmosphere is dark, its effect profoundly unsettling. ...One of the most serious and complete works by a writer who is (as yet) undeservedly little known in the English-speaking world."—Sally Laird

VICTOR
ASTAFIEV

The Cursed
and the Slain

Book One:
The Hell Hole.
Chapter One

The train crunched icily, contracting, squealing, and as though exhausted by a long run with no let up, scraping and spitting, began to relax its great iron bulk. Frozen clinker snapped beneath wheels, a white dust settled on rails; its metal parts and its carriages were spangled right up to the windows with grey beads of ice. The train, come from some unimaginably remote place, shrank in on itself, exhausted and cold.

To either side, in front and behind, all was bleakness. The place where it had stopped was wreathed in motionless fog, the sky barely distinguishable from the earth, both of them merged and fused by the freezing murk. There was something desperately alien about what was or might be there, something unearthly and desolate, and some nameless creature on the point of death could be heard scratching a failing paw with blunted claws, and piercing the frosty mist with a snapping and a decrepit wheezing like a last tuberculous cough modulating into the barely audible rustle of a soul taking flight.

It was the sound of a forest in winter, frost-bound, shallow breathing, terrified of any rash move or deep breath which might rend the trees which were its flesh to their very heartwood. Pine branches and needles, evergreen boughs, sharp from the cold, brittle, dying of their own accord, drifted down ceaselessly, cluttering the forest snow, catching on their downward flight at their fellow branches and turning into so much useless debris, a wooden detritus fit only for the building of anthills and nests for black, heavy birds.

The forest, however, was nowhere to be seen, not even its silhouette visible. It could only be imagined where the curtain of frost seemed especially dense and impenetrable. Yet a barely detectable wave was rolling in from over there, a calm insistent breath of life at odds with the deadness of the calm fettering God's earth. From the direction where the forest had to be imagined and where something could be heard breathing, from grey wilderness came what sounded like the last howl of some creature in its agony. It spread and grew louder until it filled the distant land and the invisible sky, turning ever more unmistakably into a melody to pierce the heart. That howling, coming from so far away in the fog-bound world, from the very heavens, barely penetrated the stifling, muggy carriages, but the bellowing, chortling, snorting, singing recruits gradually fell silent and strained to hear it, ever more audible, unceasing, and coming closer.

Leshka Shestakov, warm and comfortable up on the luggage shelf, uncertainly moved his cap from his ear. In this cosmic howling he began to make out the sound of marching feet, the thundering of some vast military formation, and the sound of the iron train, still rasping in the cracking frost, ceased to set his teeth on edge. He felt a chill of fear and unease run down his back, and a tremulous ecstasy. It began to dawn on the recruits that the foggy, frozen world outside the windows was not howling but singing.

All the time they were being herded out of the carriages by impartially ill-natured men in worn military uniforms, lined up alongside the white spattered train, divided into groups of ten, and ordered to fall in behind, they were turning their heads this way and that, trying to find out who was singing, and where, and why.

Only when they got close to the pine forest, its warm tree tops besieging the winter's fog, looming first black then green through the grey, motionless world, only then did the recruits see waves of human beings advancing from all directions out of the impenetrable mist, rolling in towards them beneath the trees, swaying wearily as they moved along, row upon row in close formation. Like automatons the ragged columns as they marched were exhaling puffs of white breath, which were immediately followed by the eery howling which now resolved itself into slow, drawn out sounds and words which had to be guessed at rather than heard: "Across the steppe march regiments renowned", "Once I've seen it through, Marusya, I'll come back to you, Marusya", "A fearless seagull soaring flew above the mighty ocean blue", "Never, Cossacks of Kuban, forget September twenty-one", "Ho, bold Poltava gun, four wheels made to run and run...".

The simple words of songs familiar from their schooldays and now bawled out by raw, congested throats, dealt a further blow to their already sinking morale. They felt totally cut off, filled with foreboding, and now there came this hoarse singing to the tramp of frozen soldiers' boots. The intimidating sound of marching was muted, however, beneath the forest canopy by the sand underfoot and the tops of the pine trees enclosing them overhead. The voices merged into one and seemed less harsh. The soldiers' singing sounded lustier too, perhaps because after exhausting exercises the companies were returning to barracks, rest and warmth.

Suddenly, like the shackle of a huge padlock, a wall of sound snapped shut around their hearts: "Arise, our mighty Motherland, Arise to fight the foe...". The defiant sound of advancing boots filled the world near and far, prevailing over the whole frozen, prostrate world. It nullified and obliterated all weaker sounds, all other songs, the cracking of the trees, the squealing of the sledge runners, and the whistling of far off steam engines. From all sides the thunderous crescendo of stolidly marching feet advanced, seeming even to resound from the sky welded to the earth by the stinging cold. Without realizing it, the recruits, who had been straggling along out of step, reformed and began to stamp their boots on the churned up road of sand and snow in time to that great, defiant song and they seemed to see glistening in the pits left by the heels of their boots not crushed red cranberries but the blood of trampled enemies.

The soldiers grimly lugging on their shoulders and backs rifles, machine gun mounts and barrels, trench mortar bases, anti-tank guns with bumps at the ends like the rotted skulls of weird birds which snagged overhead branches and knocked down snow on them, seemed not to be returning from exercises. They were going into battle, into bloody battle. This was not a formation trudging through pine trees and wearily planting the much repaired heels of worn-out boots in the yielding sand, but men full of strength and righteous anger, with faces scorched not by frost but by the flame of battles fought. They radiated a great potency which there was no understanding or explaining, which could only be felt, and made you draw yourself up, aware of being part of this defiant world and subordinate to it. Nothing else mattered any more, everything seemed infinitely remote, even your life itself.

When the recruits were marched down into the gloom of an underground barracks where crushed pine branches thrown on the sand formed the floor, and when they were ordered to find themselves a place on plank beds made from unstripped tree trunks barely squared on the side for sleeping on, Leshka could still hear within himself the fading echoes of that defiant "Arise to fight the foe..." He was overwhelmed by a sense of fatalism. He as an individual was no longer of significance, no longer in charge of his future. There were more important matters and causes which took priority over his little self. What mattered was the tempest, the torrent he was now caught up in. His was now to march, and sing, and fight, perhaps to die at the front together with these weary masses which carried all in their path before them, roaring out that incantation, that mighty roar of a country calling all to join to fight the foe, a country over which there hung a chilling, darksome, murky threat. How was a man to free himself of it on his own? Only in unison, only as part of a river, only as part of the melt waters of spring could he break through to the regions of light, to a different life full of the very meaning and purpose which at present were so beside the point but for which, since time began, people throughout the world have given their lives.

There came down on Leshka's soul just the spirit which is supposed to be present in barracks and prisons: a dull acceptance of everything occurring. When he was appointed to the first spell of duty as barracks orderly, to keep the barrackroom stove stoked with the raw pine firewood, he accepted the assignment without protest. Having listened to the order not to fall asleep, not to let the quarantine barracks catch fire, to make sure the recruits went well out into the forest before relieving themselves, to beat with a stick any who took it into their heads to urinate in the barracks, rifle other people's knapsacks, or, needless to say, hit the bottle, he obediently repeated the order and loudly repeated after Sergeant-Major Yash-kin that anyone who stepped out of line would be for the high jump.

The Sergeant had an armband on his greatcoat sleeve like those worn by soldiers in a guard of honour. He informed them he was the NCO in charge of the quarantine barracks guard. Yashkin had already served at the front. He had a medal and was in a reserve regiment after being in hospital. He would very shortly be returning to the front line with a draft company, glad to leave this hell hole, might the devil take it, might it go to hell, and burn to a cinder all at once, as he told them.

Yashkin was stunted, skinny, and cantankerous. He had no beard to speak of, only here and there something bristling from the sagging sledge-like hollows of his cheek bones where he had not shaved properly, and a sparse, straggly growth under his nose. His eyes were yellow and joyless, the skin beneath them minutely wrinkled, and the skin on his forehead was yellow also. He kept warm by sitting pressed up against the stove which was heaped with hot sand. His back was hunched, he whimpered like a puppy as he breathed, and he cadged tobacco, bread, and lard off them. Leshka had good tobacco, still a little bread, but no lard. He nodded towards the bulging sacks which morose-looking recruits from the Old Believer regions of the Siberian taiga sat hugging like a god-given woman, as if to say, those devils wouldn't exactly starve if they shared out some of their supplies.

Yashkin walked through the quarters, his cat-like eyes probing the recruits perched on their bunks. Many were already asleep. Wild men who had worked the gold mines of Baikit, Upper Yeniseisk, or who came from Tyr-Pont, as they called other, secret regions, sat cross-legged in a circle deep in a game of cards. One gambler was already reduced to his underpants, having staked and lost everything else. Forced out of the circle, he now stood craning his neck and giving advice and instructions from a distance to the others as to which card they should take with, which trump they should play. In a dark, far corner of the quarantine barracks, which was lit at each end by two primal tallow lampions and by the lazily burning stove with no doors, the recruits who arrived a week ago sat perched close together on the edge of their bunks, like swallows on a telegraph wire, patiently biding their time. Yashkin knew what they were waiting for.

He walked through their ranks giving warning glances, but in the gloom they all seemed not to notice him.

In the darkened depths on a lower bunk somebody was praying, "God of mercy, God of justice, deliver me not into temptation but deliver me from evil..."

"Cut it out!" Yashkin ordered for form's sake, and continued on his rounds, issuing a reprimand to anybody doing anything not in accord with regulations. Since, however, nobody in the barracks was doing anything at all, he rapidly ran out of things to reprimand.

Yashkin returned to his command post by the stove, detailing on the way back two teams to saw and chop logs outside respectively. He again settled himself on a block of wood directly opposite the hot, square opening, again spread his arms and moved his chest close to the stove, taking in the warmth, but unable to get warm.

In the barracks at large it was not exactly warm but not exactly cold either, as is usual deep under ground. The stove did little more than bring a little cheer to the dim life crammed in this airless dungeon, and even then brightened up only its immediate surroundings. The woodwork of the bunks to either side of the stove was covered in soot, but oozing sulphur made the ends of the beams stubbornly white, like bones which had already mouldered in the grave. A barely detectable whiff of sulphur and the scent from the crushed pine branches on the bunks, where the hard boughs also served in place of bedding, mitigated the smell of rot, dust, and pungent youthful urine.

The Old Believers were wagging their rumpled beards together in some kind of a meeting. One of them, a burly fellow in a ridiculous three-tiered peaked cap without a peak, hobbled over to the stove and placed in Yashkin's lap a round loaf with a nut brown crust, a piece of boiled meat, two onions and a birchbark salt box in the form of a pen case. Yashkin took out a pocket knife, cut off a hunk of bread for himself, thought for a moment, cut off another slice, and uttering the name "Zelentsov", shoved the bread and a lump of meat into hands which appeared instantly. He started peeling the onion.

"Elk meat!" Zelentsov's voice came from his bunk, followed shortly afterwards by the man himself. He sniffed with nostrils so broad they looked torn, peered round with beady but observant eyes, and demanded something to smoke from the visitor.

"We do not smoke," the Old Believer said, lowering his eyes.
"And do we not drink either?"

"On holy days we sometimes do. Beer..."

Leshka held out his tobacco pouch to Zelentsov, who lit up, weighed the pouch in his hand and, without asking, poured more tobacco out into his hand. Yashkin chewed away unhurriedly, indifferently, chomping the runners of his sledges up and down, deftly throwing rings of sliced onion from some distance into his narrow mouth ringed with cold sores. When he had eaten he looked around for someone, tugged two snoring recruits from upper bunks by their legs, and ordered them to fetch water. Two bodies lumbered to the ground. "Why us all the time?" the boys grumbled and went off clattering the billy can. The barracks door was forced open, the rasping of a saw was heard, and an eddy of chill, sweet air gusted into the barracks. All the time until they brought the water back in the iron can suspended from a bending pole a fresh draught blew from the door, and above the opening, unattainably far away, a narrow strip of grey light showed it was night.

The can, which held the same as three buckets or so, was put on the stove. The sand hissed. Hands reached thirstily out with mugs, cans, and jars. Those in charge half jokingly demanded bread and tobacco in return for the water, and when some stumped up (others did not) they too began chomping. When somebody paid in potatoes, they rolled them over into the hot sand beside the stove pipe. An appetizing aroma began to fill the place, covering the sourness and the stench.

The smell of baking potatoes drew people from the dark depths of the barracks. They crowded round, themselves producing potatoes and rolling them in until the flat top of the iron stove looked as if it were cobbled. The old stove had neither a bottom nor a door, and had already half sunk into the sand.

"Mind your backs there!" The cry filled the barracks, and reddish blocks of pine wood were rolled in banging and walloping from the door, to be followed by several armfuls more of dry chopped firewood, pine and perhaps some other kind, filched evidently from who knows where by the wily sawyers.

Yashkin moved away from the maw of the stove and a great quantity of logs was shoved into the hole, so great, indeed, that the ends stuck out the opening. The stove thought for a time before spitting and crackling and catching light, roaring gratefully as its sides grew raspberry red. The recruits surrounded it like members of its family. They munched their potatoes, asked each other where they were from, warmed and dried themselves, took stock of their new situation, and were delighted to meet people from their own village or just from the same part of the country, not yet aware that in this they were doing as the times demanded. The ties of kinship and coming from the same area would later be valued above all the transient circumstances of life, and most of all, most tenaciously they would strengthen and rule at the far away front, as yet unknown but inescapable.

The Old Believer with the remarkable hat was called Kolya Ryndin and came from Upper Kuzhebar in Karatuz, on the bank of the River Amyl which flows into the Yenisei. Kolya was the fifth of twelve children in the Ryndin family, and his relatives were beyond number.

People began teasing him. He smiled good-naturedly, baring large teeth and doing his best to join in the ribbing. When, however, a sickly lad with a head balanced on a scrawny neck protruding from a much mended quilted jacket slipped up to the stove and tried to whisk a potato away, Kolya took it from him.

"I told you, laddie, you must yet abstain a while from taking food, potatoes too, and especially one that's not yet properly baked. You'll get such runs as will blast you seven metres against the wind." Kolya paused to guffaw. "Not counting the splashes!" He continued more seriously, like a political instructor, to give a moral lesson. "Diarrhoea gets passed around, and this is a barracks, a community, and you'll be giving it to everybody." He pulled a small yellow canvas bag from his sack, sprinkled a handful of a grey mixture into a mug, put it on the fire, and added paternally, "When that's boiled, you drink it. It'll clear you up in a jiffy."

Everybody, including Sergeant-Major Yashkin, stared at this Old Believer with new interest. "What is it? What's that medicine?" they asked, because Petya Musikov, the lad with the runs, was not the only one in need of medical assistance. Along the way the recruits had bought and eaten whatever came to hand, drinking any amount of unboiled milk and water of dubious origin, and now were suffering upset stomachs.

"The fruit and dried bark of birdcherry, snakeweed, cowweed, and other herbs from the forest. When all these medicines are dried and crushed it is lastly sanctified and whispered over by Old Sekletiniya, a healer and sorceress famed the length of the Amyl River. Our taiga is rich in clever people, but none can hold a candle to Old Sekletiniya..." Kolya Ryndin pointed meaningfully towards the ceiling. "She can cure not just diarrhoea, but ruptures, even burns, and wild-fire. Everything, right up to consumption, she can cast a spell on. And she rubs bellies too."

"Bellies? Whose? What for?" Sergeant-Major Yashkin asked Kolya Ryndin amiably, his mood already changing for the better.

"Whose do you think? Not mine, to be sure. Women's, of course, to be rid of a baby they don't want."

The crowd chuckled uncertainly, and parted to make space for Kolya beside their commander. They almost forcibly made Petya Musikov and a few other ailing lads drink the scalding decoction. Someone gave Petya rusks to eat, and he crunched them loudly like a dog. Meanwhile a fight broke out among the card players. Yashkin took Zelentsov and one other solidly built lad and went to quell the unrest.

"If you don't pack that in, I'll have you out in the frost," Yashkin piped in a falsetto, "sawing firewood."

"I'd fuck your mother, General..."

"Don't go near his mother. She's a virgin."

"Yeah, seven kids and still a virgin."

"No, she only had one, but what a winner, haw-haw."

"I said I'll have you out."

"You and whose army, you gut-worm in a swoon!"

"Silence!"

"Hands off the cards, General, or I break your jaw."

"My jaw has me to look after it."

"You little shit!"

From one of the bunks a villain, bare to the waist and covered in tattoos, lunged at Yashkin, only to land with a yelp on the twig strewn floor. Yashkin, twisting the knife off him, kicked him outside. Leshka, Zelentsov, the duty soldiers and their helpers hauled two other daisies from their bunks, dragged them as their vests worked up bare backed over the splintery, crushed pine branches, and threw them too out the door to cool down. Zelentsov returned to the stove with the knife in his hand, looked at his bleeding palm, wiped it on his jacket, sprinkled it with ash from the stove, clenched it, and, baring his remaining decayed teeth in a grin, said not loudly but very distinctly to the barracks at large,

"Try it on again and this knife of yours goes in..."

The wild men went quiet and the barracks settled down again. Kolya Ryndin looked round apprehensively, viewing Zelentsov and Yashkin with new respect. What eagles were these who had no fear of wild men with knives. What people he had met up with! You could tell at a glance that Zelentsov was a seasoned lad who had seen the world, but this one, the commander, was just a little scrap of a fellow, ill looking, but he hadn't blinked an eye when he went for the knife. There's a soldier for you. He would keep the company of these men. They would defend him should need arise. Zelentsov squatted comfortably, lit up again, yawned, spat in the sand, and climbed into his bunk. Soon the whole barracks was asleep.

Yashkin lowered his soft Budyonny helmet over his eyes, buttoned it at his chin, raised the crumpled collar of his greatcoat, pushed his hands into the sleeves, lay down by the feet of the recruits at the end of a bunk with his back to the stove, and promptly began to grunt as if grumbling to himself.

"The sergeant-major is far from well," Kolya Ryndin concluded and, sitting a moment, added, addressing himself to Leshka, "I'll help you keep watch. What should he take for jaundice now? Which herb? Old Sekletiniya did tell me, but dolt that I am, I don't remember now."

"It's the front has made him yellow, the hatred and the fear."

"Is that the case?"

The watch did not hold out to morning. Leshka, slumped against a bunk upright, struggled against sleep for a long time, his head nodding, swaying, until he finally gave in. Clutching the upright, he pressed his cheek against the rough bark as his body relaxed and he sank, breathing evenly, and drifted away to his home expanses on the River Ob. Kolya Ryndin sat on his log, but eventually he too in slow motion, as if braking in flight, fell to the warm sand littered with cigarette ends, instinctively rolled a log under his head, pulled his cap down further, and immediately shook the entire barracks

with snoring so mighty that somewhere in the depths of the dug-out a recruit woke up and asked in a piteous voice,
"Oh, mum. What's going on? Where am I?"

In the morning there was great lamentation and cursing in the reception barracks, much groaning and hysteria. All the recruits' plump knapsacks had been cut open and the contents plundered, in some cases half their goodies had gone, in others not a crumb remained. The wild men were belching and scratching full bellies. Some lads quick off the mark ferreted through the barracks in search of the thieves and gave a good drubbing to any who crossed their path. In the distance Yashkin was cursing. Despite his express order and prohibition people had pissed beside the bunks and at the door. All over the sand there were small fresh pits white with salt. The dug-out smelled like a stable, despite the sergeant-major's throwing wide the pine door, through which a square of light showed it was day.

Translated by Arch Tait and Martin Dewhirst

Novy mir, Nos.10-12, 1992

Victor Astafiev

Victor Astafiev, b. 1924, lives in Krasnoyarsk, Siberia. A major "village prose" writer. Among his earlier works **King Fish** is held in particularly warm regard by Russian readers.

With **The Sad Detective** Astafiev wrote one of the first controversial best-sellers of perestroika. His latest novel is the first part of a trilogy about the Second World War.

"One more novel about the last war, but this one does not repeat what any other author has said. There are no Germans, and yet an ineluctable disaster looms over the characters.

"Astafiev breaks with stereotypes, and in so doing revives our interest in the literary treatment of the war. This proves to be just as much uncharted territory as the Gulag Archipelago...

"Several hundred young Siberians who have been called up in autumn 1942 are despondently waiting to be sent to the front, and are reaching the end of their tether in the barracks. Behind the barracks lurk the labour camps, and beyond and below them lies something even more ancient and primitive: that troglodytic, hellish existence that forms the deepest layer of our being."—Lev Anninsky

OLEG YERMAKOV

The Sign of the Beast

Part One:
The Lightest Detail,
Chapter One

And the smoke of their torment ascendeth up for ever and ever: and they have no rest day nor night, who worship the beast and his image, and whosoever receiveth the mark of his name.–
Revelation of St John the Divine, XIV, 11

This is an inventive and crafty enemy. He can creep up on you undetected. You need to be on your guard every minute, and keep on the move.

Twenty.

About turn.

Twenty.

You take twenty paces along the edge, reach the gun emplacement, about turn, take twenty paces back. Two paces are about one metre, so the length is ten metres. The height... above you is thousands and millions of light years.

The rich, aromatic blackness blinds you. It constricts your breast. Your sticky body seems trapped in a black crevice or some narrow corridor.

Twenty.

About turn...

There it is again, the rustling beyond the edge, in the chasm.

A light sound, some creature most probably. During the day they sit in their burrows waiting for the heat to be over, and at night they come out foraging. They can be all shapes and sizes. Some don't have legs. They can be round, long, narrow-snouted, many-legged, shaggy, have brown pincer-like jaws, a sting in their tail, be a soft green, tiny and heavy, large, have a warty skin, a fat tail, a massive muzzle. Almost every one of them has a few precious droplets secreted under its tongue which clear its path, sending some running and others backing off quivering.

Twenty.

About turn...

Keeping on the move only seems a good means of self-defence until you think about it. He can still get you when you are marching, take the feet from you and hurl you over the edge. And there, in the chasm, some startled creature will plunge its sting into you.

There are other techniques. You can give yourself a good shake; try shaking your head from side to side the way a horse does when a fly crawls into its eye or up a nostril; or squat down on your heels, rubbing your eyes and flailing your arms.

Squatting down with umpteen kilograms of metal on you is hard work, and dangerous. Your weary legs will crave a moment's rest when you bend them. That's when sleep can pounce, and hit you gently on the forehead. Your buttocks touch the ground, your arms fall to your knees, and your head bows to your arms.

That's when they appear...

Raising arms heavy with fatigue is not that easy, anyway, and in addition any exertion calls forth salt streams of sweat. The horse technique is useless. Your head is heavy, you feel something swelling in it, a vein suddenly filling with dark blood and bulging. One time it will burst.

That only leaves fingering your face, flicking your cheeks, pinching the skin, half closing your eyes and pressing on the eyelids.

Or you can imagine you are soaring to terrifying heights.

No, even there, up among the pale dust and the wet, warm suns and planets, he is stalking you, sleep is biding his time, waiting to pounce and gently, cripplingly, hit you on the forehead, and take the feet from you.

That's the moment they crawl to the edge...

Looking at the stars for too long gives you a stiff neck and makes your head swim. Your head swims anyway, the back of your head goes numb, from the yellow fires of daytime and the black heat at night and the clinging fragrance. The fragrance is really strong at night. In the morning there is always a breeze blowing from the east to disperse it a bit. The wind in the afternoon is no longer clean, it is hot, but at least it blows. The night is airless and heavy with the fragrance, stifling, cloying in your mouth, as if in a corridor a corpse were lying to one side in a pool of formalin, or perhaps over the edge, in an abyss full of scaly, hairy monsters with stings.

There is no body. It's unlikely. Well, there could be one, but that is not where the fragrance is coming from. Disease. One more enemy. It rules, brooding lynx-eyed over the town. The locals breathe it.

Not to fall asleep is absolutely vital.

A visitor from the steppe may crawl over the edge, or one of the seniors may come, find you sleeping, and take a swing with his rifle butt at your helmet. Or your teeth.

Twenty. About tur... Suddenly in the stillness a bird shrieks shrilly, the darkness beyond the edge comes alive, a crater rapidly deepening and widening. In the distance a wave is outlined, and unexpectedly the whole undulating horizon becomes visible, dimly lit from below. The light grows stronger, the edge of a stone mirror appears. The sky is illumined, and finally a curved sphere blotched white and blue rests on the horizon and the horizon sags. The horizon sags, rights itself, the sphere hovers over the earth, moves and begins its ascent, growing whiter, brighter, and turning into the light, flat, small moon.

The battery is seen to be standing on the edge of a gigantic plain, the long, thin barrels of its tiny guns aimed at the moon-lit horizon.

...

Stop! Who goes there? Password. Response. The old
detail leaves.
And now it's night.
Twenty paces.
About turn.
Again this space. Length ten metres. And the height above, thousands, millions of light years.

Beyond the edge monsters again rustle. Or enemies, come from the steppes together with night.

Your eyelids stick together, yawning rends your jaws.

The heat of night, redolent of disease, chokes you, sends you to sleep. No sleeping. A senior will come, and club your head with a rifle butt. Do something, rub your eyes, shake your head – but then that vein swells again, filling with heavy blood, perhaps to burst. About turn.

Staggering as if he's been at the vodka. Think up something to do. Two twos are four... five fives... It is making you dozy.

Remember something. Poetry.

...The stars are hot, and heavy; in Russia they are paler, lighter ... Listen. Intently. Primal night. And you, half-beast, must be un-sleeping, alert.

Translated by Arch Tait

Znamya, Nos. 6-7, 1992

Oleg Yermakov

Oleg Yermakov, born 1960, lives in Smolensk. He made a name for himself with **Afghan stories** based on his first-hand impressions as a rank and file soldier in the Afghan war. His collection, **Afghan Stories**, is available in English from Secker and Warburg.

The Sign of the Beast is the first full-length novel of the Afghan war. The Soviet army in Afghanistan is depicted as an image of a disintegrating society where cruel abuse of subordinates takes the place of wartime cama-raderie. At a second metaphorical level a conflict is played out between two world-views—West and East, Taoist and Viking. This theme, unfolding independently of the main story-line, makes **The Sign of the Beast** the first Eurasian novel.

"...the self-portrait of a generation that found itself left with the remnants of an empire, and which was handed weapons with which it could destroy anything in sight."—Lev Anninsky

"Yermakov describes brilliantly the mentality and behaviour of those engaged—both individually and collectively—in the "hunting" game. ...The work's metaphorical dimensions engage the reader in an endless moral and spiritual exploration."—Riitta Pittman

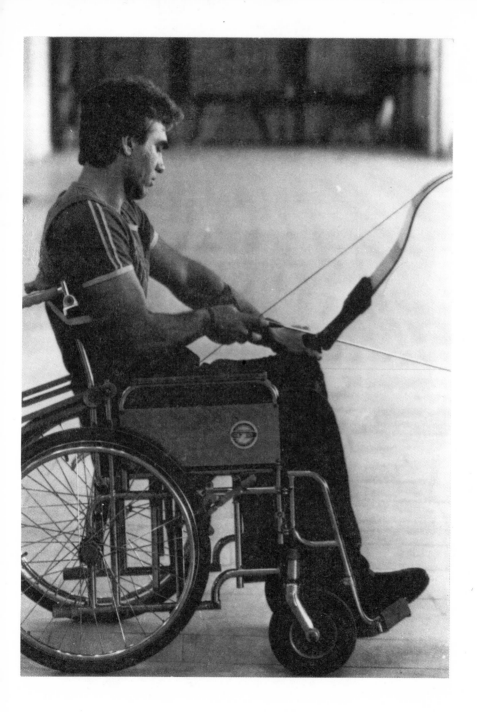

LUDMILA ULITSKAYA

Sonechka
excerpt

From her earliest childhood, even as a baby, Sonechka had been passionate about reading. Her elder brother Yefrem, the family wit, was forever repeating the same old joke: "Endless reading has given Sonechka a nose like a pear and a backside like a chair."

Alas this was no exaggeration. Sonechka's nose was indeed as flat as a pear, her backside wide and sedentary, her shoulders were broad and her legs were shapeless. Her one positive feature was her ample female bosom, which developed early and seemed ill-fitted to her lanky body. She hunched her shoulders and bent her back, wore loose, baggy garments and was ashamed of her useless endowment in front and her wretched flatness behind.

Her compassionate, long-married elder sister magnanimously spoke of her eyes, but her eyes were small, brown and wholly unexceptional. True, her slightly swollen lids were weighed down by three rows of thick lashes, but these were not particularly beautiful, just an encumbrance, since short-sighted Sonechka had since childhood worn spectacles.

For almost twenty years, from the age of seven to twenty-seven, Sonechka read continuously, plunging into books as though into a trance, which would end only with the final page. She had an exceptional talent for reading, even a kind of genius; her responsiveness to the printed word was such that fictional heroes became as real to her as actual living people, and Natasha Rostova's luminous suffering at the bedside of the dying Prince Andrey were as lifelike as her sister's blazing grief at the loss of her four-year-old daughter when the plump, clumsy, slow-eyed little girl fell down the well as she stood chatting to a neighbour.

Had Sonechka misunderstood the rules established in every art, or was this the boundless trust of one who has not reached maturity, imaginative failure liable to blur the boundaries between fiction and reality, or on the contrary such a selfless departure into realms of fantasy that everything beyond its border was robbed of its sense and content?

Sonechka's reading, by now a minor form of madness, would pursue her into sleep, so that even her dreams could be read like books. She would dream thrilling historical romances, and from the action she could guess the book's typeface, weirdly sensing where the paragraphs and censored passages were. Sleep intensified the emotional displacement of her morbid passion, and in sleep she would appear as a fully-fledged heroine or hero, balanced on the fine line between the author's intentions as she perceived them and her own aspirations for action, deeds and movement.

The New Economic Policy had run its course, and her father, the son of a village blacksmith from Byelorussia, a self-taught mechanic with a practical bent, shut up his clock workshop, overcame his native revulsion against mass production methods, and went to work in a clock factory, diverting his stubborn sould of an evening by repairing the unique mechanisms created by the skilled hands of his multi-ethnic predecessors.

Sonechka's mother, who until her dying day wore a stupid wig under a clean khaki kerchief, would surreptitiously stitch away on her Singer sewing-machine, presenting the neighbours with simple cotton garments appropriate to those poor, noisy times, whose main terror was summed up for the old woman by the dreaded name of the Finance Inspector.

Sonechka herself, after dashing through her schoolwork, would spend every remaining moment of her time in flight from the brash, sad thirties by feeding her soul on the expanses of great Russian literature, plunging into the anxious abysses of the suspect Dostoyevsky, surfacing in the dappled alleys of Turgenev, and provincial estates warmed by the generous, unthinking love of Leskov, a writer always for some reason considered second-rate.

After completing a course in librarianship, Sonechka found work in the underground repository of an old library. Here she joined a happy few who at the end of the working day would leave their dusty basement with a pang of interrupted pleasure, unsated by the rows of file cards, the blank request slips arriving from the reading room above, and the living weight of the volumes deposited in her thin hands.

For many years Sonechka considered writing to be a sacred act, regarding inferior writers such as Pavlov, Pavsany and Palama as deserving of equal respect on the grounds that they each occupied one page of the encyclopaedia. Over the years she learned to distinguish the big waves from the small, and the small waves from the shoreside foam which virtually filled the ascetic shelves in the library's modern literature department.

After serving for several years with monastic self-sacrifice in the book repository, Sonechka yielded to the urging of her superior, herself an avid reader, and enrolled in the Russian philology department at the University. She worked through the vast and rather absurd syllabus and was about to take her examinations when her world collapsed overnight as the war broke out.

This was possibly the first event in her young life to wrench her out of the cloudy realms of incessant reading. She and her father, who worked now in an instruments workshop, were evacuated to Sverdlovsk, where she quickly found herself in the one safe position in town, in the basement of the library.

It is not clear if Sonechka was merely participating in her country's time-honoured tradition of depositing the precious fruits of the spirit, like the fruits of the earth, in cold basements, or if it was a precautionary innoculation against the next ten years of her life, which she was to live with a man from the underground, her future husband, whom she met in this harsh, drab first year of evacuation.

Robert Victorovich arrived at the library one day when the woman in charge of issuing books was off sick, and Sonechka was replacing her. He was short, sharp, thin and grey, and Sonechka would never have noticed him had he not asked where the catalogue of French

39

books was to be found. There were French books in the library, but the catalogue had long ago been lost through disuse, and since there were no visitors at this late hour just before closing, she led her unusual customer down to the remote West European corner in her basement.

He stood dazed before the shelf for several minutes, inclining his head to one side with the hungry, startled look of a child before a plate of cakes. Over a head taller than he, Sonechka stood breathless at his back, caught up in his excitement.

Turning round to her, he unexpectedly kissed her long-fingered hand, and in a low, rich voice glimmering like the light of a blue lamp from a cold childhood, said, "What a miracle...! What a feast...! Montaigne...! Pascal...!" Still holding her hand, he added, "And all in Elsevier editions..."

"We have nine Elseviers," Sonechka nodded, touched, and proud of her librarianship. He gave her a strange look from the feet up, and his thin lips smiled to reveal a mouth of missing teeth. He paused, as though preparing to make an important statement, then thought better of it, and said, "Would you be so good as to make me out a reader's card, or whatever you call it."

Sonechka pulled away her hand, lying forgotten in his dry palm, and they ascended the rapacious staircase, which stole whatever little heat was left in the feet that touched it, and in the cramped hall of this former merchant's mansion she wrote out for the first time his surname, which sounded so strange to her and which in exactly two weeks would become her own. While she was writing the letters of this unfamiliar surname in indelible pencil, twisting it slightly in her worn woollen gloves, he looked at her clear brow and smiled to himself at her freakish resemblance to a young camel. A tender, patient animal, he thought. "Even the colouring - a dark umber, with warm, pink undertones..."

She finished writing, pushed back her spectacles with her index finger, and gave him a kind, questioning look, waiting for him to tell her his address.

He felt deeply confused by a powerful sensation of destiny, descending upon him as suddenly as a shower from the heights of an untroubled blue sky, as he realised that standing here before him was his wife.

The day before had been his forty-seventh birthday. Robert Victorovich was a legendary figure, but thanks to his sudden, and according to his friends, motiveless return from France in the early 1930s, this legend lived its own existence, quite independent of him, in stories and anecdotes and the deserted galleries of occupied Paris, where his strange paintings were the object of abuse, neglect, and eventual resurrection and posthumous fame. Robert Victorovich knew nothing of this. Wearing a scorched black padded jacket, a grey towel wrapped around his Adam's apple, this most successful of failures, who after serving a mere five-year sentence now had a probationary job as an artist in a works management office, stood before the clumsy girl and smiled, knowing that he was about to commit one of the episodic betrayals of which his changeful life had been so full. He had betrayed his grandparents' faith, and his parents' hopes, and his teacher's love. He had betrayed science and had cruelly and abruptly broken off friendships as soon as he felt them putting constraints on his freedom. And now he was betraying his strict vow of celibacy, which was unconnected to the vow of chastity he had taken in the years of his first illusory successes.

He was a womaniser, exploiting women and drawing sustenance from this insatiable source, yet carefully guarding against dependence lest he himself might become sustenance for that female energy which is so paradoxically generous to those who take, and so cruelly exacting to those who give.

Cocooned in a thousand volumes, lulled by the smoky thunder of Greek mythology, the hypnotic flute of the Middle Ages, the astral music of Dante, the siren singing of the clear-voiced Rilke and Novalis, and soothed by the great Russians, whose edifying melancholy was directed straight to the heart of heaven, Sonechka's untroubled soul did not notice her great moment, preoccupied as she was by the risky step of issuing books which by rights should be issued only in the reading room.

"Address," she said curtly.

"This isn't my permanent home, you see," the strange reader explained. "I'm living in the works office."

"Well give me your passport, or your residence permit," Sonechka demanded.

He rummaged in his pocket and produced a crumpled identity

document. She peered at it through her spectacles, then shook her head. "It's no good. You're not from this district..."

The kib had pointed a red tongue at him, he realised; everything had gone wrong. He thrust the document back in his pocket.

"Look, I'll take them out on my card and you can return it to me when you leave," Sonechka said in a contrite tone.

He knew then that everything would be all right.

"Only I must ask you to bring them back punctually," she urged him gently, as she wrapped the three bulky volumes in a piece of crumpled newspaper.

He thanked her briefly and left.

While Robert Victorovich was pondering with revulsion the technology of friendship and the burdens of courtship, Sonechka unhurriedly finished her long working day and prepared to leave for home. She no longer felt the slightest anxiety about the return of the three precious books she had so blithely allowed the stranger to take; all her thoughts were of the journey home across the cold dark town.

Translated by Cathy Porter

Novy mir, No.7, 1992

Ludmila Ulitskaya

A dramatist, screenplay and short-story writer, Ludmila Ulitskaya (b. 1938) has only recently begun to publish her novellas in Russia and abroad. A collection of short stories, **Les Pauvres Parents**, has just been published in French by Gallimard. This year another collection of her stories came out in Germany from Volk und Welt Publishers. See also **Glas** No.6 for two stories by Ulitskaya—her first appearance in English translation.

Sonechka is a story of a bookish girl, who unexpectedly found a husband during wartime evacuation, raised a wayward daughter, and then lost both, returning once more in her solitary old age to the addictive reading of her youth. Thanks to the decency, restraint and tolerance of the main character the effect is of a simple but accurately observed chronicle, told without tragic exaggeration.

Pervaded by nostalgia, the novella describes a tiny, fragile paradise of post-war family life in Moscow.

SEMYON LIPKIN

A Resident Remembers

Chapter One

Nothing had really changed. Now as then he shuffled down the street, his sloping shoulder brushing the buildings even though the street was wide and uncrowded. He still got dirt on his left arm, still carried books in his right. He still seemed not to notice the amused glances of passers-by, their attention caught by the odd way he walked, but also by his high, unclouded forehead and the cloudless blue eyes of a child and a madman.

He had come back to Chemadurova Buildings, one of a fortunate few of those born there who seemed likely to die there if things got no worse.

Even after a great revolution, several changes of government, the enforcement of Soviet power, and now that the Second World War had thundered off into history, the residents, even the children who were sure it had always been half demolished, all used the building's old name. One time when Lorenz was handing in some application, the secretary in the council's residences section had fluttered her painted eyelids at him with unnerving vivacity and asked, "48 Vatutin Street? In the centre, in Romanovka? There is no such street. I should know, I was born there. Chemadurova Buildings? Well, why didn't you put that down in the first place?"

The new names given to the street hadn't taken either, not in 1914 when it was renamed after General Skobelev; or in 1920 when it became Trotsky Street; or in 1928 when it was to be known as Tenth Anniversary of the Workers' and Peasants' Militia Street; or in 1941 when it was called after Antonescu; or in 1945 after General Vatutin. Pokrovsky Street it was and remained. In such cases even the most powerful authorities, even the postman, have to admit defeat and defer to the citizen.

For many years Lorenz had assumed that Pokrovsky Street took its name from Pokrovsky (Intercession) Cathedral which once divided the street into two unequal parts, one bustling with activity and the other quiet. The Cathedral had been destroyed during the civil war and a park laid out on the site in the 1920s during the years of reconstruction.

It was only recently he had read in an old newspaper that when the cathedral was built at the end of the last century, the street was already called Pokrovsky after the small church whose churchwarden Anton Sosnovik had been until his death.

You actually entered the church from Triangle Square. All there was on Pokrovsky Street was a low grey wall with a narrow gate and tiny caretaker's window. Some thin grass, always dusty, struggled at the base of the wall and had a curiously churchy smell to it, almost like myrrh or incense. Grown-ups and people going about their business simply did not notice the wall, lost among all the shops and workshops.

There was a time in our town's history when the ground floors of all the buildings were full of people trading and manufacturing things. Later, the doors were filled in with stone to a height of a couple of feet from the pavement and became windows. The shops vanished, to be replaced by flats, and only the light corrugated iron shutters, pulled down to this day with a hooked pole, hint at all the business of the past.

The offices of the stationery cooperative where Lorenz worked as assistant accountant were on Almshouse Street, on the opposite side and slightly up from the Fruit Arcade. To reach the Public Library he had to walk the full length of Pokrovsky Street.

It was only three in the afternoon. They had finished work early because the cooperative's director, Dina Sosnovik, and the head accountant had been called to the district committee of the Communist Party. Yesterday a barbed little feature had appeared in the local newspaper under the title "Playing Dirty". Among other things, the cooperative produced wooden draughts and dominoes, and the article turned on the fact that the black paint tended to come off on people's hands. There should have been little to worry about, since the cooperative itself had complained to the authorities about the quality of the paint a year ago, but was the article perhaps related to the arrest last week of Dina's mother? Oh dear, whatever could have tempted Madame Sosnovik after the tragedy she had lived through to try going back to the old ways? Dina was earning quite decently, eight hundred roubles a month. On top of that she received a further fifty roubles a month from each of three workshops. She had even once boasted to Lorenz that the money was brought directly to her home without any deductions. That was surely enough for two people to live on. Lorenz himself got by on four hundred and twenty a month. People are funny. So foolish, and so unfortunate.

Pokrovsky Street had the Fruit Arcade at one end (where the zoo is now), and the sea at the other. There was some higher symbolism to the road and its pavements linking the high funnelled steamships from distant lands which loomed up unexpectedly and magically at one end with the strident yet somehow naive luxuriance of the Fruit Arcade, that inexhaustible treasury of melons, tomatoes, grapes, plums, and apples. Pokrovsky Street symbolised a link which could never become a chain, a conjoining of free labour and free expanses, an age-old brotherhood of cultivation of the soil and sailing of the seas. Pokrovsky Street interposed between them commerce, craftsmanship, and enlightenment.

The smell of the acacias, acacias which had seen it all, was as sweet as childhood itself. How often Lorenz had remembered them in faraway Poland and Germany, and their flowers, sickly and delicate, which left a spicy coolness in your mouth for an age after you sucked them. How many times he had remembered too the buildings and the shop signs; not the new ones, but the ones with the old Russian "e" and the hard sign at the end of words, both abolished after the revolution. The war had been over for several years now. Many of the buildings were mere shells. Others, like the red, three-storey one with the winter balconies, or the long narrow one which used to house the bar and later the tobacco factory club, had disappeared completely and now had low grass growing on their desolate sites. The bar had been on the first floor, the ground floor being Nazaroglou's Oriental Sweetmeats. A wide awning jutted far out above its windows, and the dark shadows of the acacia flowers on its grey canvas made patterns like ancient cuneiform. How many familiar faces he could still see. They would gather of an evening in the bar, Cybulski the huge, shaggy locksmith; Dimitraki the joiner, small, parchment-faced, his black hair in a brush cut; Ionkis the ladies' tailor, elegant and self-assured. Sometimes Mr Kaempfer would come, a "semi-intellectual" as he proudly styled himself; and Mr Lorenz, the accountant, his father, with him, Misha, in tow. He would listen raptly, sipping his tea through loaf sugar, eating hot poppy seed bagels while they talked and talked about the Kaiser and Lloyd George, Poincare and Milyukov, Chkheidze and Lenin.

The author of a certain popular novel mercilessly satirises these impotent windbags in their pique waistcoats, blethering on with such aplomb on political topics. How little our clever satirist knows! To this day he, Mikhail Fyodorovich Lorenz, a man with a university education, whose papers in their time were deemed worthy of publication in the Herald of Philology of the Academy of Sciences, was amazed at their grasp of immensely complex situations, at the wit and sagacity of these evening conversations in the noisy, cheerful saloon of that bar with its fog of perspiration and aromatic cigarette smoke hovering under the low ceiling. And who is to say that that was not true freedom: hard-working people putting on their, possibly tasteless, waistcoats of an evening, sitting in a bar drinking tea, eating poppy seed bagels, and fearlessly propounding whatever political opinions they chose.

The bar is gone now, and gone too the factory club where Rachel ruled supreme; but those are other memories.

Mere shells, two-storeys, three-storeys high. The town couldn't be said to have suffered badly in the war, but Pokrovsky Street had borne the brunt. What life, though, he imagined in the dead, gaping windows, how many faces of people near and dear to him, or not near but still dear. People thought him odd, "malancholy", as they say hereabouts. He knew people laughed at him, but how he loved them all, the living and the dead. He was flesh of their flesh, and sometimes felt that he too had been taken out and shot, he too had been burned, had hidden underground; he too had come out with them into the light of day, afraid of the bright, unwonted sun, gripping at the stones.

His memory was exceptional. It struck his teachers and schoolmates as magical. It retained now the way the street had looked almost thirty years earlier. At just this spot there was always an appetising smell from Pirozhnikov's bread shop. But how many of the traders' names were Ukrainian, Jewish, Greek, Polish, Turkish, Armenian, and yet for all that he insisted that the town was purely Russian. Russia was more than central Russia and the Volga, demure birch trees overhanging ponds, log huts and haylofts and hoping for the best. Russia was also the living embroideries of Mordovia. Russia was her own endlessly colourful, energetic history; her first satirist, the Moldavian Antioch Kantemir; the Ethiopian lips of Alexander Pushkin, her greatest poet; her great marine explorer, Vitus Behring from Denmark; and Admiral Pavel Nakhimov, hero of the siege of Sebastopol, and the descendant of a Christianised Jew. Russia was her bank, the Credit Lyonnais; her Belgian tram company; her German-educated Decembrist revolutionary, Pavel Pestel; her theosophists and decadents; her marauding Cossack gaidamaks and her bolsheviks. And Russia was him, Russia was also Mikhail Fyodorovich Lorenz. She was even that renowned oculist, that star in the firmament of the city authorities, Sevostianov, a member of the Jew-baiting Union of the Russian People under the Tsar, vice-chancellor of the University during the period of Romanian rule, and today's Stalin Prize laureate.

Lorenz walked past a tall building very dear to him. It occupied an entire block and seemed, from Pokrovsky Street, to have survived well. You couldn't tell that the two-storey wing at the back had been destroyed, where they, the Lorenzes, used to live; where ill-starred Volodya Varuti's art folder used to lie on the window sill; where Cybulski thought his thoughts, and Rachel hummed to herself; and where the smell of sour cabbage soup wafted from the window of the yardkeeper, Matvey Nenashev. Now only a charred wall, exposing the vulnerable interior, fronted on to Nikolaevsky Avenue. The downstairs windows and door into what used to be Madame Chemadurova's shop supplying church plate, the same Madame

Chemadurova who owned the whole building, were blocked with porous stone; and the basement where Madame Sosnovik and Dina hid for three years had gone. On Albania Lane nothing remained of the house at all, not a brick or a beam. Nothing was left of Dimitraki's carpentry workshop, the Kaempfers' apartment, or Belenky's furdressing works. Now all of them who were still alive and now lived in two once luxurious flats, one above the other, which had belonged to the Pomolovs and the Kobozevs, and whose windows looked on to Pokrovsky Street. On the ground floor in years long past people had bought knitwear, drap, and cheviot wholesale or retail in Kobozev's huge textile shop. Now that, and the premises next door which had belonged to ladies' tailor Ionkis, housed an official institution with a long, unpronounceable name made up of abbreviations.

Did Lorenz notice Dina's balcony was on the verge of collapsing? Or that the spring sun was already beating against the wall while meat, bought with tremendous difficulty, had been left hanging in a string bag from a nail? Neither Dina nor her mother were at home, of course. The balcony did not collapse and Lorenz passed safely beneath it, feeling the warmth from his old home on his shoulder.

Bright posters advertising the cinema, the circus, and the theatre were pasted on hoardings concealing the derelict plots, but for him there was nothing derelict about the place where a compact Italianate house with four high windows had stood, a neat brass plate, like a barrister's, on the stained glass double doors, reading, "Antoine. Coiffeur". Antoine the coiffeur had voluntarily come out of those gleaming doors to go on his last journey, merging with the doomed crowd waiting mindlessly, dully in expectation of something by the police station. Old Chemadurova, small and fat, froze into immobility on the steps, whispered something with her white, flabby lips, and either waved him goodbye, or perhaps made an ineffective sign of the cross over him. For the first time he had not dyed his great main of hair or his goatee beard, and everyone could see that the fiery-eyed, handsome octogenarian had long been grey. Most likely, however, nobody noticed. Only he, malancholy Lorenz, standing across the street by the statue of Laocoon and his sons with the serpents winding round them, could think at such a terrible moment about Anton Sosnovik's coiffure. That sculpture still stands out white against the greenery, and even today you can see the marble plaque on that side of the street with its inscription. Incredible that it should have survived the occupation.

Here, in the former police station, in January 1920 Denikin's butchers brutally martyred the following Young Communists:
Raya Lyubarskaya
Leo Himmelfarb
Konstantin Pomolov
Boleslav Blizhensky
Alexey Kalaida
Boris Vargavtik.

Why is there not another inscription beside it in memory of other martyrs? Perhaps because space would have had to be found for not six but 160,000 names; and then there would have had to be a third list, of many thousands of other victims martyred by other butchers.

Here now was the park where the Cathedral had stood, all white roundness bathing in the azure of the sky. Here the bustling part of the street ended, with Genrikh Shpekht's shop. Who could forget Shpekht's? Anybody Lorenz's age had felt his heart pounding as he entered that stately realm of exercise books, pens, pencil cases, satchels, rulers, and buckles bearing the crests of the high schools. Perhaps only the young louts of inner city Romanovka did not enter there, but even that is unlikely: in our town all the children went to school. At the till in the depths of the shop sat Martha, the proprietor's daughter, her yellow face, scrawny plaits and meek, pretty eyes like emblems of the straight and narrow path and virtues of learning. A tall man, with only a few buck teeth remaining and wearing check trousers and a jacket of black alpaca wool, advanced radiantly to greet the customers. Exultation was in his chestnut-coloured eyes:

"Bonjour, Madame Pzheradskaya! You've brought your youngest? Your grandson? I never would have believed it. In all seriousness! Monsieur Bakalyar! Where have you decided to send your heir? To the Commercial College? Come now, he has such ability, the whole town is talking about it. Ah yes, of course, they won't allow us into the high schools. Oh, these Volunteers, I can tell you... Young fellow, please don't touch that."

The children supposed this person to be Genrikh Shpekht, and when Lorenz boasted that he lived in the same building as he did,

49

and that his name was Kaempfer, and that he was Shpekht's sales assistant, they just laughed at him. They had often laughed at him...

A few steps more. He crossed a wooden pavement and the character of the street changed abruptly. A distant view of something out of the ordinary, something eternally new. The sea. There had never been shops or workshops in this part of the street, but something legitimately born with them: the University.

Visitors admired our town for its European appearance, but Lorenz had always felt that the sacred culture of Europe was to be found not in the classical porticoes of the banks on Cardinal Street or the great dock installations, but here, in the stones of the University's austere buildings. The cognoscenti did not deny the local architecture its elegance, recognising the pleasing blending of pillars of different orders, but they spoke of eclecticism. They were wrong. It was not eclecticism but a considered synthesis. Behind the ordering of these buildings lay the probing intellect and incendiary writings of Renaissance Italy, the French Encyclopaedists, and the sages of Germany.

Once, after the revolution of February 1917, little Misha Lorenz had been walking here with his father, and students had come towards them in their crumpled forage caps and light grey double-breasted tunics. "Comrades," Misha heard a bearded student say, his face like a picture he had seen of the wild-eyed writer Vsevolod Garshin, "Momentous news: Grigulov has signed up with the God-seekers!"

"Papa, what are God-seekers?"

For some reason the phrase was etched into his memory for the rest of time. Like all children he imagined that life never changed. It was only he who would change, growing up and becoming tall, and a time would come when people would say, "Comrades! Momentous news: Lorenz has signed up with the God-seekers!"

He did grow up and become tall, and he went in through the massive portals of the University only to find that it was not he, Misha Lorenz, but life which had changed. A flaming August was burning to its close behind him, but inside all was stony coolness. Although he had passed the examinations brilliantly, he looked in vain for his name on the typewritten list pinned up alongside an old bolshevik propaganda newspaper. He was the son of an accountant.

What right had he to higher education? A year later he did matriculate for all that. Rachel managed to help with a letter to Grinev, a member of the Central Committee of the Communist Party.

He did not change, but life did, and then a war broke out which some in the town had been fearfully expecting, and half hoping for. Our town became Transnistria and Lorenz was summoned to the vice-chancellor's office by Professor Sevostianov, who declared, "My dear young colleague, I know it all. The Bolsheviks' scholarly satraps treated you most unjustly."

This expression too was etched in his memory, uttered as it was on the very day the condemned were led off to be massacred. The following morning Lorenz left his native town. He had never been back inside the University.

For some people the towns and houses they have lived in, and indeed the people they lived among, are like a cigarette packet, of interest only while it still has cigarettes in it. You may even jot down the odd address or telephone number on it, but when the cigarettes are finished, the packet is thrown away, out of your pocket and out of your thoughts. Perhaps, in all truth, Lorenz's life was not all that full, but buildings, flats, streets, and people he barely knew, with whom, indeed, he had only the most tenuous links, did not fade from his heart and mind. They were constantly alive within him, and the associations he made between them changed constantly and fantastically. Perhaps that was why an idea would so often fragment into dozens of associations with him, the links falling away: something which could make it far from easy to talk to him. Dina, smiling archly but affectionately, had passed on to him Madame Sosnovik's judgement: "Misha has a heart of gold, Dina, but say what you like, he is downright malancholy". Now fleeting, insubstantial memories of the University had been stirred up and came flooding back. It struck him, although he subsequently discovered he was not the first to note it, that west of a crooked line described by the Rivers Danube, Pripyat, and Vistula the letter 'r' does not tolerate being followed by a soft vowel but mutates into a 'zh' sound. He saw again the staircase where he had bumped into his army instructor, and endured his taunting with shameful subservience. "Take a look at him, will you? Looks like he's been jumped, and beaten up with an old sack!" The quiet, cold technician's room, with its window looking out on to the roof of the pavilion in the municipal park where people sat at the tables eating colourful ice creams. (Alas he never did rise higher in the scholarly hierarchy than technician.) The creaking bookcase: Potebnya, Veselovsky, Gerber's Die Sprache als Kunst.

The University too, it seemed, had gone. As a part of European culture, at least, it was done for, apparently for good. And if it was still his life blood, who was to know? "What's it to us?" they might ask in our town.

He was coming closer to the sea. Before turning along Sebastopol Road to the library he sat down on a stone bench. It had been there since the trams terminated here. For as long as he could remember there had never been a day, rain or shine, when two or three people were not to be found sitting on that bench, no matter what time of the day he came by. Who were they? Lay-abouts, sight-seers, dreamers? Bewitched all of them, evidently, not by the port siren but by the mysterious siren of the sea. This was not a place for nannies with prams or women on their own. (Couples came only at night.) It was always men, once in bowler hats and panamas, later in flat hats, now in forage caps or fur hats. Heaven knows, the great attraction of the cities of Europe (which are not at all the asphyxiating octopuses naive Verhaeren represents them as being) is precisely their sightseers and dreamers. Happiness is being able to work for a few hours each day, to live without needing a police registration or internal passport, to be able to wander through a town, dreaming and thinking. Especially looking down on the sea.

The sea surrounds our town on three sides. There is a world of difference between the open sea and the sea beside a coastline, where it takes on the characteristics of the coast. Like molten steel, like a dull liquid it churns at the foot of factories and mills. Its waves echo with the multi-ethnic voices of children and adults, the bustle of kitchens and courtyards as they rush up the sandy beach bearing melon skins, swirl around the overturned piles of collapsed jetties, and pour into sockets for hooks. As monotonous as life in a barracks the sea flows along past sheer yellow cliffs on top of which suntanned coast guards play football in their underpants, their green peaked caps thrown down on the sand. Like Moldavians in their carts, like rustic oxen the sea plods obediently in from the direction of the steppes, murmuring sleepily in marshy coastal dells. It grinds like grey metal, and sprays like sparkling black coal, rises like flour in canvas sacks, and gleams like mother of pearl fish scales by moorings and harbours and in the port.

But over the high seas no one has dominion. If the sea beside a coastline takes on the characteristics of the coast, people on the high seas take on the characteristics of the sea. As in the time of Theseus, so today the sea is a cloud-like swell, now docile, now threatening, but always signifying freedom. Lorenz was single, as yet without ties (Dina was energetic, but would leave him alone eventually), and he hadn't even any distant relatives. What was to stop him from leaping that moment over the low parapet, slithering down over the mossy stones, climbing through the hole in the stone wall, skirting the customs sheds, and flinging himself headlong into the pure lilac sea, flinging himself out of the autocratic realm of necessity into the turbulent anarchy of freedom? What was to stop him?

"Himself! It can only be himself!" he heard a heavily nasal voice exclaim.

Lorenz raised his head to find himself under scrutiny from a single clouded but crafty eye (where the other should have been there was a repulsive pit), by a rangy, long unshaven man in a torn greatcoat, a cap which had lost its peak, and galoshes pulled directly on top of footcloths. He exhaled a smell of vodka through rotten teeth.

"You don't wish to recognise me? You are right, ramoli, quite gone to the dogs. We're admiring the sea? Well we might. To the right, long boats and dikes, shades of brown, beyond which, violet and grey. To the left ruins of the Turkish fort, arcade of the palace. Terrible thing nostalgia. Believe me, I know. Let me give you a clue: Volodya Varuti? The soirees at Lily Kobozev's?"

Lorenz had already recognised him. It was Likhodzievsky, a painter who used to earn a bit with Volodya Varuti painting propaganda pieces for Soviet holidays; a fop from the local jeunesse doree. "If ever I think of marrying," Lorenz recalled him saying, "I shall select my wife on the beach. No two ways about it. How otherwise can you be sure you won't marry one with toes which overlap?" Even in those days Likhodzievsky had talked through his nose, for effect, most probably. But Lorenz could remember much worse things about him than that.

"Good Lord, what has..."

"The War. I sank. I work as a casual porter at the terminals, carting the baskets of fat Jewesses home from the bazaar for them. You were in the war too. You know the score. And while you and I were shedding our blood for the motherland, Volodya Varuti was drawing cartoons of Stalin for Mayor Pynti's newspaper. They gave him fifteen years. Should have been more."

"Yes. It was dreadful."

"Do you remember, we used to joke about him being the illegitimate son of a Romanian viscount. Some joke. His Romanian blood told in the end."

"Well, you know, General Vlasov who commanded the anti-Soviet volunteers..."

"Was a Jew. Real name Waldman. Used to be in the Cheka executing counter-revolutionaries. To the point: are you back at the University?"

"No, I work in a cooperative, as an accountant."

"Well you might. Everyone's got to live. No two ways about it. I was going to ask you for a fiver, but as you're working in a co-op, give us a corner. Slang for twenty-five. Or are you a bastard?"

Lorenz pulled three roubles out of his side pocket.

"You're a pal. Same address? Chemadurova Buildings? I'll be round to trouble you. Adieu in English."

Likhodzievsky did not, however, depart just yet.

"Good parties those were at Lily's," he said suddenly, raising the eyebrow over his empty eye socket and shifting his foot around in the overshoe. "Where is she, by the way? Don't know? I still remember something you once said. I'm not sucking up to you, although I've nothing against sucking up to people, but I don't have to, do I? You've already given me money, and you will again."

"What was it I said?" Lorenz asked, smiling somewhat wanly. Crippled and penniless though he now was, might Likhodzievsky still be dangerous?

"Remember it word for word, and just think how many years have passed; and a war. We've all been well shaken up. On that carefree summer evening you said, "The concept of realism should be replaced by the concept of literature and art for God and human beings. This naturally means that socialist realism is literature and art for the Devil and inhuman beings. Modernism is idolatry, and idols can be beautiful or monstrous". I've remembered it right? What talent! I refer to myself."

He moved over to the parapet, a one-eyed tramp who retained the swaggering gait of a young dandy. He did what Lorenz would have liked to have done in the first place: leap over the parapet and slither down to the port and the boat terminal.

Lorenz recalled that Dina Sosnovik had asked him to buy a loaf on the way back (a round one, though, from a proper bakery). He had no money left. Again she would be saying, "Misha, you are so educated, but you don't know anything".

The siren sounded. Was that three thirty or four? Four most likely. Time to get to the library.

Lorenz had seen a great change come over the Public Library. There were fewer and fewer eccentric readers. Even in the 1930s there had been oddballs: the dark-browed young man with the Christ-like face, who walked barefoot in a long smock which came down to his heels; the top-hatted Armenian in his morning coat, emphasising an extraordinary resemblance to Pushkin by wearing sideburns; the mathematician, a round-shouldered country lad, who insisted he had made a major discovery. People wanted rare books then: magazines were only read to kill time. There was a spacious smoking area in the basement beside the toilets, a true political club and academy of sciences. Some readers headed straight for it, including some who were non-smokers, and spent long, pleasurable hours there. Now only schoolchildren and students came to the Public Library, and occasionally respectable, neatly dressed academics; and all that was asked for were the current textbooks. There were no fanatical bookworms any more, just long queues where the conversation was barely literate. Lorenz was not engaged in serious study either. He read old, pre-revolutionary magazines and newspapers, burying himself in the remote past and memories of life as it used to be. And who is to say it is not memories such as these which give birth to the future?

Translated by Arch Tait

Novy mir, Nos. 9-10, 1992

Semyon Lipkin

Semyon Lipkin was born into a Jewish family in Odessa in 1911 and has personally experienced most of the events described in his A Resident Remembers.

Until perestroika, when his poetry and prose were first extensively published in Russia, he was principally known as the outstanding translator of many Central Asian epic works. Vasily Grossman's **Stalingrad**, Lipkin's reminiscences of his close friend, the author of **Life and Fate**, was published in 1986 by Ardis.

A Resident Remembers is an original blend of fictionalised autobiography, vivid sketches of life in old Odessa, and reflections on the nature of history and society. It traces the life of the inhabitants of Mme Chemadurova's house in Odessa through the first half of this century as they encounter a succession of conquerors and occupiers, Bolsheviks and Ukrainian nationalists, Romanians and German Nazis. It ends with the return of the hero, a Russian German, Lorenz, in 1945 to find his childhood home in ruins.

Sleeper at Harvest Time
by Leonid LATYNIN

Translated by Andrew Bromfield
256 pp. Illustrated with 12 woodcuts by Timur Iskhakov
Zephyr Press, 13 Somerville, MA 02145, USA

Writing in incantatory, magical style, Leonid Latynin invokes the entire history of Russia in the story of Emelya, born of the sorceress Leta and fathered by a bear in the deep pagan past. Emelya traverses the ages, witnessing the major catastrophes that befall Russia, including its violent conversion to Christianity and the rise of the wounded civilization in post-apocalyptic Moscow in which citizens are segregated according to blood type, and can only mix below the surface in the pitch blackness of the ruined Metro. Through Emelya, Latynin makes Russian history the novel's protagonist, embellishing it with a reworking of myths and folktales and with an underlying theme of human sacrifice.

THE RUSSIAN EDITION OF THE BOOK IS ALSO AVAILABLE.

GlaShort List

VICTOR PELEVIN

Omon Ra

excerpt

I don't remember the exact moment when I decided to enroll in a flying school, probably because this decision had ripened in my mind – and in Mitiok's – long before we graduated from high school. For a little while we faced the problem of choice – there were a lot of flying schools around the country – but we decided everything very quickly once we saw a coloured double-page insert in the magazine "Soviet Aviation", all about life in the Lunar Village at the Maresiev Red Banner Flying School in Zaraisk. We immediately felt like we were there among the crowd of students, among the yellow-painted plywood mountains and craters, we could see our future selves in the close-cropped young men turning somersaults on the gymnastic turnstile and dousing themselves with the water captured and frozen by the camera as it fell from the large enamelled basin that was such a tender peach colour you immediately remembered your childhood, and somehow the colour made you trust the picture more and made you want to go to Zaraisk.

I remember the town of Zaraisk. Or rather, I can't really say I either remember it or I've forgotten it – there's so little in the place either to forget or remember.

Right in the centre was a tall bell-tower of white stone, from which long ago some princess leapt on to the stones below, and despite all the centuries that had passed, the townspeople remembered her for it. Next to the tower was the history museum, and not far from that were the telegraph office and police station.

When we got out of the bus, a nasty slanting rain was falling, and it was cold.

We went to look for the other bus to take us further, to our destination, and found the same one in which we'd arrived. It turned out we needn't have got out, we could have waited out the rain in the bus while the driver was having his lunch. Small wooden houses began drifting past the windows, one after the other, then they stopped and the forest began. The Zaraisk Flying School was in the forest, well away from the town. It had to be reached by walking about five kilometres from the final bus stop, which was called "Vegetable Shop" (there was no shop anywhere near, but we were told the name was left over from before the war). Mitiok and I got off the bus and set off along a road which led us deeper and deeper into the forest, and just when we were beginning to think we were going the wrong way we suddenly came up against gates made of welded metal pipes, with large tin stars on them; on both sides the forest ran up to a tall fence of grey, unpainted planks with rusty barbed wire coiling along its top. We showed the sleepy soldier on guard duty our warrants from the district military enlistment office and the passports we had received only recently; we were admitted and told to go to the club, where a meeting was about to begin.

Immediately to the right of an asphalted roadway leading into the centre of a small settlement was the beginning of the Lunar Village I had seen in the magazine – it consisted of several long single-storey barracks buildings painted yellow, a dozen or so tyres dug into the ground, and a special plot designed to look like a panoramic view of the surface of the Moon. We walked past it and came to the garrison club, where the boys who had come to enrol were crowded around the columns. Soon an officer came out, appointed someone sergeant, ordered us to register with the examination committee and then go and collect our kit.

Because it was hot the examination committee was sitting in a lattice-work pavilion in the yard of the club – three officers drinking beer and listening to quiet eastern music on the radio as they gave out numbered squares of cardboard in exchange for passports. Then they led us over to the edge of a sports-field overgrown with grass that was waist-high (it was obvious no-one had played any kind of sport on it for about ten years), and issued us with two general-army tents, which we were to live in during the exams...

I can hardly remember the actual exams. All I do remember is that they weren't difficult at all, and there was no chance to fill up the answer paper with all the formulae and graphs that had absorbed the long days of spring and summer spent poring over the pages of textbooks. It was no problem for Mitiok and me to get a passing mark, and then came the interview, which scared everyone more than anything else...

"Do you realise how difficult it is to fly into outer space?" asked the little old man with the scar on his forehead, wearing tattered technician's overalls, who was conducting the interview, "and what if your Motherland requires you to lay your life? What then, eh?"

"If it comes to it..." I said with a frown.

He stared me right in the eyes for maybe three minutes.

"I believe you," he said. "You can do it."

When he heard that Mitiok, who had wanted to fly to the Moon since he was a baby was joining too, he noted down his name on a piece of paper. Mitiok told me afterwards that the old man spent a long time asking him why he particularly wanted to go to the Moon.

Next day after breakfast, lists of the successful applicants appeared on the columns of the garrison club: my name and Mitiok's were beside each other in the list, out of alphabetical order. Some of the boys trudged off to appeal, some of them jumped up and down for joy on the asphalt crisscrossed with white lines, and high above it all I recall the white streak of a vapour trail in a colourless sky.

Those of us who were enrolled as first-year cadets were summoned to a meeting with the flight-training staff – the teachers were already waiting for us in the club. I remember heavy velvet drapes and a table across the full width of the stage, with officers sitting at it looking strict and official. The meeting was chaired by a youthful-looking lieutenant-colonel with a skinny pointed nose: while he was talking, I imagined myself in flying-suit and pressurized helmet, sitting in the cabin of a MiG fighter covered in blotches, like expensive jeans.

"O.K. boys, we don't want to begin by talking about scary stuff, do we? But you know well enough we don't get to choose the times we live in — the times choose us. Maybe I shouldn't be giving you this kind of information, but I'm going to tell you anyway..."

The lieutenant-colonel paused for a second, bent down to the major sitting beside him and whispered something in his ear. The major grimaced, rapped thoughtfully on the table with his pencil, and then nodded.

"Right," said the lieutenant-colonel in a quiet voice, "at a recent closed session of the political instructors of the armed forces, the times we are living in were defined as a pre-war period!"

The colonel paused, waiting for a response, but clearly the audience hadn't understood a thing — at least Mitiok and I hadn't.

"Let me explain," he went on, even more quietly. "The meeting was on July fifteenth, right? So up until July fifteenth we were living in a post-war period, but since then — a whole month already — we've been living in a pre-war period, is that clear or not?"

For a few seconds there was silence in the hall.

"I'm not saying this to scare you," the lieutenant-colonel went on, in a normal voice now, "but we have to remember the responsibility we bear on our shoulders, don't we? And make no mistake about it, by the time you get your diplomas and your ranks, you'll be Real Men with a great big capital M, the kind that only exist in the land of Soviets."

Then the major stood up.

"Boys," he said in a melodious voice, "although it would be more correct now to call you cadets, but I'm just going to call you boys anyway. Boys! Remember the story of the legendary legless pilot immortalised by Boris Polevoi: "The Story of a Real Man". The hero our college is named after! Despite losing both legs in combat, he didn't lose heart, he rose again on artificial legs and soared up into the sky like Icarus to strike at the fascist scum! Many people told him it was impossible , but he never forget what was most important — that he was a Soviet man! And you must never forget this, never, wherever you are! All of the flight-training staff and I personally, as assistant flight political instructor, promise that we will make Real Men of you in the shortest possible time!"

Then they showed us our places in the first-year cadets' barracks we were being moved into from the tents, and took us to the mess-hall, where the dusty MiGs and ILs dangling on strings from the ceiling seemed like immense flying islands beside the squadrons of swift black flies. After we'd eaten we felt really sleepy; Mitiok and I barely made it to our beds, and I fell asleep straight away.

The next morning I was woken by a loud groan of pain and confusion right in my ear. In fact I'd been hearing the same sounds in my sleep for a long time, but I was only jerked into full wakefulness by a particularly loud and piteous wail. I opened my eyes and looked around. The beds round about were alive with a strange squirming and muffled bellowing – I tried to prop myself up on my elbow, but I couldn't, because I was bound to the bed with broad straps: the most I could do was turn my head slightly from side to side. From the next bed I met the pain-filled eyes of Slava, a young village boy I had got to know the day before, and the lower part of his face was hidden by a tightly-tied piece of cloth... I tried to open my mouth to ask him what was wrong, but discovered that I couldn't move my tongue, and I had no feeling at all in the lower part of my face, as though it had gone numb. I guessed that my mouth must be gagged and bound too, but before I could feel surprised, I was struck by horror – where Slava's legs should have been, the blanket fell straight down in an abrupt step, and the freshly-starched blanket cover was stained with red blotches like the marks left on cotton towels by melon water. What was even more terrifying – I couldn't feel my own legs and I couldn't lift my head to look at them!

"Platoon five!" – the words thundered out in a sergeant's fruity bass, replete with an infinitude of allusions – "to the dressing station!"

About ten men immediately came into the ward – they were second and third year students (or more correctly – cadets in their second or third year of service, I could tell from the stripes on their sleeves). I hadn't seen them before – the officers had said they were out helping with the potato harvest. They were wearing strange boots with tops that didn't bend, and they walked unsteadily, holding on to the walls or the ends of the beds. I noticed how pale and unhealthy their faces were, they seemed to bear the imprint of long days of interminable torment, to have been recast in a fixed expression of preparedness.

The cadets wheeled the beds out into the corridor one after another, with the first-years bound on to them moaning and squirming, until only two were left in the room – mine and one by the window, on which Mitiok was lying. I couldn't get a proper look at him because of the straps, but I could see out of the corner of my eye that he was lying quietly and seemed to be asleep.

They came for us about ten minutes later, turned us round feet first, and wheeled us along the corridor. One cadet pushed the bed while another walked backwards and pulled it towards him; it looked like he was backing down the corridor and warding off the bed as it pursued him. We trundled into a long narrow lift with doors at both sides and went up, the second-year student backed away from me down another corridor, and we stopped beside a door upholstered in black with a large brown plaque that I couldn't read because of my uncomfortable position. The door opened, and I was rolled into a room with an immense crystal chandelier in the shape of an aircraft bomb hanging from the ceiling, and the upper section of the walls decorated with a band of bas-relief ornamentation made up of sickles, hammers and urns entwined with grapevines.

They took my straps off, and I propped myself up on my elbows, trying not to look at my legs. The person sitting at the desk was hidden from me by the open pages of a copy of *Pravda*, from the front of which a wrinkly face with radiantly kind eyes stared straight at me. The lino on the floor squeaked, and Mitiok's bed came to a halt beside mine.

The newspaper rustled a few times as its pages were turned, and then sank down on to the table.

There in front of us was the little old man with the scar on his forehead, the one who had grabbed me by the arm during the interview. Now he was wearing the uniform of a lieutenant-general with brocade at the button-holes, his hair was neatly brushed down, and his gaze was clear and sober. I noticed that his face seemed like a copy of the one that was looking at me from the front page of *Pravda* just a minute before.

"Now boys, since you and I will be seeing quite a lot of each other for quite a long time, you can call me Comrade Flight Leader," said the old man. "Allow me to congratulate you on the results of your exams – and the interview in particular," the old man winked. "You have been registered immediately for the first year course at the secret space training school of the USSR Committee of State Security – so you'll just have to wait a bit before you become Real Men. Meanwhile get ready to go to Moscow. I'll see you there."

I didn't realise what he'd said till we'd been taken back to the empty ward along those long corridors, where the lino sang its quiet song of nostalgia beneath the tiny castors of the bed.

Mitiok and I slept the whole day – it seems they'd drugged our supper the previous evening (I was still sleepy the next day), and that evening a jolly yellow-haired lieutenant in squeaky boots came for us, and laughed and cracked jokes as he wheeled our beds out on to the asphalt parade-ground in front of the concrete sea-shell of the variety theatre, where several senior generals with kind intelligent faces, including Comrade Flight Leader, were sitting at a table. Of course, Mitiok and I could have walked there on our own, but the lieutenant said that this was standing orders for first-year cadets, and he ordered us to lie still so as not to upset the others.

All those beds stacked up against each other made the parade-ground look like the yard of an automobile factory or a tractor plant: a subdued groaning traced a complex flight path above it – dying away in one place, it sprang up in another, and then in a third, as though some huge invisible mosquito was darting about above the beds. On the way out the yellow-haired lieutenant told us that a combined graduation party and final state exam was about to begin.

Soon we were watching our lieutenant, the first of about fifty like him, as he danced the "Kalinka" for the exam committee. He was pale and nervous, but he performed with incomparable mastery, to the sparse accompaniment of the assistant political instructor's accordion. Then the same dance was performed by all the others, and by the end I was bored stiff watching them. I turned to look at the sports field immediately beside the parade-ground – and suddenly realised why it lay under such a thick covering of wild grass.

I lay there and watched the stems swaying in the wind. The grey, rain-cracked fence topped with barbed wire just beyond the ruined soccer goal-posts seemed to me like the Great Wall, still stretching, despite all the warped and missing planks, all the way from the fields of distant China to the town of Zaraisk, making everything that appeared against its background look Chinese – the latticework pavilion where the exam committee worked when it was hot, the obsolete fighter-plane, and the ancient general-army tents I could see from where I lay on my bed.

Translated by Andrew Bromfield

Published in Russian by Text Publishers, Moscow, 1992.

Victor Pelevin's *Omon Ra* is a strange and compelling story of one man's fascination with space – which takes him from his Moscow childhood dreams of flight to the moon, through the training ground of a Soviet Flying School and KGB headquarters, to selection as a cosmonaut for despatch on his final mission, for the greater glory of the Motherland.

But all is not what it seems... For Omon, the novel's hero, each new step in his journey brings a new revelation – and further disillusionment of his ideals about the preeminence of Soviet space achievements. The ironic detachment of Victor Pelevin's narrative exploits to the full the absurdity of his subject, with an ingenuity characteristic of a writer who is establishing a reputation as one of the most promising figures of his generation – one whose philosophic concerns go beyond the particular details of his subject matter.

The extract printed here opens with the arrival of Omon and his childhood friend, Mitiok, at Flying School. The examinations which mark the beginning of their journey will end with an unexpected twist – one which is all the more horrific for the casual banality of its setting.

Omon Ra will be published by the London-based publishing house, Harbord Publishing, in September 1994, in a translation by Andrew Bromfield. Appearing in a single volume with another novella by Pelevin, *The Yellow Arrow*, it will be the first title in a contemporary fiction list which will introduce English-language readers to the best of writing from Russia and Europe.

For further information about future titles, contact
Tom Birchenough at Harbord Publishing,
58 Harbord Street, London SW6 6PJ.

Tarzanka

The wide boulevard with houses ranged along its sides brought to mind the lower jaw of an old Bolshevik who had come to democratic views in his declining years.

The oldest buildings were from Stalin's time – they reached upward like wisdom teeth stained by many years of cheap tobacco smoking. For all their monumental size they appeared fragile, dead, as if the nerve had long ago been replaced by fillings. In places the old structures had been destroyed, and crudely fashioned, eight-story pre-fab apartment buildings stuck out like false teeth. In short, it was a gloomy sight.

The only bright spot on this joyless landscape was the business center that had been built by the Turks, looking, with its pyramid shape and crimson neon brilliance, like a huge gold fang spattered with drops of fresh blood. And like a bright dentist's lamp, hung on a special bar so that the light fell directly into the patient's mouth, a full moon shone over the city.

"Whom should I believe, what should I believe?" said Pyotr Petrovich, turning to his taciturn companion. "I am a simple man. Maybe even a fool. I am trusting, naive. You know, sometimes I even believe the things I read in the newspaper."

"The newspaper?" repeated his companion tonelessly, adjusting the dark hood covering his head.

"Yes, the newspaper," said Pyotr Petrovich. "Any one, it doesn't matter. You know how it is, you're riding in the metro, someone is sitting beside you reading, you just lean over a little bit, just take a peek, and already you start believing what you see."

"Believing what you see?"

"Yes, you really believe it. Anything at all. Except, maybe, God. It's too late for me to start believing in God. If I suddenly started to believe it would be somehow dishonest. I didn't believe my whole life long, then as I turn fifty I just up and get the faith. What did I live for then? So instead you believe in herbalife or in the separation of powers."

"What for?" asked his companion.

"He's a gloomy sort," thought Pyotr Petrovich. "He doesn't speak, he kind of croaks. What did I have to be so open with him for? I really don't know him at all."

For a while they walked along in silence, one after the other, moving lightly and barely touching the walls with their hands.

"What do you mean, what for?" said Pyotr Petrovich finally. "It's like holding on to something on a bus. It doesn't really matter what, as long as you don't fall. What was it the poet said: 'to rush into the night and the unknown, peering hopefully through the black hole of the window.' So there you are walking along, looking at me and probably thinking: 'So, brother, you're a romantic in your soul, although you don't much look like one.' That's what you're thinking, isn't it?"

His companion turned the corner and disappeared from view. Pyotr Petrovich felt that he had been interrupted in the middle of an important phrase and hurried after him. When he again caught sight of the dark, hunched-over figure up ahead he felt relieved and suddenly thought, apropos of nothing, that his companion in his pointed hood looked like a burned-out church.

"What a romantic you are, brother," muttered the figure.

"I am not a romantic at all," protested Pyotr Petrovich vehemently. "You could even say that I am the complete opposite. I am an extraordinarily practical person. I am all business. You hardly ever think about what you're living for. Certainly not for business, the hell with it. No, not for business, but for..."

"For...?"

"Maybe so that you can walk out of an evening and breathe freely, to feel that you are part of the universe, a small blade of grass, so to speak, in the concrete.... It's just too bad that it is very rare that I feel this so deeply, that it penetrates into my heart. It's probably because of that..."

He raised his arm and pointed to the huge moon shining in the sky, and then realized that his companion was walking on ahead and could not see his gesture. But he must have had eyes in the back of his head or something, because he echoed Pyotr Petrovich's movement almost simultaneously, also extending his arm upward.

"At such times I start to think, what do I do with the rest of my life?" said Pyotr Petrovich. "Why do I so rarely see things the way

I do now? Why do I constantly choose the same thing all the time – to sit in my cell and gaze into the darkest corner?"

These last words with their unexpected accuracy gave Pyotr Petrovich a bitter kind of pleasure, but he suddenly tripped, began to flap his arms, and immediately lost the theme of the conversation. With a monkey-like movement of his torso he maintained his balance, bracing himself against the wall with his hand, while his other hand almost broke a nearby window.

Beyond this window was a small room, lit by a reddish nightlight. It seemed to be a communal apartment – there was a refrigerator among the furniture, and the bed was half-shielded by a wardrobe, so that only the naked, skinny legs of the sleeper were visible. Pyotr Petrovich's gaze fell on the wall above the nightlight, decorated with a multitude of photographs. There were family portraits, pictures of children, adults, old men and women, and dogs; in the center of this exposition was a graduation photo, where the faces were placed in white ovals, which made the whole thing look like a carton of eggs that had been sliced in half. During the second that Pyotr Petrovich was looking into the room, a face yellowed with age managed to smile at him from every oval. All the photographs seemed very old, and from all of them came such an air of a well-lived life that for a moment Pyotr Petrovich felt nauseous, turned quickly and proceeded on his way.

"Yes," he said after he had taken a few steps. "Yes. I know what you are going to say, so don't bother. See, I knew it. It's life experience. We are simply losing the ability to see anything else around us except for dusty photographs from the past, hung in space. And so we look at them, look at them and think, why is it that the world around us has become such a garbage heap? And then, when the moon comes out, you suddenly understand that the world doesn't have anything to do with it, it's just that you yourself have become this way, you just don't know when or why..."

Silence descended. His look at the room – especially those egg-yolk faces, had had a very sobering effect on Pyotr Petrovich. Taking advantage of the fact that no one could see him in the dark, he opened his eyes and mouth very wide and stuck out his tongue, making his face look like an African mask. The physical sensation from this grimace diverted his attention for several seconds from the melancholy that had taken hold of him. He immediately lost the desire to speak – moreover, the whole long conversation, extending over several hours, suddenly seemed stupid and unnecessary bathed as it were in the dim red nightlight from the communal apartment. Pyotr Petrovich glanced at his companion and thought that the latter was too young and not at all bright.

"I really do not understand what we have been talking about," he said in an exaggeratedly polite tone.

His companion did not respond.

"Maybe we should be quiet for a while?" suggested Pyotr Petrovich.

"Be quiet," muttered his companion.

2.

The further Pyotr Petrovich and his companion walked, the more beautiful and mysterious the world around them became. There was really no need for speech. A narrow road lay beneath their feet, shining silver in the moonlight, the constantly changing color of the wall stained first one shoulder, then the other, and the windows floating by were dark, in the manner of the poem that Pyotr Petrovich had recited. Sometimes they had to climb, sometimes they descended, and sometimes, in some silent compact they would suddenly stop and freeze for a moment, gazing at some particularly wonderful sight.

The distant fires were especially beautiful. Several times they stopped to look at them, and each time they stood for a long while gazing – ten minutes or more. Pyotr Petrovich was thinking vague thoughts, almost inexpressible in words. The fires, it turned out, did not have any particular connection to people and were part of nature – either a particular stage in the development of rotting logs, or else stars that were retiring. The night was very dark, and the red and yellow points on the horizon seemed to outline the dimensions of the world around them – without the fires it would have been impossible to determine where there was life, or whether there was life at all.

But his companion's soft steps always brought him out of his reverie. As soon as his companion started off on the path, Pyotr Petrovich came to and hurried after him. Soon the photographs from the window behind were completely forgotten, and his spirits rose again, and the silence began to wear on him.

"And, anyway," thought Pyotr Petrovich, "I don't even know his name. I will have to ask."

He waited several seconds and then asked, very politely,

"Ahem, you know what I was thinking. We've been walking along, talking and talking, and we haven't really even introduced ourselves."

His companion remained silent.

"But, in general," said Pyotr Petrovich in a conciliatory tone, when enough time had passed for it to become clear that there would be no answer, "that is probably as it should be. What do you care about my name, hmm, it is just an empty sign... if you really know someone, and if he knows you, then you do not really talk to him anyway. You think all the time: what does he think of you? what is he going to say about you? But when you don't even know who you are speaking to, then you can say anything you want, because there are no brakes. How long have we been talking? Two hours? Right? You see, and I have been talking almost the whole time. Ordinarily I am a rather quiet man, but now it's as if I have just burst. Perhaps I do not seem very intelligent to you and all that, but I have been listening to myself all this time – especially when we passed those statues, remember? When I was talking about love... yes, I have been listening to myself in amazement. Can it really be true that I understand so much about life, think about it so much?"

Pyotr Petrovich raised his face to the stars and sighed deeply; across his face, like the shadow of an invisible wing, passed an ethereal smile. Suddenly he noticed on his left a small movement, barely noticeable. He shuddered and stopped.

"Hey!" Lowering his voice to a whisper, he called his companion. "Wait! And be quiet! You'll frighten it. It might be a cat... yes, it is. There it is, you see?"

The hood turned to the left, but Pyotr Petrovich, no matter how hard he tried, could not catch a glimpse of his companion's face. But it seemed that he was looking in the wrong place.

"There it is!" said Pyotr Petrovich in an urgent whisper. "You see the bottle? About a half-meter to the left of it. It's moving its tail. So, how about on a count of three? You go to the right, I'll go to the left. Like last time."

His companion shrugged his shoulders coldly, then nodded reluctantly.

"One, two, three!" counted Pyotr Petrovich, and threw his leg over a low tin barrier that weakly reflected the moon's light. His companion followed him instantly, and they dashed forward.

Pyotr Petrovich felt happiness for the umpteenth time that night. He ran under the night sky, and nothing bothered him; all of his problems, which had made his life unbearable a day or two ago, suddenly disappeared, and no matter how hard he tried he could not remember even one of them. Over the black surface under his feet three shadows rushed simultaneously – one, short and dense, was born of the moon, and the other two, asymmetrical and sparse, came from other light sources – probably from windows. Turning to the left, Pyotr Petrovich saw that his companion had turned to the right at the same angle, and when the cat was between them, he turned to it and picked up speed. The figure in the dark hood immediately executed the same maneuver – his movements were so smoothly coordinated to Pyotr Petrovich's own that a vague suspicion pricked at Pyotr Petrovich.

But right now he didn't have time for that. The cat remained seated, which was strange, since cats did not usually allow people so close. The last one, for example, the one they had chased forty minutes or so ago, right after the statue – did not let them get within ten meters. Anticipating some kind of trick, Pyotr Petrovich slowed down, began to walk, then stopped altogether a few steps away from the cat. His companion echoed his movement and stopped at the same instant, about three meters away.

What Pyotr Petrovich had taken to be a cat turned out to be a plastic bag. One of the handles was broken and flapping in the wind – that was the tail that Pyotr Petrovich thought he had seen.

The companion faced Pyotr Petrovich, but his face remained shaded – the moon was in his eyes, and his companion presented that same dark sharp-pointed silhouette. Pyotr Petrovich leaned forward (his companion leaned at the same moment, so that they almost bumped heads). The bag opened, and something soft fell out of it and plopped on the spongy black surface. it was a dead cat, half decomposed.

"That's disgusting," said Pyotr Petrovich and turned away. "I should have known."

"Should have," responded his companion like an echo.

"Let's go," said Pyotr Petrovich and went over to the tin border at the edge of the tar paper field.

3.

They walked in silence for several minutes. Up ahead of Pyotr Petrovich the dark back continued to bob up and down, but now he was not at all sure that it was really a back and not a chest. He half closed his eyes, looking down, trying to get his thoughts in order. All that he could see was the silver road under his feet – the sight of it calmed him, even hypnotized him a bit, and gradually a kind of clarity, not quite sober, flowed into his consciousness, and his thoughts rushed around one after the other with no effort on his part – or, to be more accurate, it was always the same thought about the one in front of him, constantly replacing itself in his head.

"Why does he always repeat my movements?" reasoned Pyotr Petrovich. "And everything that he says is just an echo of my own words. I would have to say that he is acting like a reflection. And there are so many windows around! Maybe it is just an optical illusion, and I am a bit upset, and I am just imagining that there are two of us? There are so many things that people once believed that turned out to be just optical illusions! Almost everything, in fact!"

This thought gave Pyotr Petrovich an unexpected boost. "Yes indeed," he thought. "Moonlight, the reflection of one window in another and the provocative smell of flowers – and you can't forget that it's July – can produce such an effect. And everything he says is just an echo, a faint echo. Of course! he always repeats the words I have just said!"

Pyotr Petrovich looked up suddenly at the regularly bobbing back in front of him. "Besides this, I have read many times," he thought, "that if anyone embarasses you or outsmarts you, there is always the possibility that it is not a separate person, but your own shadow or reflection. The thing is that when you are motionless, or performing some routine, monotonous action, without any thought – for example, when you are walking along and thinking – your reflection can seem to be an independent entity. It can begin to move a little bit out of sync – you won't really notice. It can begin to do things that you are not doing yourself – but only, of course, if it is something unimportant. Finally, it can become very bold, and begin to believe that it really does exist, and then begin to act against you... as far as I know, there is only one way to determine whether or not it is a reflection – you have to make some sharp and definite motion, so that your reflection will have to repeat it. Because it is; after all, just a reflection, and it has to obey the laws of nature, at least some of them... so, I have to try to distract him with conversation, and then do something really unexpected, sharp, and watch what happens. I can talk about anything at all – the main thing is not to think about it too much."

Clearing his throat, he said,

"It is a good thing that you are a man of few words. Listening is also an art. It makes the other guy open himself up, talk, and they say that the quiet ones are the most reliable friends on earth. You know what I'm thinking?"

Pyotr Petrovich waited for a question, but there was none forthcoming, so he continued:

"I am thinking that I really love a summer night. Of course – it is quiet and dark. Beautiful. But that is not the main thing. Sometimes it seems to me that there is part of my soul that sleeps all the time, and only on a summer's night does it wake up for a few seconds, to look out and remember how it was, long ago and far away... the dark blue of the sky... the stars... the mystery..."

4.

Soon it got noticeably more difficult to walk.

The reason for this was that around yet another corner they ended up on the dark side, where the moon was blocked by the roof of the house across the street. Right after this Pyotr Petrovich was seized by melancholy and indecision. He continued to speak, although forming the words was agonizing and distasteful. It seemed that something similar was happening to his companion, because he stopped holding up his end of the conversation with even short answers – sometimes he just muttered something unintelligible.

Their steps became shorter and more cautious. From time to time the companion in front even stopped to think about where to go next

– he was always the one to make the decision, and Pyotr Petrovich could do nothing but follow after him.

A square of bright moonlight appeared on a wall in front of them, coming through the break in the houses opposite. Once more raising his eyes from the now dim silver road under his feet, Pyotr Petrovich saw a thick coil of electric cable hanging by the wall. A plan instantly formed in his head, a plan that seemed to him extraordinarily natural, and not without a bit of wit.

"Aha," he thought, "This is what I can do. I can grab hold of this thing and kick off from the wall. And if he is really a reflection or a shadow, then he will have to show himself. That is to say, he will have to do the same thing I am doing, but without the cable, and to the other side... Even better – yes! Why didn't I think of this earlier! Even better, I could just swing right into him. And if he is a reflection, or some other kind of bastard, then..."

Pyotr Petrovich could not really complete the thought, but it was clear that this was the way to either confirm or dispel the suspicion that was torturing him.

"The main thing is to do it suddenly," he thought, "to catch him unawares!"

"By the way," he said, shifting smoothly onto a new theme in their long conversation, "water skis are fine, but the most surprising thing is that even in the city you can get closer to the primitive world, if you just get away from all the bustle for awhile. We, of course, cannot manage this – we are too set in our ways. But children, I assure you, do it every day."

Pyotr Petrovich paused, giving his companion time to answer, but he kept silent. Pyotr Petrovich continued:

"I mean, their games. Of course, they are often ugly and cruel; sometimes you even get the feeling that these games arise from the filthy poverty that today's children have to live in. But I somehow think that it is not poverty that is to blame. It isn't the fact that they can't have a motorcycle or a skateboard. For example, there is this thing called a tarzanka. Have you ever heard of it?"

"Heard of it," his companion muttered.

"It is a cable that they tie to a tree, to a thick branch, the higher the better," continued Pyotr Petrovich, peering at the square of moonlight and calculating that there was less than a minute to go before they reached it. "Especially if the tree is near a precipice. The main thing is for it to be really steep. Even better if it's near water, then you can dive. They call it a tarzanka because of Tarzan, there was a movie where Tarzan was always swinging on these vines. It's really easy to use these things – you just grab the rope, push off with your feet, and make a long, long arc, and if you want, you let go and fall into the water. To tell you the truth, I've never swung on a tarzanka, but I can really picture that second when, after hitting the surface with a loud slap, you slowly sink into the glinting darkness, into cool peace... Oh, if only I could find out where these boys fly to on their vines..."

His companion stepped into the pool of moonlight. After him Pyotr Petrovich also crossed the moonlit boundary.

"And you know why I can imagine it?" he continued, anxiously measuring the distance to the cable with his eye. "Very simple. I remember once in my childhood jumping off a diving board into a pool. I hurt my stomach, of course, when I hit the water, but I understood something very important at that moment – something that later, when I had come up out of the water, I kept saying to myself: "Don't forget, don't forget." But by the time I had climbed out onto the side, all I could remember was thinking, "Don't forget.""

At that instant Pyotr Petrovich drew even with the cable. He stopped, touched it with his hand, and made sure that it was firmly anchored.

"Even now, sometimes," he said, getting ready to jump, his voice becoming quiet and sincere, "I feel like just taking off, with my feet off the ground. It's stupid, of course, childish, but I still think you would understand or remember something major. Well, here goes, with your permission..."

With these words Pyotr Petrovich took a few quick steps, kicked off heartily and soared into the warm night air.

His flight (if you could call it that) did not last very long. About two meters away from the wall executing a turn on his axis, he flew forward and crashed into the wall right in front of his companion, who took a frightened step backwards. But Pyotr Petrovich lost his balance, and had to grab him by the shoulder, after which, of course, it became clear that what he had in front of him was no reflection and no shadow.

All of this was very awkward, accompanied by a lot of puffing and panting. The companion reacted to the surprise very irritably. Brushing Pyotr Petrovich's hand from his shoulder, he jumped back, pulled the hood from his head and cried out sharply:

"What are you trying to pull here?"

"I'm very sorry," said Pyotr Petrovich, feeling himself turn crimson, and glad of the darkness around him. "Honestly, I didn't do it on purpose. I..."

"What did you tell me?" interrupted his companion. "You said everything would be quiet, that you were not violent, that you just had nobody to talk to. Isn't that what you said?"

"Yes," babbled Pyotr Petrovich, burying his face in his hands. "I said that. I really did, how could I have forgotten... But these stupid thoughts came into my head — that you were not you, you were just my reflection in glass, or my shadow. It's funny, isn't it?"

"I don't think it's funny at all," said his companion. "Have you finally remembered who I am, at least?"

"Yes," said Pyotr Petrovich, and made a strange movement of his head, as if he were bowing, maybe, or just drawing his head into his shoulders.

"Thank God. And so you decided to jump on me to see whether or not I was a reflection? And you kept blabbing about the tarzanka to throw me off? "

"No, of course not, what are you saying!" cried Pyotr Petrovich, taking one hand off the electric cable and placing it on his chest. "That is, at the beginning, maybe, I really did want to distract you, but only at the beginning. But when I started talking, I immediately began to think about something that had bothered me my whole life. As if I were making a confession...

"You say some pretty strange things," said his companion. "I am even starting to fear for your sanity. Just think — we walk for two hours side by side, talking, and after this you seriously think that you are faced with your reflection. Could this happen to a normal person?"

Pyotr Petrovich gave this some thought.

"N-No," he said, "it couldn't. I know it looks really strange from the outside. A talking reflection, that walks with its back to you... Some kind of tarzanka... but you know, it all seemed so logical that if I could tell you how my thinking progressed, you wouldn't be so surprised.

He raised his eyes. The moon over the roof opposite had gone behind a long, ragged cloud. For some reason this seemed to him a bad omen.

"Yes," he began again. "If you analyze the subconscious motivation for my actions, then I, it seems, just wanted one second of triumph..."

"As for the reflection," interrupted his companion, raising his voice, "I could maybe accept that, okay. But what you were saying about the tarzanka seems even stranger to me. That business where you let your feet leave the ground and understand something major. What is it you want to understand, really?"

Pyotr Petrovich raised his eyes, met his companion's gaze, and then immediately transferred his glance to his companion's shaved head.

"What do you mean, what," he said. "It makes me uncomfortable to utter banalities. Truth."

"What truth?" asked his companion, putting the hood back up over his head. "About yourself, about others, about the world? There are lots of truths."

Pyotr Petrovich again sank into thought.

"I guess, about myself," he said. "Or, better, about life. About myself and about life. Of course."

"So, should I tell you?" asked his companion.

"Well, go ahead, if you know," answered Pyotr Petrovich with sudden animosity.

"Aren't you afraid that this truth will be like that cat in the bag?" asked his companion, with the same harsh tone, gesturing with his head to a point further back.

"He is insinuating something," thought Pyotr Petrovich. "He is making fun of me. He is putting psychological pressure on me. But he has picked the wrong person. And what kind of sadism is this, anyway? So I grabbed his shoulder, I apologized for it."

"No," he said, squaring his shoulders and directing his gaze right into his companion's eyes. "I am not afraid. Go ahead, say it."

"Okay then. Does the word 'sleepwalker' mean anything to you?"

"Sleepwalker? That's someone who doesn't sleep at night, who walks out on ledges... I know. Oh my God!"

5.

The sudden awakening was much like the jump into cold water that Pyotr Petrovich kept trying to tell his merciless companion about – and not only because it was cold. Pyotr Petrovich looked under his feet and saw that the thin silver road that he had walked for so long was, in fact, a rather narrow tin ledge, bent dangerously under the weight of his body.

Under the ledge was emptiness, and beyond the emptiness, approximately thirty meters below, burned streetlights, doubled by their reflections in puddles, the black crowns of trees shook in the wind, the asphalt glowed grey, and all of this, as Pyotr Petrovich realized to his terror, was absolutely and definitely real – that is, there was no possibility of ignoring or getting around the fact that he, in his underwear, barefoot, was standing high above the sleeping city, by some miracle keeping from plunging downward. He was keeping himself from falling by a miracle – there was nothing for his palms to grab on to, except for the minute roughness of a concrete wall, and if he just leaned out a bit from its cold damp surface, the implacable force of gravity would draw him downward. Not far from him there was an electric cable – but in order to reach it, he would have to take several steps along the ledge, and he could not even think about doing that. Looking down, he could see a parking lot far below, and cars the size of cigarette packs, and a penny-sized spot of empty asphalt, left, it seemed, especially for him."

The main testimony to the fact that this nightmare was genuine was the smell of burning garbage – a smell that immediately removed all question and that seemed to contain a self-sufficient proof of the ultimate reality of a world where such odors are possible.

A wave of panic swept through Pyotr Petrovich, washing everything else away in a fraction of a second. The emptiness behind his back sucked at him, and he flattened himself against the wall just like a political campaign flyer from a little-known party with absolutely no chance of success.

"Well, how do you like it?" asked his companion.

Pyotr Petrovich cautiously – so as not to look again at the chasm beneath his feet – glanced at him.

"Stop it," he said, quietly but very insistently. "Please, stop it. I'm going to fall!"

His companion snorted.

"How can I stop it? It's not happening to me, it's happening to you."

Pyotr Petrovich understood that his companion was right, but in the next second he understood something else as well, which filled him instantly with indignation.

"That's pretty low," he yelled, terribly upset. "You could say that to anyone, that he is a sleepwalker and is poised over emptiness, and just cannot see it! On a ledge... but we were just... and here..."

"That's right," nodded his companion. "You can't imagine how right you are."

"So why did you do this to me?"

"You know, I just don't understand you. First you say one thing, then another. You were just going on and on about flying on a tarzanka. I was really touched, believe me. Then, you wanted to hear the truth. This, by the way, is not the final truth."

"So what do I do now?"

"You? Nothing," said his companion, and it suddenly became obvious that he was not holding on to anything and was even standing a little bit at an angle. "Everything will work out."

"Are you making fun of me?" hissed Pyotr Petrovich.

"Of course not."

"You are a villain!" said Pyotr Petrovich with impotent rage. "Murderer. You have murdered me. I am going to fall."

"Well, now it's starting," said his companion, "insults, hatred. In a minute you'll jump on me again, or you'll start spitting at me, like some do. I'm leaving."

He turned around and calmly began walking away.

"Hey!" yelled Pyotr Petrovich. "Hey! Wait! Please!"

But his companion did not stop – he just waved a pale hand weakly in farewell, the hand that protruded from the sleeve of his garment – a cassock or a long dark raincoat, it was hard to tell. A few steps and he had turned the corner and disappeared from view. Pyotr Petrovich closed his eyes again and leaned his damp forehead against the wall.

"Well, this is it," he thought. "Now it's really over. It's the end.

My whole life I've been thinking, how will it happen? And, it turns out, it will be like this. I will start to sway, I'll flap my arms, and... Calm down, Pyotr, calm down. I wonder, will I scream? Pyotr, Pyotr, calm down... Don't think about it. Think about something else, anything else, just not about that. Please. The main thing is to keep calm, at any price. Panic means death. Think about something pleasant... what can I think about? Just today, for example, what was nice about it? Maybe the conversation near the statue, when I was telling that shaven-headed guy about love... Oh, God, I've thought about him again. What an idiot I am. I couldn't just keep walking, looking around and enjoying life. No, I had to start thinking about whether he was a shadow or a reflection. So I got what I deserved. I should read a lot less nonsense. But who is he, anyway? That's the hell of it − I did remember just a little while ago. Or maybe not, maybe I didn't remember, maybe he said himself... Where did he come from?"

Pyotr Petrovich opened his eyes for a second and saw that the wall near his face was yellow and shining − the moon had once again emerged from behind the clouds. For some reason this made him feel better.

"So," he continued his train of thought, "where did I meet him? Before the statues, that's for sure. When the statues appeared he was already beside me. And we chased the first cat before the statues. Yes, that's right − at first he just wouldn't agree to it. And then I just burst − I began to talk to him about nature, about beauty − but I knew I shouldn't talk, that I should keep it all inside me, if I didn't want people to just spit into my soul... Who is it in the Bible... don't cast pearls before the swine, they will just stamp them into the ground, isn't that right? Life is like that. Even if some little thing makes you happy, like how the moon lights up the statues, you have to keep quiet. You have to keep quiet all the time, because if you open your mouth you'll be sorry. But it's interesting, I've known this for a long time, but I still suffer for being too trusting. Every time I just wait until they spit in my soul... And that guy was just a bastard, bastard! Then he has the nerve to say that it will all work out. So patronizing... The hell with him, really, I've been thinking about him for ages, and now the moon is hiding. I am giving him too much credit."

Pyotr Petrovich turned away from the wall, looked up and smiled weakly. The moon was shining through a small fluffy hole in the cloud and seemed, because of this, to be its own reflection in a non-existent pool. The city below was quiet and still, and the air was filled with a barely discernible scent of God knows what grasses.

Somewhere in a distant window Sting began singing in a pirate bass, perhaps too loud for the night hour. It was "Moon over Bourbon Street" – a song that Pyotr Petrovich remembered and loved from his youth. Forgetting everything, he began to listen, and in one place even began blinking rapidly, remembering something he had forgotten long ago.

Gradually the pain and the hurt subsided. The quarrel with his casual companion seemed more and more insubstantial with each passing second , until at last he could no longer understand why he had been so upset just a few minutes before. When Sting's voice began to weaken, Pyotr Petrovich took his hand from the wall and even tapped his fingers a few times to the beat of the despairing English words:

> *And you'll never see my face*
> *hear the sound of my feet*
> *while there's a moon over Bourbon Street.*

At last the song was over. Sighing, Pyotr Petrovich shook his head to clear it. It was time to go home.

He turned back, stepped around the corner, and lightly jumped down a few meters where the going was easier. The night was still just as mysterious and tender, and he really did not want to let it go, but he had a lot to do the next morning, and he had to get at least a little sleep. He looked around for the last time, then glanced up, smiled and slowly picked his way along the glimmering silver strip, kissing the night wind and thinking that, in essence, he was a completely happy man.

Translated by Jean Mackenzy

Victor Pelevin

Born in 1962, Pelevin graduated from the Moscow Aviation College and worked at a design office for a while before beginning to write professionally. He has been one of the most talked about authors of recent years, his stories first appearing in the Moscow literary magazine **Znamya**, and then in book form with Text Publishers.

Omon Ra can be compared to Zamyatin's **We**, Orwell's **1984** and Bradbury's **Fahrenheit 451**. In 1994, **Omon Ra** is coming out in German translation from Reclam Publishers. His other novel, **The Life of Insects**, published in **Znamya** in 1993, has been nominated for the Russian Novel Booker Prize.

"Pelevin takes off on a flight of imagination into space beyond the ideological and material expanses of Soviet reality. The story is firmly rooted in the tangible, yet the protagonist's aspirations and ambitions—to leave earth for the moon—constantly and ironically undermine the import of the surface story, thus suggesting endless paradoxes between the Soviet dream and reality."—Riitta Pittman.

To this we would only like to add that criticism of the various phenomena of Soviet life is still very germane, because Russians haven't stopped being Soviet overnight. Much of what was poisoning life in Russia is still present, and still needs to be examined and dealt with.

Victor Pelevin's collection of short stories
BLUE LAMP
won the 1993 "Little Booker" Prize.

The "Little Booker" prize, worth 2,500 British pounds and sponsored by an anonymous donor, is awarded for a different category of literary and publishing endeavour each year. The first year "Little Booker" prize was shared by two small literary journals: *Solo* (Moscow) and *Vestnik novoi literatury* (St Petersburg). The second year it was for a collection of short stories and was won by Victor Pelevin. The 1994 "Little Booker" prize will be awarded to the provincial journal that has done most to promote literature in the provinces.

ZUFAR GAREYEV

The Park
Two characters

The Watchman Potemkin

There was once a certain watchman called Potemkin. One day on returning home from work – at about nine o'clock in the morning – he discerned that it was stuffy in his apartment, and as a result, psychologically oppressive. In order to let some air into the apartment, he opened the windows. Meanwhile he sat down in the kitchen and began drinking beer, adding to it small amounts of a stronger liquid.

"To cheer me up," the watchman said to himself. An hour later he sensed in his head a deep-set mental heaviness, an intellectual stagnation, a kind of drowsy buzzing. The watchman Potemkin passed about twenty minutes in this state, but he didn't start feeling any more cheerful, even though he tried launching into a dance to liven himself up. The sensation of drowsiness began acquiring density and settling down inside Potemkin like an overfed pig.

After half an hour spent staring into a plate on which nestled a lump of meat as dreary as a yawn, for the sake of variety he began glancing out of the window in an attempt to provide his mind with some nourishment. But his eyes described nothing beyond the window, even though they almost tumbled out of their sockets precisely in order to obtain a closer look at the surrounding reality. However, it contained no objects capable of mental interpretation by Potemkin. Then the watchman Potemkin began staring curiously at the ceiling.

After almost fifteen minutes had passed, the watchman's lower jaw began to droop, and his mouth began to assume the form of the letter "O". Amidst the luxuriant growth of hairs in the watchman's nose there was born a subtle, whistling music, beautiful in its own peculiar way: a couple of flies darted into the watchman's nostrils and observed the birth of the music through the dense undergrowth.

The watchman sneezed and thought: "What the hell's that..." He moved his fingers expressively through the air: the conceptual volume contained between them was something like a cube, and a sphere, and a cone, or even a cylinder, and yet somehow neither the first, nor the second, nor the third, but most precisely and above all a quite obvious "what the hell." Then the watchman Potemkin barked out of the window on the seventh floor: "We'll see about that!" – as though he was struggling with the forces of the absurd. He roared out cheerfully and merrily, like some unknown animal:

"Give us something sour."

This attracted the attention of public inspector Kuzkin who soon arrived and said, in the first place:

"Why, comrade Potemkin, in the ragingly beautiful, furious space decorated with many-coloured flags in honour of the day of such-and such and so-and-so – the broad-flapping canvases of which can be seen from your window... "

In the second place, he said:

"Why do you, comrade Potemkin, blatantly ignoring the instructions of your wife concerning the carrying down of the dirty laundry to the appropriate place, of which you were informed in a note, thrusting which under your gaze I myself colour in shame for you, for mist clouds your glasses and in the effort to read what is written you break out in a hot sweat, and in the effort to make sense of what you have read you turn greener than grass, as you take on this labour of Sisyphus..?"

In the third place, he continued:

"Why do you, comrade Potemkin, forgetting the potemkinesque

norms and laws of our communal life, lay claim to the dishonourable role of a scab on the healthy body of our collective?"

In the fourth place, he concluded:

"Why did you, in short, get yourself drunk?"

Having unburdened himself of these questions, Kuzkin rose and assumed an expectant pose, the meaning of which was: "Now let's have a look at you, you fine goose! Got soused as a herring first thing in the morning, and now you're howling for the whole block to hear? And you think there's nothing we can do about you? You're wrong there, brother. You may be sitting drunk in your apartment right now, but in a minute you'll go outside and threaten someone's life with criminal danger! And they'll say inspector Kuzkin slipped up! They'll say: Where was inspector Kuzkin? What was he up to?"

"Alright now," Kuzkin thought to himself, "the best thing would be to send you off in good time for preventive treatment, and nip you, Potemkin, in the bud..."

But how could he realise his plan? In order to send Potemkin off for forced treatment, he had to apprehend him, not in a flat, but in a public place.

Then Kuzkin began luring the watchman outside.

"Eh, my friend! My brother!" Kuzkin exclaimed, and put his arms round Potemkin.

"My brother! My friend!" mumbled Potemkin, tossing back his crazy head in warm emotion and peering attentively at his newly-acquired bosom-buddy. Then he barked in a joyful voice: "Give us something sou-ou-our..." Meanwhile Kuzkin nudged him towards the door, until eventually they found themselves in the lift. Once they were out in the yard, Kuzkin dispatched the zig-zagging watchman into independent motion, whistled on his white whistle and immediately detained him.

The Charwoman Tolubeeva

The charwoman Tolubeeva, a sullen and stubborn old woman, resembled a mound of earth heaped up roughly in the form of a human figure. Her lowly philosophy of life did not, alas, resemble a swift flying bird or a ringing melody. Her thoughts were like millstones which painstakingly ground down even abstract concepts into the flour of practical needs.

She was swabbing away with her mop in the foyer of the theater, glancing now and then at the door into the hall which was filled with the rumbling and clanging of one of those fiery artistic productions. She thought: "Fine lot they are, with their culture! Big swells! We've seen plenty of their kind!" Tolubeeva's thoughts crawled on, in their paunchy, heavy fashion, for another two or three centimeters, and a remarkable insight began to take shape in her head. The essential element of this insight was that they were simply afraid that charwoman Tolubeeva might somehow get rich.

Charwoman Tolubeeva began answering them in spirited style: "What would I want with getting rich? How could I get rich on a rise of 5 and 20 roobils?" Then she went on to ponder: "Why'm I any worse than they are? The fancy buggers just come straight in and sit down! And here you are hunched over slaving away all your life long – and no respect for it, no thanks, no rise! Don't suppose they'd want to take a mop in their hands even for a moment! They're not interested in flogging and slaving away, in slaving away and swabbing seven blasted leagues of dirty damned floors, somebody else's floors that mean nothing to you, floors you hate with all your heart – like I do e-ve-ry si-ngle da-ay..."

The monologue was crowned with something between a sigh and an exhalation: aagh-ma! o-ogh! The etymological roots of this sigh stretched far back into the history of folk culture: behind Tolubeeva's massive back there appeared the glimmering light of summer lightning and burning barns. Men in long peasant coats and women in peasant headdresses ran towards the burning manor with pitch-forks and rakes held at the ready. "Ogh, we'll kill that dratted bloodsucker," they said, "we'll kill 'im!"

Then the charwoman Tolubeeva noticed Kolya Stepanchikov coming out of the auditorium. She straightened up vigilantly from her bucket and mop, she was on her guard. Any fool could see that this young lad was out to get up to *no good*. She cut across the empty foyer and set off after Kolya in prophylactic pursuit. She knew for certain that once he was out of the theater the hooligan intended to take some chalk out of his pocket and write something on the wall like "MEAT," or "STABLE," or "VASYA SPAT HERE".

She was astonished when it didn't happen the moment Kolya emerged from the theater. "Agha!" Tolubeeva punctuated her moment of insight with an exclamation.

Kolya Stepanchikov himself added to the tension of the situation: for some reason he glanced around stealthily, and that expression on his face – "Is anyone following me?" – definitely added impetus to Tolubeeva's repressive intentions. "Agha!" – her insight was finally complete. "A punk! That's what he is, a punk!" For some reason the thing Tolubeeva feared most in the world was punks. "I know what plan you've got in mind, my wee lad!" she thought, and wagged a threatening finger.

The distance separating the two antagonists was easily bridged telepathically, and the stream of vigilant thoughts emanating from Tolubeeva flowed across into Kolya's foolish head, where it gathered into a dark gloomy cloud above the sky-blue flowers that were already there. The flowers began to chirp and twitter:

"I'm not going to do anything criminal, you've no need to worry, Mrs. Tolubeeva..."

Innocence personified, Kolya threw back his head to look at the sky and changed his route slightly. With a camera-face expression, he began to move in the direction of the statue "Girl With an Oar." But the charwoman Tolubeeva, moved by a fragment of thought still lodged in her head, stole after him.

She moved out in pursuit of Kolya from behind the statue "Alarm and Storm-Clouds," which represented a certain highly vigilant watchman of the male variety, peering out into the treacherous distance from under shaggy eyebrows. The watchman's head was framed in stone clouds.

The charwoman Tolubeeva moved in Kolya's direction from out, as it were, of this atmosphere of alarm, although undoubtedly the real cause for alarm was herself. Her face had assumed a resolute expression, and her squat form, inaccessible to reproduction by any degree of sculptural skill, somehow even assumed a certain threateing poise, a certain "I'll fix you!" attitude, even a certain resilience.

Kolya moved away from the "Girl With an Oar" and Tolubeeva moved towards the "Girl With an Oar," leaving behind, as it were, the stage of alarm and moving into the phase of determination, as a result of which any startled conscious observer was well able to conjecture that the second was approaching when the mimic force of decisive will which was dawning on the face of Tolubeeva would precisely equal the powerful pelvic determination written on the face of the girl with the oar.

Of course, the clear danger was represented by the former, but as a result of its combination with the psychological pressure of the latter, the air was suddenly permeated with a nascent atmosphere of slaughter. Physical reprisal! Young Kolya Stepanchikov's heart shuddered and began to dart this way and that in his narrow ribcage. "My God!" he thought.

The small square in front of the theater building was immorally empty. However, the cheerful sounds of the choir could be clearly heard coming from the theater, and the sun still shone in the sky. A metaphorical coalition could be cobbled together.

Kolya's awareness of his surroundings began to grow a bit stronger, and he spoke: "Are you alarmed because you think that I... er... are you genuinely prophylactically concerned?"

This was probably an unnecessary question; in the formal space it had a hopeless sound. But the charwoman Tolubeeva, strangely enough, responded.

"Me?" she said. "I'm not doing anything. But what did you have in mind, eh? You think this is a place..."

Tolubeeva shifted her mop from her right hand to her left:

"... you think this place, this temple, this gallery of the arts, this treasure-house of regional culture, is a place where you can... you know... get away with the dirty business you had in mind, you nasty little boy, you filthy dog..."

From her exalted feelings for the arts which Kolya Stepanchikov had intended to irrigate, a song was born in her heart. No, it was a Russian epic poem! Its menacingly triumphant metre blended with the choir in the theater, Tolubeeva's voice singing the solo lead:

> *"I'll get you now!*
> *See how your streamlet silvery,*
> *silvered and silvery,*
> *glinting in the sun's rays playfully,*

swift and topsy-somersaulty,
I will cut off with a belt
from behind on a soft spot.
Ho, a belt on your pink little bottom,
Like two little baby's pinkies!

"Oh, I'll belt you hard!
I'll make it sting!
I'll slap you loud!
Then you'll shut off
your glinting streamlet silvery,
You'll cut it off,
my stupid little puppy,
my foolish one,
my little baby,
my wee laddie,
like a fairy-tale!"

Translated by Andrew Bromfield

From: Zufar Gareyev, *Multiprose*, a collection of short novels, Moscow, 1992.

Alexander Petrovich's Allergy

an excerpt

Houses smelled of late apples. They fell from out of somewhere, most likely, their high flight had been cut short by time. Most likely, they never reached the tender, frightened hearts, however eagerly the hot langorous fingers out of which they fluttered tried to catch them. They fell and fell into our houses, rustled behind our backs, vanished behind doors.

Yes, yes, that was time itself that let them fall absent-mindedly into people's houses. These red tart-smelling apples contained the summer. As always, we let the summer slip, and now it was passing silently through our houses, throwing its hands up to its temples, let the apples fall and, without glancing back, went on its way. We followed the apples with our eyes, we did not take them in our hands, they were on the far side of our possibilities, they had their own road: they rolled into the following summer, rustling on thresholds, in stairwells and entranceways. And we sank helplessly into chairs – our heads hitting the high rigid backs, our arms dangling down to the floor.

During these vermilion days yet another disaster befell Alexander Petrovich, caused by the fear that always visited his poor soul at this time. At this time, when the skeletons of yesterday's luxuriant trees, that has now been devoured by time, stand immersed in the air's limpid formalin, and human throats behind the windowpanes drag out their miserable heart-rending life.

Fear drove Alexander Petrovich out into the street: he went out into the booming city in search of colors and beauty.

Before him lay a silvery aluminum day at its very inception. Nothing reminded you of summer anymore. The streets were filled with durable clothes. He walked along many streets. In the end, he was ready to run around the city just to find someone somewhere by the Metro selling apples or oranges. But, strangely enough, on that particular day for some reason no one was selling anything by the Metro: when your turn in line comes nearer and nearer, minute by minute and – oh! – whole armfuls.

To come home and, before eating them, carve up the fragrant hunks – split them in half, thrust them open in the quietly creeping life of the room: table, chairs, tattered couch, scraps of newspaper, cloudy bottles. To thrust open the immense hemispheres, oneself in the center – like a tsar. You destroy yourself, melt, becoming longer together with the streams spurting up from them.

But that day for some reason no one was selling anything on the streets.

In the street crowds, only humanity's youths and young women wore light, pretty clothes. Humanity's youths and young women, oblivious of the glitter on the trees, merrily crisscrossed the icy hard little puddles with their slim feet, ate ice cream as if nothing had changed, drank sparkling water from water machines kissing successions of tiny carbonated bubbles, strolled along the streets, revealing the moist enamel of their teeth to the invigorating air through incidental smiles: they glanced at posters, stood before bright store windows, squinting into the reflected sun, exchanging leisurely remarks, gently enveloping each other in the steam billowing out of their clean lungs. In the unprepossessing crowd, they seemed like beings from another world, they were not made for the stuffy stores, or the train stations, the pharmacies, or the horrible baggy coats and muskrat hats and rucksacks. Their cold-sensitive ankles, tucked inside white socks, light swift legs arrayed in vivid fabrics. Alexander Petrovich was touched by their bright faces, – and he fleetingly fell in love with one of the groups of young people, virtual adolescents.

The group had come out of the Metro and was moving along the street. Humanity's youths wore colorful caps with tassels.

"I came out to find apples, but instead found those to whom they are offered," Alexander Petrovich reflected with the cold approval of an aesthete. Thus he unexpectedly found himself a captive of classical love.

He followed the youths at a distance, listening closely to their staccato banter which to his ears, according to all the laws of love, was like music. Their laughter, too, reached his ears; it hurt the amorous Alexander Petrovich: you see, Alexander Petrovich did not have a chance, according to the laws of this forbidden love, of being noticed by them, let alone being liked by them even a little.

However, he was soon noticed. A short November day was drawing to a close, and in the crowd it was impossible not to notice the one whose lips burned brightly, smeared with the cherry-colored sunset.

He had been noticed: the youths glanced back more and more anxiously at their pursuer. In a flower store, into which they had taken themselves without obvious purpose, the group erupted in loud laughter, openly scrutinizing him. In this laughter, he detected insolence, defiance. But then they dashed out of the store: perhaps they were afraid Alexander Petrovich would buy a bouquet and present a brightly burning flower to each of them for all to see?

Alexander Petrovich went out of the store, too, but he didn't see them anywhere, they had vanished. With reverence, he imagined

91

how they had gone home and were now bent over their slates, diligently doing their assignments.

And only one of them – the shrewdest one, as Alexander Petrovich later judged, and the most seductive, with that freshness of face which recalls feminine beauty, with those golden ringlets around the forehead which Zeus no doubt admired time and again while dallying with the stolen Ganymede – only one of them remained and he was waiting, or so it seemed, for Alexander Petrovich.

He made as if to walk away, but turned and smiled over his shoulder. In this smile Alexander Petrovich read liking and even a slight coquetry, which was quite surprising. He went after him, but the youth quickened his pace; at the building entrance he again turned, and again the smile of liking rolled across his pretty face. Alexander Petrovich continued in pursuit with the fearlessness of an aesthete; he hastened toward the entrance and, before running inside, plucked a flaming red apple from the sunset. He threw his arm up high into the air, in celebration, and strode into the entryway, illuminating its crannies with sparkling, hissing light.

The one for whom the apple was intended flew easily up the stairs and vanished. Alexander Petrovich began to mount the stairs after him, despite having noticed, out of the corner of his eye, just this. The vanished youths had not gone home, they were not bent over their slates, breathing gently, brushing soft curls out of their eyes. The entire group had materialized behind his back. They too began to mount the stairs, avoiding touching the railing in those places where it had been set on fire by the burning hand of Alexander Petrovich.

Finally he stopped to catch his breath. The faces of the adolescents who had overtaken him were sullen, rapt. Alexander Petrovich noticed that these faces were gradually becoming flushed with anger.

And here he understood everything.

"Hey, what do you... ," he asked, sensing danger.

At this point the false Ganymede ran down the stairs and stood in front of Alexander Petrovich. His face was filled with such hatred and aggression that, without saying a word, Alexander Petrovich retreated. Disgraced, he went back down the stairs and tossed the wrinkled apple into a trash bin.

And then, in the city, winter suddenly set in. The snow fell in drifts, drain pipes froze, dogs died.

The snow and frost smell of cold and nothing. They have forgotten about you because of the winter, because of the frost, the night, the pale blue stars.

Translated by Joanne Turnbull

From: Zufar Gareyev, *Multiprose*, a collection of short novels, Moscow, 1992.

Zufar Gareyev

"Zufar Gareyev is an outstanding "new" writer, notable for his linguistic virtuosity—especially his use of slang, neologisms, and linguistic corruptions—and his understanding of the fantastic, grotesque, double-think world that Soviet communism created (especially as viewed, in its twilight days, from the vantage point of the underdog or outsider—the cleaners, stokers, nightwatchmen, dropouts, tramps). His prose displays an extraordinary dynamism and presents, in a cartoon-like effect, snatched scenes and conversations, banal and fantastic, run through in a kind of hilarious fast-forward."—Sally Laird.

See also Gareyev's stories in Glas No.1 **When Other Birds Call** and in Glas No.4 **Facsimile Summer**. His story **The Holidays** will shortly be appearing in **Grand Street** (New York). His novel **Multiprose** have been published in Germany by Piper Publishers.

ALEXEI SLAPOVSKY

This Isn't Me

An adventure story

Chapters 20-22

In Alexei Slapovsky's novel Nedelin, a modest intellectual leading an uneventful life, finds he has the alarming gift of being able to transmigrate into the body of another person if both of them wish to change places. His first experience has taken him into the body and life of Victor Zapaltsev, a Saratov mafioso. In his next he changes places with the General Secretary of the Communist Party of the Soviet Union.

Nedelin was renting a room in Pitsunda on the Black Sea. He had acquired faded jeans on a beach near Sochi, a light blue T-shirt on the beach at Gagra, snugly fitting trainers, also on the beach at Gagra, and that was also where he had acquired the bag now slung over his shoulder which contained cigarettes, a bottle of wine, and two hundred honestly earned roubles. A trader had been desperate to get a truckload of fruit unloaded at the market in Gagra and paid very good money. Nedelin liked that and had unloaded three more trucks before the locals spotted him, explained his mistake, and encouraged him to leave. He was thinking of taking it easy for three or four days in Pitsunda before moving on, and toying with the idea of high tailing it across the border, not for any political reason, as was common enough in those years, but simply

94

in order to see the world. To the question of what he would do once he got there, with no knowledge of the language and customs and no money, he did not for the moment address himself.

Today's programme was a simple picnic in the surrounding woods with a young lady picked up on the beach the day before. The young lady was married and, as it happened, was called Lena.

Nedelin was exuding a confidence soundly based on the readiness with which this Lena had agreed to join him. Her husband was going over to Gagra to get train tickets because they were having to cut their holiday short. Mother-in-law had fallen ill, the silly old moo, and sent a telegram saying she was at death's door.

They wandered along paths and woodland tracks until they came to a seemingly endless fence, at which point they turned aside. Lena was all for walking on and on. She seemed much given to small talk. They came out to a small clearing with lush, thick grass.

"Right," Nedelin said. "That's it. We're here."

"We'd better stop then," Lena consented. "This looks a nice place for sunbathing!" In a trice she had stripped to her bikini, set herself down opposite Nedelin, and was waiting for him to open the wine. The polythene stopper wouldn't yield. Having no knife, Nedelin tore at it with his teeth. He tried to melt it with a match. Lena laughed. He looked at her white teeth, the way she threw back her suntanned neck, and the way this puckered the hollows by her throat. He cast aside the recalcitrant bottle and fell upon her, pressing his lips to her neck.

"Yes! Yes! Yes! Oh, please!" she moaned, helping him to slip off her bathing costume and shuffle out of his own clothes at the same time.

"Yes! Yes! Yes!" she murmured, laughing, as Nedelin readied himself for that first virile thrust, her long groan of anticipation preparing to turn into a cry of ecstasy...

"On your feet!" Nedelin was lashed by the shout from above. He leapt off Lena, tripped, and blundered about in the bushes in a rush to get his clothes. He pressed the bundle to his person, and saw Lena hastily putting on her bikini and other things.

The thickset man standing in front of them looked completely out of place in this setting in his suit, collar and tie, and shiny black leather shoes.

"What, what's going on?" Nedelin demanded, recovering some measure of composure.

"Never you mind about that," the besuited citizen half-whispered for some reason.

"We are married, you know," Lena said.

"That's as may be. Just clear off at the double."

"All right, we're just going," said Lena. "Much I care! What's so special about here anyway? Why shouldn't we stay if we want to? Oo-ooh," she added suddenly, "This is..."

"Ye-es," the Suit mimicked, at the same time awarding her a smile of approbation.

"This is what?" Nedelin asked in bewilderment.

"Explain it to him," the Suit said to Elena.

"Yes, of course. Come on. I'll tell you afterwards."

Nedelin's deep rooted sense of anti-climax turned rapidly to exasperation.

"Why should we leave?"

"Because big brother says so!" the Suit remarked, exchanging a glance with Lena. "Look, mate, I hate to spoil your *matrimonial* pleasure but..."

"Not so fast. Are you trying to tell me there's anything illegal in what we were doing?"

"You were behaving entirely naturally. Carry right on, mate. Only not here."

"And why not?" Nedelin demanded.

"Don't you know where you are?" the Suit asked, nodding vaguely in some direction.

"No I don't, and I don't give a monkey's!"

"All right, that's enough of that. Move on right now."

"Who the hell do you think you are?" Nedelin yelled, sitting demonstratively. "I am not going anywhere!"

"What?!"

Voices were heard. The Suit blenched.

"Do me a favour, mate."

"And you do me a favour, *mate*," Nedelin said with heavy emphasis. "Piss off! Understand?"

"Right..." The Suit looked round anxiously before quickly pulling out a red identity card. He was evidently about to flip this open and display it to Nedelin, but Nedelin turned away.

"Fuck your fancy ID. This is public land, not private property."

"A national park," the Suit corrected him, registering rapidly increasing concern.

"So what? We're not vandalising trees or lighting fires."

The voices were coming nearer.

"Right, that's it," said the Suit, pulling out from under his arm an improbably real-looking black pistol.

Lena gave a shriek and clutched Nedelin's arm.

"Let's go! This is... I'll tell you afterwards. You really don't know? What an idiot I am, I thought..."

"Go on then, shoot!" Nedelin said. "Shoot! What's stopping you?"

The Suit was patently distraught.

"Look, you're only being asked to move twenty metres away from this clearing. Is that too much to ask? You can come back in half an hour and bonk till daybreak for all I care."

"What did you say?"

"Oh, love each other, then."

"Say you're sorry."

"All right, then, I'm sorry."

"Without the "All right, then"."

"I'm sorry."

The Suit was panicking now, constantly looking behind himself. Then he said,"Ssshit! You have landed us in it now," and tucked the pistol back under his arm.

A couple of dozen people emerged into the clearing. In front lumbered a stout old man wearing white trousers and a white shirt and with a rifle slung over his shoulder. Behind him and to either side walked identical looking members of his staff.

The Suit was shifting from one foot to the other and turning paler by the minute. Another Suit stepped briskly up to him looking daggers, but said nothing and only glanced towards the approaching old man.

The old man, completely unaware of the situation, came up to Nedelin and Lena and suddenly held out a hand for them to shake. They shook it.

"Enjoying yourselves?"

"Yes... You know, somehow... The air... The scenery..." Lena mumbled in confusion.

Nedelin was also in some confusion, having recognized the old man as the country's present Chief, evidently vacationing at a government dacha hereabouts. He realized now that the citizen in the suit had been clearing the way for the Chief's constitutional.

"The pine trees here are magnificent!" the Chief pronounced, and his retainers immediately smiled and beamed approvingly at the pine trees, as if in recognition of the effort they had made to please the old man.

"Does this belong to you?" The Chief indicated a bikini top lying in the grass which Lena had overlooked in her haste.

"Yes," she said and made to pick it up, but somebody's arms restrained her because the Chief had himself taken a step in that direction. He lifted it and, holding it in two fingers, returned it to Lena.

"Thank you," said Lena.

"Not at all. How is your holiday going?"

"No complaints," said Nedelin.

"How's the supply situation? Do you have enough to eat?"

"Certainly do," said Nedelin with an upbeat gesture, as if to say, "Need you ask?"

The retainers were visibly relieved.

"But things could be better?" the Chief asked with a populist twinkle.

"Perfection knows no bounds," Nedelin answered rather well, as the last shadows were dispelled from the retainers' faces.

"You must be on a diet," the Chief said, turning to Lena. "What a neat little figure you've got!"

"It's just the way I am," Lena said.

"Lucky you!" the Chief said to Nedelin man to man, and winked. The retainers also laughed, very man to man.

SUDDENLY

"Where did that mirror come from?" Nedelin asked unevenly.

The Chief responded, also rather shakily,

"You wanted it."

"What's going on? What's happening?" Nedelin demanded nonplussed.

"Enjoy the rest of your vacation," the Chief said, walking away.

The retainers followed in his wake, puzzled by this strange dialogue.

"Where are you going?!" Nedelin shouted. "Arrest him! What's going on? What's happened?"

"Let's be on our way," the Chief said. "Let's be on our way. They need to be alone."

Nedelin rushed after him, but found his way barred by a man in a suit who locked him in an iron embrace.

"Where do you think you're going, mate? Have you taken leave of your senses?"

"Are you calling me "mate"?" Nedelin demanded, shocked and outraged. He was, of course, as our reader has already discerned, not Nedelin at all but the Chief who had transmigrated into Nedelin. And he collapsed in a dead faint.

"See to him, miss," the man in the suit said to Lena.

* * *

Lena managed somehow to bring her companion round. He came to, but started saying things which gave her a nasty turn. He said he was the Chief, and there must have been a misunderstanding, and he absolutely must get back to the government dacha straight away as he had a government telephone call to take at twelve o'clock, and then he had to receive the Minister of Heavy Industry, then have lunch, then have a game of table tennis, then sign his assent to various documents, then... And besides, what would his wife say when she arrived tomorrow evening?

Lena realised that as a result of their extraordinary encounter her would-be lover had lost his wits. Her first thought was to bolt for it, but she was after all a kind woman and, at some risk to her reputation, walked the Chief back to Pitsunda, soothing and humouring him the while. She phoned for an ambulance from a public call box. This arrived half an hour later and the Chief was taken away. The ambulancemen were obliged to report the incident to the police and duly did so, to the considerable satisfaction of the latter. The lunatic was identified as Nedelin's earlier double, Victor Zapaltsev, speculator, fence, and general hard man with links to the drug trade and many other felonious activities, currently being sought the length and breadth of Russia. They had long been on to him. The Saratov police had been closing in when, literally one day before he was due to be arrested, he had vanished, telling his wife, who was an honest woman, that he was flying to Sochi. To keep their consciences clear, since quite obviously no criminal would ever go where he said he was going, they requested the Sochi police to join the search, and they soon had him tracked down to one of the local hotels through information received from a reception clerk who drew their attention to a person living beyond his means; but Zapaltsev had again gone into hiding, and for a period of time they had lost the scent. The noose had been tightening once more when this hardened and experienced criminal decided to head them off by resorting to a technique far from new in the criminal world, namely seeking refuge in a lunatic asylum.

The investigating magistrate was a middle-aged man who had seen it all, but even he was amazed at how artfully Zapaltsev entered into his role, to the extent, apparently, of worrying little that he might evade a criminal sanction only to find himself arraigned on serious political charges. He certainly had a nerve. Even a real lunatic wouldn't get away with imagining he was who Zapaltsev was pretending to be. Perhaps he really had lost his marbles. The psychiatrist called in was given a very clear remit: he was to catch out the simulator. The psychiatrist was baffled. On the one hand the patient's reactions were all normal, while on the other he couldn't be faulted in relation to his mania. In fact the psychiatrist found the suspect's general demeanour and his outbursts of supremely authoritative rage so authentic as to be profoundly unsettling. He said to the magistrate, "This Zapaltsev... If he is Zapaltsev..."

"What's that?"

"All right, forget the if. Your Zapaltsev really does seem to have gone off his rocker. Let's face it, he's going to be incarcerated one way or the other, if not by you then by us. We don't let people get out either."

"All right then," said the magistrate. "But you carry the can."

"Have I ever let you down?" the psychiatrist asked rhetorically.

After the Chief had been injected with tranquillizers and recognized the tragic inevitability of what had befallen him, he was introduced to the other patients. They accepted him matter-of-factly, evidently seeing no grounds to doubt he was who he said he was. The only untoward occurrence came from one particular scrawny individual who circled restlessly before finally coming up to him.

"Hello, there," he said. "I'm Marx-Engels-Lenin-Stalin. Look at me in profile."

The Chief looked.

"Recognise me?"

The Chief decided not to disabuse him.

Towards evening the scrawny patient became very active, assembling people into groups and obliging them to march past the Chief shouting slogans and greetings, waving flags, and raising propaganda banners. They used spoons in place of flags and open books from the hospital library in place of banners. He then composed a telegram of greetings to the Chief pledging to meet even higher targets under the five-year-plan. Somebody tried to object and was vigorously and expeditiously brought to order. The offending party thereupon undertook to meet even higher targets and everybody cheered. Then the scrawny patient barked, "Bring me an armoured car!" They wheeled over the black grand piano from its corner, singing in unison "Hostile winds gust overhead," followed by a chorus of "Hey, little apple, rolling, bowling to the loony bin!" The scrawny patient leapt up on to the piano and announced in his best Lenin accent, "Comwades! The wevolution pwedicted by the bolsheviks, is iwwevewsibly wealized." This said, he became violent and pointed at the Chief, screaming, "Ecrasez l'infame! Throw him overboard from the steamship of the Revolution! Kill him! Unmask the scum and dehabilitate him!" They all fell upon the Chief, who started trying to explain to the comrades their error in not taking full cognisance of the circumstances of the present moment in history. A burly orderly made a timely appearance.

"More hot air in the Constituent Assembly?" he asked in a resounding voice and moved in on the scrawny patient, adding laconically, "The sentries think it's time everyone went home."

The scrawny patient leapt down from the piano and covered his head with his arms. The Chief shuddered. He had read in Gogol and Chekhov about lunatics getting beaten, but surely that did not go on in the land of the Soviets! The orderly did not, however, beat the scrawny patient but merely towered over him, intoning,

"Here is an important Government announcement, broadcast over all radio stations of the Soviet Union. Today at five zero zero hours Greenwich Mean Time the life of You Know Who drew peacefully to its close!"

The scrawny patient twitched convulsively and fell to the floor, immobile. The orderly removed his white cap. The patients began to cry, some lining up in a guard of honour while others raised the motionless patient and bore him to his place of rest on the piano. The orderly appeared satisfied, but added in parting,

"In view of a paradox of history fully in accordance with government planning, the revered deceased will be honourably re-interred in his Kremlin fucking wall."

The scrawny patient quickly jumped up and ran off somewhere to hide, evidently aware that the process of re-interment would be very unpleasant. The dispirited patients, deprived of their fun, wandered back to their corners.

The Chief pondered day and night, night and day over what had happened but could come up with no explanation. He vaguely recollected something about transmigration of souls. Something to do with India, was it? But that was all ridiculous religious thinking, not a scientific view of the world. He would do better not to give himself a headache speculating about that but work out how he could prove he really was the Chief. The Chief, dammit! He had somehow been transferred into the body of an ordinary person who must be traced. The matter must be investigated thoroughly and the necessary measures taken! But first he needed some way of convincing everybody. The Chief remembered a children's book called *The Prince and the Pauper*, written by some American. The Chief had had a hard childhood, very active, and he had never got round to reading this book at that time. On one occasion, however, he had been intending to give it to his grandson (a de luxe edition, specially printed) and had started reading it himself. He had read and read, unable to put it down. The phone had rung to advise him that the car taking him to his grandson's birthday party was at the door, but he had carried on reading. His wife had rung from the next room to ask whether they were going or not. He said he was on his way, but carried on reading. His personal physician, Academician Mengitis, had rung to ask how he was feeling, and he replied that actually he wasn't feeling all that well and everybody should be advised accordingly. He didn't need any treatment. He would just lie down for a bit. Everything was fine, he just needed to lie down for a bit. His wife should be told to go without him and buy a present somewhere on the way.

He read through the night, irritably registering the growing concern centred on his private office, conscious of distant comings and goings. Nobody dared disturb him, however; only his wife rang every hour. He told her drily, "I'm working." This was wholly plausible, because he had an important meeting arranged for the following day, but at the same time not entirely plausible, because he had not worked at night for a long time. His main obligation on such occasions consisted of looking fit and well. He read all night but did not finish in time, since he always had been a slow, serious, meditative reader. He rang the secretariat in the morning and gave instructions for the meeting to be set back two hours. The Minister of Agriculture heard of this by chance and, suspecting that the Chief had received some important foreign policy communication which, no doubt, everybody else knew about only as usual they were keeping him, the Minister of Agriculture, in the dark, he lost no time hinting to the Minister of Defence that actually he too was fully briefed about certain events. The Minister of Defence thought it no coincidence that the left side of his head had been feeling numb since the previous evening. How come some prissy little Minister of Agriculture knew something he didn't know? Could this be the Minister of Light Engineering up to his old tricks again? And might not he, as Minister of Defence, be accused of not being on the ball? Hastening to his quarters he gave immediate orders for all units to be put on red alert. In many units and subdivisions red alert was understood to mean full combat readiness, because everyone had long ago forgotten the difference, if indeed there was one. Underground silos slid open, the heads of missiles appeared. This was instantly registered by spy satellites and the information transmitted to the headquarters of the probable adversary. The probable adversary opened his silos and got his strategic bombers airborne. These began circling like so many vultures in the vicinity of our borders awaiting the order. In response the entire complement of our regular airborne forces was scrambled and submarines directed to their appointed stations. Trotskyites proclaimed the outbreak of world revolution. The heir to the Russian throne, vacationing in Cannes, received a telegramme consisting of the single word "Soon!" All hell broke loose in the world's stock exchanges; the shares of companies whose production processes were dependent on Soviet oil plunged; banks folded in quick succession; somebody shot himself; arms factories in Saratov received notice of possible evacuation; the old grannies of Saratov, who knew absolutely nothing of all this, nevertheless began instinctively hoarding bread to make rusks; and as usual processed cheese disappeared from the shops. A Saratov TV and radio reporter, Alexei Slapovsky, hearing some nonsense about an atom bomb heading towards Saratov from Florida, sat down moodily to put together yet another programme from the letters and complaints of workers in which he would mercilessly expose the shortcomings of community and other middle management officials; he went out now and again to the corridor for a smoke and to give further thought to an idea for a comic but sad novel titled *This Isn't Me*, only somebody suddenly phoned. Having talked at some length with this somebody while conspiratorially shielding the receiver with his hand, he said to his boss, a lady, not looking her in the eye, "I've just got to check out an urgent complaint...", and left the office.

At the appointed time the Chief entered the committee room looking pale. Those assembled broke out in a cold sweat.

"My heart was affected," the Chief said. "Right, shall we get started?"

The red alert was called off; missiles were again concealed in their silos, aircraft recalled to their bases. The top brass inspected the grey hairs they had acquired in those hours. The heir to the Russian throne, by then already in Paris, received a telegramme reading, "We wait". The shares of the affected companies rebounded dramatically, as a result of which a few more banks folded; somebody else shot himself; the old grannies of Saratov fed re-hydrated rusks to the pigeons; but processed cheese did not re-appear. Quite independently of these events Saratov TV and radio reporter Alexei Slapovsky came home drunk, late, and waving an upraised finger in the air, twisting the words from his wet mouth with difficulty, mooed, "*This Isn't Me*! Please remember that!"

"Don't worry. I'm remembering," his long-suffering wife Lena replied.

Well, then. Thinking back to *The Prince and the Pauper*, the Chief recalled that the Prince persuaded everybody he really was the Prince by telling them where the Great Seal of England was kept (which he used for cracking nuts, or was it the Pauper who used it for cracking nuts? He would have to read it again.) So he, the Chief, should remember something too, which only he could know and which would authenticate his credentials. The only trouble was, he did not have a Great Seal. In.fact, he did not have even a key to a secret safe, or indeed a safe, because he lived openly and open-heartedly. Perhaps he could reveal his knowledge of some Great Official Secret? But which?

There were military secrets. They landed on the Chief's desk in the form of black files with five stars on the cover to signify ultimate secrecy. The title page bore the inscription, "In strictest confidence. Seen only by..." followed by the signatures of five or six authorised individuals apart from whom nobody in the whole world knew the contents of the document. The Chief had now, however, to admit to himself that he could remember sod all of what was in all those secret diagrams, tables, and maps. He did remember an arrangement of circles like the constellation of the Little Bear on a map of either East or North Siberia, and remembered drawing attention to the fact that this was a bit of a give-away. His remark had been taken as requiring action, and six months later it was reported that the bases had been redeployed as economically as possible at a cost of five (or maybe it was eight) billion roubles, and that the configuration no longer bore a resemblance to anything whatsoever. The astronomical atlas had been checked specially. As to what the little circles were and what bases they might have stood for, that he couldn't for the life of him recall.

The Chief took a look in the hospital library and, would you believe it, he found *The Prince and the Pauper* by the writer Mark Twain. He revelled in it for two days. Then he read *The Mysterious Island* by Jules Verne. That was five days of sheer pleasure. Then *The Children of Captain Grant* by the same author. That, however, was the last interesting book in the library, which occupied half a glass shelf in the dispensary. There remained only much thumbed books of no interest to the Chief: two or three foreign novels, two or three whodunnits, four copies of M.Dolomakhamov's 967-page novel *The Mountains Bloom*, three copies of Pushkin's *The Captain's Daughter*, and eighteen miscellaneous but pristine volumes by Shitov, a Soviet writer to whom the Chief thought he might have presented a State Prize a few years ago. Quietly and tactfully, in order not to rub the staff up the wrong way, the Chief asked if he might attend the head doctor's clinic. His request was granted. The Chief asked the doctor for permission to ring through on the secure Kremlin telephone network to the Kremlin library to have books by Jules Verne, Mark Twain, and that author who wrote about Winnie the Pooh, donated as charitable aid for the mentally handicapped. How great was his astonishment to learn that the clinic was not connected to the secure telephone network, and that there was nothing the head doctor could do to help him. The head doctor readily agreed that the library was very thin. How many times had he written applications and made representations, but his only concrete achievement had been a promise to send them the complete collected works of Lenin.

The Chief was genuinely upset. The psychiatrist felt sorry for him and brought him a book which belonged to his son: *Urwin Deuce and His Wooden Soldiers*. The Chief accepted it with immense gratitude and almost with a bow. He immediately made a dust jacket for it and soon, as a reward for his carefulness, began regularly to be lent books from the head doctor's own library: Jules Verne, H.G. Wells, and even the one about Winnie the Pooh.

The Chief became the clinic's most tractable inmate. He never recalled his mania, and would wake to birdsong early in the morning with a cloudless smile on his face. He would wash cheerily, have breakfast, and sit down avidly to his latest book of adventures and excitement. On one occasion he unexpectedly saw himself on television, that is, the person he used to be. He became restive and started looking around wild-eyed. The orderly moved towards him. The Chief covered his eyes with his hands, shouted something, and ran from the television room.

Another time, when he was covering a book in newspaper, he suddenly saw his own face on the front page, and beneath it the text of an important political speech. He read only a few lines before throwing a fit.

From then on he steered clear of the television, never touched a newspaper, and dug up from somewhere a special loose leatherette book cover which he guarded jealously. When a patient known as the Fireman ran down the corridor shouting "Fire! Fire!" he did not rush like the others to rescue his pathetic worldly goods from the ward. He took only his book in its cover and waited placidly, either for the fire, if there really were one, to be over, or to be told it had been a false alarm.

He was happy.

* * *

Nedelin meanwhile took to being the Chief like a duck to water. The Chief's life was determined not by consciousness but by routine, to which many hands contributed. All that was needed was to observe and comply.

If members of his bodyguard appeared bearing flippers and masks, this indicated it was time to go and swim in the sea in a small enclosure, or go out fishing on a military patrol boat. Fish were caught at an amazing rate, and Nedelin suspected that frogmen down below were affixing a supply of previously caught fish to the hooks, but this in no way reduced the pleasure of the angling. The frogmen evidently knew what they were doing and would wait for a time, allowing anticipation to build up before attaching a fish and – tug, tug.

If his bodyguards and other members of the staff all appeared wearing official suits, this indicated a reception or similar engagement in the offing.

Nedelin was regularly brought dossiers of documents which he was supposed to consider, signing his assent to them or not. For the most part these were lists of awards and he signed willingly, having first learned to forge the Chief's signature.

But he wanted the big time. He wanted Moscow.

Then the vacation was over, and Nedelin was indeed conveyed to Moscow.

Here he had an immediate opportunity to make his mark. An important meeting attended by delegates from every part of the country was scheduled for the following day and he was due to make a speech.

His hour had come.

It was hot. Nedelin felt like taking off his jacket and tie and to hell with it. He pictured the state's twelve most powerful people appearing in public in their shirt sleeves and with their collars casually unbuttoned. This would be enough on its own to jolt people into wondering whether new times were not at hand. It would instil optimism.

"It's hot," Nedelin said.

Everybody agreed with him.

Nedelin removed his jacket and tie and unbuttoned his top shirt button.

The Minister of Agriculture, ever quick on the uptake, did the same. The others, turning away in embarrassment, as if they were not merely taking off their jackets but stripping naked in public, followed suite. The Minister of Defence had a problem since he was wearing dress uniform and could hardly remove his tunic; however, he whispered something to his orderly, a ranking general, who disappeared to return with a summer semi-dress uniform which had a lawn shirt of a delicate green hue with epaulettes. The ideologist held out longest of all, unbuttoning and re-buttoning his jacket, tugging at the lapels and looking imploringly at Nedelin. Nedelin only pulled a disapproving face at him. The ideologist removed his jacket and, for the first time in his life, blushed.

They all immediately looked quite unmilitary and unusually approachable. The bell rang for the meeting to begin and they crowded round the door, leaving a passage for Nedelin. They would wait a few minutes more to allow the expectancy to grow, prompting an ovation when the Praesidium finally appeared.

Hearing a sound like quiet surf on the other side of the door, Nedelin became suddenly nervous and afraid of something. He felt awkward. His fingers automatically did up his top shirt button, his hands groped on his chest and somebody immediately handed him his tie. He put it on, wriggled his shoulders, and was handed his jacket. He put it on.

Drenched in sweat from the shock they had been subjected to, the most powerful people in the country fell over themselves getting properly dressed again.

Nedelin was angry with himself for this unexpected weakness. He resolved to even the score by now saying openly to the entire nation,

"That's it, people. Rock bottom. We've finally managed to totally wreck the country."

He strode out to the lectern.

Endless applause.

Turning into an ovation.

The hall rose to its feet.

They all began chanting adulatory slogans.

How wonderful it would be, Nedelin thought, if all this were deserved, if he had earned such respect. How wonderful it would be to enjoy this love of himself. Our people are good-hearted; they know how to feel gratitude. It was not, of course, him they were applauding but the greatness of the state. And was it not a great power? Was not this hall (Nedelin cast his gaze over its stately vastness), was it not symbolic of that greatness? He raised a hand, quieting the ovation, paused, and then said:

"Comrades! On this momentous day..." That much he managed without the prompting of his notes, that much came from the heart. His throat contracted in a spasm of emotion, and from then on, to calm his agitation, he kept to the text.

"No," he thought, watching the video recording of his speech afterwards, "if there is such unanimity among our people all is not yet lost. The need is only to direct that unanimity into a sensible channel. There is much that is bad, very much, even, but... but what is essential is to listen again to what ordinary folk have to say. How, though, are you to do that if you are always surrounded by officials, always in your official setting?"

He decided to resort to the traditional ruse of rulers who want to know how they are being viewed and to seek the counsel of ordinary folk about the good ordering of the state. He would go out secretly among the people.

He called the Captain of his bodyguard and ordered him to bring a thick grey wig, false beard and moustache, and dark glasses. The Captain duly carried out the order.

"I want to take a walk through the streets," Nedelin told him.

"Without an escort, with respect, quite impossible!"

"All right. Just don't crowd me too obviously."

"Sir!"

The Captain of the Guard ran after Nedelin, ran carefully round him so as not to jostle him, and barred his way out of the government building.

"With respect. We are unable to allow into or out of the building an individual lacking personal identification and of unknown appearance."

"What do you mean?" Nedelin asked in amazement. "This is me!"

"Sir! I am not, however, at liberty to disregard instructions."

"Here, look at my identification. Look at it!" Nedelin waved his Party card at him.

"With respect. That person is of a different appearance."

"I'm wearing a wig, you lunatic. I put the disguise on in front of you."

"That's as may be, but having regard to the discrepancy between your appearance and that of the person depicted on the identification document..."

"Here! Here!" Nedelin tore off the wig, beard and moustache, and removed his spectacles.

"Pass," said the Captain of the Guard saluting.

Nedelin pulled the wig, beard and moustache back on.

"With respect, halt!" The Captain instantly barred his way. "In view of your unknown appearance... my instructions..."

"Idiot!"

Nedelin tore off his disguise and left the building without further hindrance. A car drove up and the Captain of the Guard opened the door.

"I want to walk," Nedelin said.

"With respect. Quite impossible. Persons will crowd round you desirous of expressing their heartfelt appreciation. And there's no telling what might happen to you in a crowd."

"What? Who could want to make an attempt on my life in my own country, you oaf. Do the people love me or do they not?"

"Of course. But on rare occasions alcoholics are sometimes to be found in the streets and all manner of insane persons. And foreign agents. Biding their time."

"Well, what do you think I've got a wig for? And a false beard?" Nedelin donned his disguise yet again.

"With respect, I am obliged to detain you as a person of unknown appearance loitering in the vicinity of a government building."

"You utterly ridiculous goat!" Nedelin shrieked. "It's me, for heaven's sake."

"I appreciate that..."

"That's it. I'm going for a walk."

"Quite impossible," the Captain of the Guard exclaimed in desperation.

"Who says I can't. I already am."

Nedelin managed only three steps before the Captain of the Guard gave a command, two sturdily built young men of identical appearance ran up, seized Nedelin, twisted his arms behind his back, and frog-marched him away. They took him to a small windowless room and beat him up, but not too brutally, out of respect for his age. It still hurt. Nedelin delivered himself of an incoherent expletive and ripped off his beard, wig, and moustache. The sturdy young men recognised him, released him, and sprang to attention, but without trepidation. What, after all, has someone to fear who has merely been carrying out orders conscientiously?

Groaning, clutching his abdomen, and swearing dreadfully, Nedelin tottered back to entrance of the building with the full intention of firing the idiot Captain of the Guard on the spot and sending him to a corrective labour camp for fifty years. The Captain stood awaiting him, pale but resolute. He saluted.

"Permission to report? A person of unknown appearance and harbouring unknown intentions was detained by the entrance to the present building. Measures have been taken and the danger liquidated!"

"If you so much as cross... If I ever catch sight... I hope you..." Nedelin clutched at his heart. People ran up, caught him, raised him up carefully, carried him off.

It has to be remarked that Nedelin had been feeling worse with every day that passed. *Mens sana in corpore sano*, the saying goes, and conversely spiritual health brings with it physical health. For this reason Nedelin, his soul transmigrating into the Chief's body, seemed at first not to notice the ills to which all flesh is heir. He had, of course, to accustom himself to someone else's old, flabby body, but he did not feel particularly frail. Those around concurred that the Chief had returned from his vacation refreshed, rejuvenated, and remarkably full of energy, the old bastard. For all that, after an important and demanding speech he would immediately be conscious of his liver, and kidneys, his heart, and his joints...

Barely recovered from his heart attack, Nedelin demanded to be kept informed of current state and government business. It wasn't so much that he desperately wanted to get back into harness, but by now he felt under an obligation. It was his duty, even when ill, to keep hold of the strings and levers of the world process. He had no right to relax. Of the events of special importance one stood out as supremely important and harrowing. There had been an explosion at a major enterprise which had caused extensive damage. Lives had been lost. Nedelin called in the Minister of the industry concerned and, holding his heart, said to him:

"Well?"

"Prophylactic measures not implemented... A concatenation of objective circumstances..." the minister mumbled.

"You!" Nedelin screamed at him in fury, his eyes widening like those of the eponymous hero of the film *Peter the Great*. "Wretch! You craven wretch!" He ground his teeth and tore at his pyjama collar, seized a cup in his trembling hand, and flung it at the Minister. "You've put those people in their graves, you cur! You shall gnaw your own carrion, you knave!"

Everybody who heard of this exchange, and by one means or another many of the most powerful people in the state did get to hear about it, and indeed many of the second and even third most powerful people, everybody who heard of it said to themselves, "Ho! Verily! Things are tightening up again, and a good thing too and not before time!" They took it upon themselves to call their subordinates curs, wretches, and knaves, and to throw a variety of objects at them in the process. This spread to the very lowest links of the chain of command, where people really did have things to yell at other people about, and for a long time after that extravagant and unbalanced shouting was to be heard throughout the land as various items of crockery flew through the air towards blameworthy and blameless heads, and children conceived during this time were born completely round-eyed, their eyes wide with rage or perhaps astonishment.

The pain in his heart got worse and worse, until Nedelin suddenly realized that matters had gone too far and he really could be about to die. The whole force of his illness came crashing in on his consciousness, as if the Pale Horse had somehow miraculously passed soundlessly through the chambers, and unexpectedly kicked his door open with its iron hoof, neighing and baring its great red teeth. How terrifying it was, Lord, how terrifying.

He rang the bell and heard hurried footsteps.

"I am dying," Nedelin whispered.

And die he did...

The reader will wish to now that Nedelin is resuscitated and continues in varying health for thirty-one chapters more.

Translated by Arch Tait

First published in Russian in the Volga monthly, Saratov, 1992.

He Says, She Says
A novel in forty-nine chapters

Chapter One

He's a photographer, she's an employee of the district sanitary service; he's in his mid thirties, she's just a little younger. They have fallen in love with each other – which is what concerns us here.

Chapter Two

She says:

"While examining the sanitary conditions in public catering enterprises in the course of carrying out my professional duty, I constantly encounter dirt and filth of various kinds. What has happened to me could be called a professional health hazhard. Of course, I could change my job, but I can't be sure that my sickness would not simply follow me, since, in the first place, dirt in one form or another is to be found everywhere, and in the second place, I've got used to being ill..."

Or:

"Perhaps the real nightmare is not so much that there's dirt and filth everywhere, but that I am astonished, genuinely astonished and even a little shaken if I suddenly come across something that's, you know – clean... it might be a beautiful bed of flowers or a child with a clean-washed face, or maybe a shop window that is actually transparent. The one comfort is that it's only temporary: they'll trample down the flower-bed, the child will smear his face with sand and snot, a drunk will lean up against the window and puke all over it – and of course no-one will wash it again until the second coming..."

Or:

Don't talk of love, that stuff sticks in my throat –
Let's take the case of my very own spouse:
He offered me his love as one holds out a coat,
The way bright shining hope might be held out.
But just as any tree-stump sheds its bark,
His feeling's waste-products were swiftly shed,
Now he always complains of the stress of his work,
And he won't wash his feet before he goes to bed,
So I close my eyes tight and never make a move.
I know that I shall never fall in love –
Some far less fancy name will have to do
For this thing there is between me.and you.
And it really amounts to nothing at all –
I'm not going in for any more falls:
Slim, neat ball-room feet are a loo's greatest dream –
And I only dream of a love that's ideal!

Or:

"I don't know how to explain it, but I do know that there won't be anything between us, because I would have to be re-born, I'd have to change everything – my appearance, my name, everything, do you understand?"

He says:

"A photographer's profession, like any other, leaves its mark on a man, there's no such thing as an entirely safe profession. You may wonder what's harmful about photography. Allow me to explain. While gazing into the faces of people who come to have photographs taken for their documents – and that is what I do, I don't have the necessary equipment and materials for artistic work, and perhaps not the ability either – so, gazing into these faces, by the bright light of the lamp, I notice that very few of these faces are kind or beautiful. If anyone appears attractive, I only have to enlarge their image and project it on to a screen to be convinced that they too are ugly, just as the giants appeared ugly to Gulliver, with their faces furrowed by cracks like ravines and the pores of their skin like cesspools in their reddish-greenish-bluish flesh."

Or:

"No, honestly, I swear. I even had the idea, merely as a matter of sporting interest, of trying to find a face, or rather, not find one, but wait for a person to come in with a face which would make me want to hang their photograph on the wall and look at it. It wouldn't have to be a really handsome man or a beautiful woman, just a face I could look at and think: now that's a real human being! There hasn't been a single face like that! Not a single one, in all the ten years I've spent in this lousy studio! I admit we're not a high-class establishment, we don't do wedding photos and such things, but we get a hundred-odd clients every day, and in ten years there hasn't been a single one! Monsters, nothing but monsters, I have a collection of monsters of my own now, for consolation, if you like, something I can look at and admire..."

Or:

> *Books lay it all out in poetic style,*
> *But still, for love the same old truths hold good:*
> *And your wife's sweaty armpit, in a while,*
> *No longer stirs the passion in your blood.*
> *And what about those glossy colour pix*
> *Of naked bodies in a magazine?*
> *Though you may strain to spot the printer's tricks,*
> *There's not a single blemish to be seen.*
> *But let those beauties step out of the page*
> *You'll see the laddered tights, the pimply skin,*
> *The skinny, bony legs, the breasts betraying age,*
> *And catch that arm-pit odour once again.*
> *Love's harvest is like reaping in the sands...*
> *N'est-ce pas?*

Chapter Three

She came to have her photograph taken for her office pass. Three centimetres by four with one blank corner. As he photographed her he noted that her face had pretensions (but without any aggression) to intelligence and beauty, and he looked forward to how he would enlarge this face after work and, as always, in the place of intelligence and beauty would see ugliness and stupidity.

But the negative turned out to be ruined – not just fuzzy in places or spotty, there was nothing at all, just a dirty-white surface, charcoal dissolved in milk.

He apologised and said he would photograph her again – for no extra charge, of course. She shrugged: it was the same old story: waste-products, nothing but waste-products and filth everywhere.

He did everything according to the rules, all the other negatives that day developed and held their images the way they were supposed to, capturing for ever those self-important faces that still looked somehow scared of something or other. But Nechaev knew what it was they were scared of – the mystery of an apparently simple process. After the flash and the click, you carry on living, changing, growing old. After all, every second that passes finds you a different person, and now your image has been torn apart from you, it is no longer you, but someone who has been left far behind in the distance, someone who has died there. All the negatives, all the photographs came out right – except for hers. No outline, no shadows, just a smooth dirty-white surface, milk mixed with charcoal.

She said:

"Listen, if this is your way of trying to get to know me or something, then it's stupid. It's not funny."

He said:

"I'm not after anything, and I certainly don't need you. I just can't make it out. All of them turned out right except yours. It's ridiculous."

"So now you're saying it's my fault?"

"I'm not saying anything. I'll give you your money back if you like."

"No, never mind. It's bound to work the third time."

Chapter Four

It didn't work.

Chapter Five

She said:
"Maybe this is how you amuse yourself? Maybe it's some kind of hobby of yours?"
He said:
"Look for yourself! Just to be sure I photographed you three times! Here are the photographs of the others, before and after you – they all came out! And here are your negatives, all three of them are blank. Now do you understand?"
"I don't understand a thing."
"Neither do I!"
"Am I supposed to be some kind of phantom, then?"
"I don't know. When did you last have your photograph taken?"
"A long time ago. I can't remember when. Wait now... No, it really was a very long time ago. I can't stand having my photograph taken. It was a long time ago. My wedding photograph would be almost the last one."
"Haven't you had any photographs taken with your children, with your daughter or your son, whichever you have? Mothers love to be photographed with their children."
"I haven't got any children."
"Oh, I'm sorry."
"No need to apologise. I'm not sad about it. I'm not sick. I don't want children, so I don't have any."
"Then you just take your money and go to a different studio. I'm beginning to like you, and that makes me furious. As if you were some great beauty!"
"Have you tried looking at yourself lately? You've got hairs sticking out of your nose."
"I hadn't noticed. What else?"
"Your ears are repulsive, the lobes grow into your cheeks. I hate ears like that."
"They're just very close, they don't grow into them. Alright, then.

What else? You've got me interested now. You don't hear things like this everyday."

"What else? You got a tooth missing on the left side. I can see the gap when you smile."

"Am I smiling?"

"Well, for a moment I thought that grimace was a smile. You think it's an ironical grin, you're quite sure it's an expression of intelligent sarcasm, but all you're really doing is showing off the gap in your teeth."

"Alright, but then your pearlies aren't exactly flawless."

"At least they're all there."

"And you've already got folds in your neck. You're getting old, madame, old."

"Alright. What else?"

"You're hiding all the rest. But I can see it, I've got a professional eye. You've gone flabby, madame, flabby and fat all over."

"That's not true. I'll accept the truth, no matter how unpleasant it is, but that's not true. I still go ballroom dancing."

"I can imagine it. Elderly female book-keepers skipping about with bald, bandy-legged accountants."

"I'm not a book-keeper."

"So much the better."

"What do you mean, so much the better? Are you going to take my photograph?"

"I'll take it. If I have to ruin ten negatives, I'll take it. Then you'll see yourself for what you're worth!"

"If you would be so kind."

Chapters Six to Eight

Whether it worked this time or not is none of our concern. As previously stated, what concerns us here is love.

Chapter Nine

She said something like:

"So, we like each other then. We love each other, eh? Although that's impossible but we won't even touch each other until... there's nothing left, that's when... We could perhaps go away to some other town. I don't know. So there'd be nothing left. Otherwise it'll just be filth."

"We really should break free. To make everything ahead clean and pure."

"That's impossible."

"Then what are we supposed to do?"

"How should I know. Let's just try."

"What?"

"What?"

"I don't understand."

"What was that you asked?"

"Who, me?"

Chapter Ten

He tells her:

"Yesterday I spoke with my wife. I said I've found a woman, I'm sorry, set me free. So I won't have to pretend, so... She said: you swine, you libertine, you scoundrel. I said: you've no right. She said: I'll show you what right I have. Then I..."

She interrupts him:

"I don't want to listen to this filth."

He's astonished:

"What do you want me to do about it? I'm just telling it the way it was. Or would you prefer it like this:

"Is the mistress at home" I asked the doorman, handing him my fur coat and telling him to shake off the snow thoroughly.

"She is, sir," Vasily said gloomily, and I glanced in bewilderment at the severe expression on his face, thinking to myself, 'Does he sense something, then?'

I glanced into the nursery. Nickolas was already sleeping, the nanny forestalled me and shielded the small bed with her body:

"Christ be with you, master. You be just in from the frost, the choild'll catch a chill."

"The word is child, nanny, not choild," I corrected her.

"At's what oi said: choild," said nanny, not understanding my comment, not really even hearing it.

119

I went to see Kitty, irritated beforehand at her invarying question: Why so late? – but at the same time cherishing this irritation, which would support me in conducting the forthcoming conversation. In any case, one should not give free rein to one's feelings. Humility, certainly, but inflexible firmness.

"Why so late?" asked Kitty, wrapping her peignoir around herself in a chilly fashion.

"Business!" I answered briefly – and immediately regretted pronouncing the habitual word. I should not have answered like that, without answering her question. With a serious expression on my face, I should have taken her by the hand, sat her down and begun: Listen to me, Kitty... but now, after the usual bravado declaration: Business! – the words to follow were already on the tip of my tongue: "I'm beastly tired and beastly hungry! Why don't we ask Marfusha to heat up the samovar?"

"You're very quick to bother the servants in the middle of the night," said Kitty, but then she went and gave the instructions.

No, I must smash all this, smash it, or the enchanted circle will never be broken!

I paused deliberately and walked about the room, rubbing my hands together, then gently sat her down in the armchair and said:

"Listen to me, Kitty..." Her eyes suddenly filled with tears. She could sense it. But these tears helped me. They created a mood in my heart which made it possible for me to go down on my knees before her and say:

"Kitty, I beg you, please. Grant me my freedom!"

"No, no, no," exclaimed Kitty. "You are joking, you are drunk, I will not listen to you, no, no, no!"

"I implore you, Kitty! This is inhuman, this... "

"No," she said, gasping for breath. "No, no, no! Who's there? Come here and defend me from this terrible man. I am going to faint!"

"Hey there! Anyone! The mistress is unwell!"

My call brought the footman Grishka, blowing his nose on the floor, jangling the keys of the Mercedes and sipping gin and tonic.

"Whatyer yelling at?" he asked disdainfully. "People needs their rest, and you go yelling like that. When did anyone last flatten your face for you, you rotten bugger?"

Then he squirted out a long stream of spittle on to the carpet, went up to Kitty and pulled up her skirt.

...

Chapter Eleven

She tells him:
"About midnight, knowing that I stay reading till late, he knocked at the door of my room:
"Can I come in?"
I let him. He came in, avoiding looking me in the eyes, the way he does when he has lost heavily at cards. But this time it was not a question of cards.
"Forgive me," he said to me, "but my work has clearly taught me to be blunt and direct, which may make me appear rude to you. But I can no longer speak in any other way. You have grown cold towards me. What is the reason? For more than three months you have not let me near you. At first you cited illness. But now I can see that that is merely a subterfuge. I ask you please to explain yourself."
To be honest, I had hoped that this conversation would take place later, not today. I said:
"Please, Andrei, leave me alone, I have a terrible headache, let us postpone this discussion at least until tomorrow."
"I see. So there is after all something to discuss?"
"Unfortunately yes."
"What do your words mean, explain them to me," he said with that sharp impatience which has obviously been developed in him by his period of service as a head of department. Oh, I can imagine how his subordinates tremble at his appearance, how timid they become at his glance and his word — for how long is it since I myself ceased to tremble when he addressed me with that refined politeness of his?
I made up my mind.
"I must tell you, Andrei. That is precisely it, I must tell you — and I ask you to accept my words with the dignity which becomes a rational person such as you are, and for which I admire you beyond measure. I have fallen in love with another man."
There was a pause.
"How's that?" he exclaimed at last, having thought through the

structure of his speech and now setting it forth point by point. "To hold in contempt my position in society and your own obligations as the wife of a man occupying a certain position in society, a position which could be shaken as the result of a scandal! To hold in contempt the obligations, if not of a mother, then of a mother-to-be! To despise the duty of a Christian woman who considers herself devout!"

I got to my feet, drew myself erect and replied:

"You stinking bastard! Quit that babbling! I'm sick to death of you, you lousy pest!"

He grabbed me by the throat, pressed me up against the wall and yelled:

"Who've you got tangled up with, you slut? Answer me!"

But I'm not such a pushover, I gave him a fine belt across the bonce and smacked my knee up into the spot where the balls bounce, he doubled up, I belted him again a couple of times on the kisser, he reached for a knife, I reached for the frying-pan, he went for me, I went for him:

"Go on, hit me!"

But he stabbed wide with the knife, and he was as drunk as hell, and I clocked him with the frying-pan. I took a look at him, and – Oh, lordie, lordie! – his eyes were closed and he wasn't breathing! I looked at his head, and there was a great gaping hole in it! And buckets of blood! I came over real dizzy, I thought: I've gone and killed him! It's the camps for me now, alright, my life's finished!

Chapter Thirteen

He asks:

"But what happened, seriously?"

"Seriously, nothing serious. He doesn't want me, what he needs is a simple, caring kind of woman who'll feed him and wash his clothes and so on – who'll bear him children, he wants children."

"My wife's exactly like that. Simple and all the rest. I tell you what – why don't we introduce them, eh?"

"It's a crazy idea."

"Why? Anything's possible in these healthy times."

And he couldn't calm down. He went on fantasizing.

One day his jealous wife Katya came to the photographic studio and discovered her Nechaev and the woman Tanya kissing each other. She was not only jealous, but vengeful. No, she would not sear the face of her rival with nitric acid, her vengefulness took a more Soviet form: bringing the facts to the attention of public opinion. However, nowadays public opinion seems to have grown entirely indifferent to morality, since the public is itself amoral. All that was left was to go to the seducer's husband. So she went to Andrei and said: "My dear sir, are you aware that it is your wife's intention to lure my husband Nechaev away from the bosom of his family?"

"Indeed, no," Andrei replied.

"Then know, you oaf!" said Katya, "that your wife is a perfect bitch, and if, you louse, you don't take measures to deal with her, I shall take measures to deal with both of you, I won't give you bastards a moment's peace, what sort of man are you anyway, if you can't even control your own woman?"

His hands on his hips, Andrei replied:

"That's none of your bloody business, you should keep better control of your own man instead of yelling and screeching like a rusty old chain-saw. It's obvious why your husband likes a bit on the side, with a voice like that you should be working the Bering Straits ferry, calling the passengers on the other side. You repulsive cow."

"And you're a little shit!"

"And you're a filthy slut!"

And she went for his eyes with her nails, and he tore himself away from her and threw her out of the fifth-floor window.

Or:

Nechaev, working as a free-lance street photographer, photographs Tanya and Andrei, promising to forward marvellous colour prints to their home address. He writes down the address, then later turns up there to apologise because the prints didn't come out, but says that now he will photograph them again in their home. He takes their photograph, then starts up a conversation with Andrei, for instance about his hobby – what does he really enjoy? Fishing?

"No."

"Chess?"

"No."

"Does he collect matchbox labels?"

"No, no, no!"

"What then?"

"Nothing."

"Okey. I'll still make friends with him one way or another."

We all get to know each other, both families. We go for trips out into the country. We drink wine. We leave them alone together. They start hugging and kissing for all they're worth.

"And if they don't?"

"They start hugging and kissing, then we appear out of the bushes: "Ah, so that's how it is! Even though it hurts, we'll let you have your love, but we're leaving you behind and setting out into the blue distance with tears of pain blinding our eyes!"

Or:

...

Chapter Fourteen

He says:

She's called in my mother- and father-in-law. To put the pressure on and make me feel guilty. My mother-in-law had a separate little talk with me.

When we were alone, Efrosinia Dmitrievna remained silent for a long time, pursing her lips drily as she surveyed me out of the corner of her eye, or rather not me, that is, not my face, but rather, apparently, my clothing, and I even began searching for some element of disarray in my dress, but I could not see any.

"Well now, my dear," said Efrosinia Dmitrievna, "I've seen a good deal of life, the Lord be praised, I've set up two sons and two daughters, and I still have one more to give away, as you know, and I'll do it right and marry her to a good man. All the rest are well married to good people. But I've been disappointed in you – and I've only myself to blame."

"Efrosinia Dmitrievna!" I exclaimed angrily, wishing to cut her short and make her see reason straight away.

"I have been Efrosinia Dmitrievna for sixty years now!" she replied grandly, going against her usual custom of knocking off ten years of her age. "Just you listen to me, you fine game-cock! You'll have your turn. So, my friend, it seems you have acquired a fancy-woman – silence!" She halted the cry that was ready to burst forth from my chest. "You call her whatever you like, but I say she is a fancy-woman! Because I have no other word for a person who way-lays a married man. Now listen to what I have to say. I know very well what you are thinking: now the old woman will demand that I put an end to this business straight away! Oh no! I saw what my own dead husband used to get up to. I saw it, but I was clever, I knew what to do: let him run wild. If I'd gone making a fuss over every one of them, he'd have left me for the first one that made up to him, I know what men's pride is like, no sooner do you start nagging them than their pride wells up, only for a minute maybe, but a minute's long enough for them to run off. No, it's but safer to hush things up. So this is what you should do: tell Katya that it's all over, that you've thought better of it and put the nonsense out of your head, and you and your fancy-woman – silence! silence! – you just have all the good times you want. And what you really want, my dear is another month, perhaps two."

"This is vile", I exclaimed, unable to restrain my indignation.

"Allow me to be the judge of that," she cut me off sharply. Then she added: "Let me also remind you, my boy, that the doctors have recently pronounced sentence on me. Nothing lasts for ever, but it is hard to think that there is only a year or so left... As you are aware, my second husband has his own capital. But everything that belongs to me will go to my daughters. I had been intending to leave you about two million dollars. Provided, of course, that everything remained as it was. As far as I am aware, your affairs are not going too well."

"My share dealings are perfectly sound," I laughed. I felt free without her millions and mentally thanked my father for leaving me a sound business and not just dead capital.

"I have heard your shares are high. Of course they are, I arranged. for them to be bought up. But tomorrow they could be dumped on the exchange at a cheap rate, then the panic would begin, everyone would try to get rid of them, and in three days you would be ruined."

I was obliged to gulp down a sizeable whisky in order to restore my presence of mind.

"I would lose a hundred thousand," she said with a smile, seeming to anticipate the loss as though it were a gain, "but you would be left without a cent. As far as I know, this woman of yours has nothing either, apart from her professional qualification and her career. But that can be set right: tomorrow the city council will pass a resolution cutting back the public health services. The poor dear will be left without a job, just like you." The old woman smiled, baring her brilliantly white false teeth, dead matter in living flesh, and at the sight of those teeth I pulled out my revolver...

Chapter Fifteen

"But seriously?" Tanya asked.

"Seriously? Nothing serious happened. She just screeched and mumbled a bit."

"You louse! That's the only word for you – louse! And why have you uncovered the child's throat like that, left it wide open to the frost? It's ten degrees below out there. Give him here, let him hear, let him know his father's a louse, what a louse! Let the poor little orphan know, now you'll grow up without a father and you'll end up in prison, and you stop bawling, it's your own fault, you don't take any real interest, you can't be bothered to go round and see what the louse is up to, and you be quiet, no-one's talking to you, that's it, my little love, you run, don't eat the snow, you run, my love, what a louse, what a little shit, it makes me sick to look at you, I could kill you, I'd scratch your eyes out, you louse, you just make a mess of other people's lives, you louse..."

And she took me, unresisting, by the scruff of the neck, dragged me over to the kitchen table and held down my hand on the table-top while she hacked off my fingers in a violent frenzy, she cut off my ears and my nose and then began putting them through the mincer. She called her husband, my father-in-law: there, try that. My father-in-law chewed on the minced meat and said thoughtfully: could do with a bit more salt, then he said to his daughter: never you mind, love, we'll break him, we'll break him up and break him down, and then he said to me:

"Well, what've you got to say?" A hiccup. "Don't you give a damn for anyone else?"

"Let me go away, let me disappear, I can't go on!"

"Go away? You'll be put away. At public expense."

My father-in-law bared his teeth in a grin – and suddenly his face seemed to turn to stone, only his lips moved, all the rest was dead. He spoke in a whistling whisper:

"You remember we drank beer at the christening? With my neighbour Leonid Ilich?"

"Well?"

"What did we talk about?"

"How can I remember that?"

"I don't remember either. But I do remember that you had an argument with him. And you shouted: "You're wrong, Leonid Ilich!" You listen to it: "Leonid Ilich is wrong!" And now you just remember who else is called Leonid Ilich. And just you think what would happen to a man who shouted out that Leonid Ilich was wrong in front of witnesses!"

I burst out laughing, but my father-in-law went on looking at me with his stony face, and suddenly I felt a sensation like frost biting into my spine and I realised that this man was capable of anything.

"That's right," he said.

"Go on then! Inform on me!"

"They'll take note of that, too," my father-in-law said viciously. "They'll take note that you call bringing the facts to their notice in good time informing. You may not be afraid for yourself, but have some pity on your wife. Have pity on the child, he'll be a son of an enemy of the people."

I didn't answer him. I just went out and slammed the door behind me.

That night I couldn't sleep. I was waiting for something, and it came. The tramp of boots in the entrance-way, the peremptory knock at the door.

"Stop it, stop it, I can't take any more!" shouted Tanya. "I can't hear any more of this! It's filth, nothing but filth!"

"But people died!" Nechaev reasoned sagely.

"What business that is of mine?" asked Tanya. "It's difficult enough just trying to work things out with myself."

Chapter Sixteen

She says:

"I think I've worked things out. I told my husband everything, explained it all. Told him I couldn't and all the rest."

"And what did he say?"

"Nothing in particular..."

He looked straight at her, right through her, with eyes that were white from fury, alcohol and cocaine.

"So..." he said, turning away his eyes and gazing thoughtfully out of the little window, beyond which the pawns and knights in which he took no interest moved in turn.

"So..." he said cautiously, the way one tests the keenness of a sharpened sabre with one's finger.

"So!" he cried out wildly, pawing the air clumsily as he got up from the table to advance on me. "You've decided you want to be free to go rushing across the steppes in a wagon like some travelling whore?"

"Wake up, Andrei," I said, tightening my shoulder belt and straightening up my revolver. "You're wallowing in the petty-bourgeois bog, you don't even look like a human being any more. I'm ashamed for you! I shall not be a travelling whore, but a free woman of the new world, galloping on my fiery steed across the steppe to greet a new life in which there will be no more slaves and masters, in which everyone will be equal, pure and beautiful, in which woman will be man's comrade, and not the object of filthy erotic manipulation!"

"Scum!" he squealed, and threw himself at me, but the barrel of my parabellum dug into his ribs.

"I'm not afraid!" he growled. "No woman's going to frighten me! You won't dare!" He dashed at me in an attempt to grab me by the throat. I stepped back and struck him on the temple with the butt of my mauser. He slumped on to the floor. Paying no attention to him, with a light heart and a light spirit I walked out on to the porch. The wind ruffled my head-scarf and I laughed as I tore it from my head, then waved it in the air as I ran after my comrades, shouting: "Hey! Hey!.."

"Alright, alright," said Nechaev. "But seriously?"

"Seriously? Nothing really serious."

She was standing close. Nechaev couldn't resist, he embraced her.

"No," she said. "Please, please. Not here, not now."
He says:
"We're going to the seaside to relax. By car. Tomorrow."
She says:
"OK."

Chapter Twenty-One

...

He says:
"No, I can't believe it..."
She says:
"I can't. The smell of petrol makes me sick. The seats are dusty and filthy. I can't."

He says:
"We should have stayed in town. We'd have got into a hotel somehow."
She says:
"We can't help it now. Let's sleep."
...

Chapter Twenty-Five

...

He says:
"Not too bad as hotels go, eh?
She says:
"It's awful. Sheets someone else has already slept in... And maybe they didn't just sleep..."
"They've been washed."
"So what?"
...

Chapter Twenty-Six

...

He says:
"There. Our home for an entire three weeks."

She says:

"Where's that stench coming form?"

"The landlady's boiling cabbage for schi."

"That word's venomous. That word stinks. Schi."

"I always say tasty schi's the dish for me. Well then, shall we go to bed? We were up at half past five."

"I suppose so. Turn the other way."

"Good God, I can't understand you. After all, sooner or later – what's the problem? Is the yearning body not capable of boxing the cantankerous intellect's ears?"

"Behind the door there are voices and the shuffling of feet, and someone's plump, greasy whisper – darling, climb in! And the rhythm of love is an uneven champing, and all is filth and filth, and filth, and filth... I'm sleeping, I'm sorry."

...

Chapter Twenty-Nine

...

A beach. The sun. The sea. She says:

"Well? have you had a good look at me?"

"You are divine!" he says in his dark glasses.

"Let's go home," she says. "I want to go home."

...

Chapter Thirty-Four

...

... there will be everything – later...

Chapters Thirty-Five to Forty-Nine

She has a special job to do – inspect the snack-bar in the circus. She goes on a Saturday, during the matinee performance.

The music taunts her with its childish, carefree rhythm, she goes in through a door and finds herself close to the floodlights. Then she sees Nechaev nearby with a boy and woman, with his wife. Nechaev is talking to his wife, and from the way he is talking with her, she suddenly realises without any doubt that he has deceived her, that he has never even spoken with his wife about leaving for good because he has finally found a pure and radiant love.

She walks along the street in the falling snow, not blaming Nechaev, because she hasn't said anything to her husband yet either. In fact, she doesn't even have a husband.

1992

Translated by Andrew Bromfield, 1993

Alexei Slapovsky

Alexei Slapovsky was born in 1957 in Saratov and has been living there ever since. He graduated from the Department of Philology, Saratov University, taught at school for a few years and is currently deputy editor-in-chief of **Volga**, a literary monthly published in Saratov, in which most of his works have appeared. When he offered his stories to **Znamya** in Moscow he immediately attracted the attention of readers and critics alike. Slapovsky is very prolific, both as a dramatist and a prose writer. His plays have been produced in many countries, including the Eugin O'Neill Drama Festival in USA and this year he won the first prize of the European Drama Festival in Kassel (Germany) sponsored by Bern Bauer Verlag. His plays usually have a cast of two or three characters and a minimum of sets.

This Isn't Me was nominated for the Booker Russian Novel Prize last year, while all the three of his novels, published in 1993, have been nominated this year. Slapovsky has been highly praised in the Russian press for the originality of his ideas and imagery, great power of observation and startling insights into the current state of Russian society, as well as his apparently straightforward and elegant style and professionalism. His other works include: **The First Second Coming (200 pp), Who's Going to Kill the Bride (160 pp.), Happy New Year! (130 pp.), The Coded One (100 pp.), The War of the Idiots (100 pp.), On a Dusty Winter Day (80 pp.).**

VALERY RONSHIN

Living a Life

Trostnikov rented a room on the fourth floor of an old three-story building. In order to get to his room, one had to cross the ground floor, where lived the girl Inna, who for several years now had been waiting for True Love; the second floor, where lived Professor Elenev with his young wife Muse (who was by profession an art critic and by calling a train station whore); and the third floor, where lived the snitch Parfyonov, who would snitch on everybody, one after another in a row. After that it was necessary to go up by a narrow iron staircase, coil oneself to the left, go up again along another narrow staircase, this time a wooden one, coil oneself to the right and lean on a dirty door, upholstered in simple sacking.

Beyond this door, in an always filthy room, on an always unkempt bed, lay the always sleepy Trostnikov.

He did not, on principle, want to do anything. Because he was a philosopher.

From time to time he got various ideas into his head. Usually other people's. Trostnikov carefully noted them down in a big notebook.

The first idea in the notebook was this: *Life is a dream.*

And so he slept. Three days at home. And three days at work. Trostnikov worked as a watchman at some office where no one really did any work. There he had a personal trestle bed. On this very bed, Trostnikov worked... In the corridor hung a board with a list of employees. Personnel flow was high. People came... left... came... Trostnikov carefully noted with a pencil: *fired... on vacation... dead... on sick leave... skipping work...* Granny Manya lingered in the office longer than anyone else. She had come here as a 17-year-old girl, and now she was already going into her seventh decade.

In her own way, Granny Manya was also a philosopher. No matter what she talked about, she would invariably talk about death. Granny Manya would always begin from far away.

"How the world has changed," she sighed gravely. "I'd crawl across the front line, I'm dragging a wounded man, the bullets are whistling: fyoot! fyoot! fyoot! and I'm dragging him and I don't think about how they can kill me..."

"Well, just what are you telling me all this for?" Trostnikov lazily asked from his trestle bed.

"For no reason," Granny Manya philosophically answered. "I'll die soon. Then you'll remember me: that's what kind of person she was, let her rest in peace."

"Of course," said Trostnikov, and thought to himself, *The hell you bugging me for, you dumb old bag.*

Besides Granny Manya, the alkie Grisha and the ex-pilot Rusanov, also an alkie, had worked here for more or less a long time. They mainly drank face lotion. And if they were short of money, then they'd drink foot lotion.

Opposite the office, across a dirty little river, there was a children's toy factory, surrounded by a high wall. At night military vehicles would drive into the factory...

The day was ending. Time stood still. The clock on the central square had been showing 10 minutes to three for about a year. Professor Elenev was appearing on television. He was shooting the breeze with an intelligent expression on his face. Trostnikov walked along the street. As usual when there weren't other people's ideas in his head, he had to think his own.

Is today Monday or Wednesday? he racked his brain.

At an intersection, Trostnikov saw the girl Inna. She was looking into a puddle on the asphalt.

"Look," said the girl Inna, "the clouds are reflected in the puddle."

Trostnikov had a look, but he didn't see any clouds at all. An ordinary mud puddle. The soaked-through butt of a cigarette floated on the top.

"Is today Monday or Wednesday?" asked Trostnikov.

"Today is Sunday," said the girl Inna. "And yesterday, coming out of the doorway, you ran into me and didn't even notice."

Trostnikov looked at her, not understanding what she had just said.

Yep, he thought. *If your head has trouble grasping things, then there's nothing you can do.*

A little drizzle started.

"I don't like umbrellas!" The girl Inna jumped for joy. "I love rain!"

She spread her arms and began to spin round and round.

Is she drunk or what? thought Trostnikov, puzzled.

"I have all the defects of the world in me," said the girl Inna, having stopped her spinning. "That's why sometimes in my soul I feel really, really miserable."

Trostnikov started showing off his intelligence.

"Everything in life is relative," he said with importance. "For example, in relation to some poor devil, who right now is freezing in Siberia, you're quite well off, even. But if we compare you with the princess of Liechtenstein, then she'll probably have it better than you."

The girl Inna grew a little sad.

"You just said that I'm not a princess, and I'm a little hurt. Every woman wants to be a princess."

"People were too fruitful and multiplied," sighed Trostnikov. "You can't be a princess for everyone."

"But only for one?... The only one!... My beloved!..." she imploringly gazed into Trostnikov's face.

"Well... maybe. I don't know."

This foolish conversation was already tiring him. He wanted to get to bed and lie down as soon as possible.

He quickened his pace. The girl Inna did not lag behind.

"You've been living in our building for three years already," she said with offence in her voice. "And we don't know anything about each other. Even that unpleasant old man Parfyonov always questions me in detail on what I'm reading, where I'm going, who I'm seeing. Even Professor Elenev's wife once told me, 'You, my sweetheart, have a major screw loose.' And you never ask anything...''

"It doesn't matter! Doesn't matter!" Trostnikov waved the girl Inna away like an annoying fly.

He practically ran.

"For a woman it does matter a lot," said the girl Inna, barely keeping up with him. "You just say, 'Hello, Inna,' when we meet. And then I'll feel good."

The trolleybus was already driving off. Trostnikov jumped up onto the footboard.

"Oof," he wiped the sweat from his brow. "Pain in the ass stupid girl."

...A yellow filth spewed from the smokestacks at the children's toy factory. Time continued to stand still. The manager Ivlyev came. In his childhood he took ballet lessons. Then he drank himself to ruin and became a manager. Ivlyev walked with his head thrown back and, in the fashion of Napoleon, with his palm stuck behind the cuff of his jacket. Approaching Trostnikov, who lay on his bed, he poked a dirty index finger on Trostnikov's knee and demandingly said:

"You're a watchman! And you're obligated! obligated! to roam your duty area, answer telephone calls, and sweep the floor!"

"Fuck off!" answered Trostnikov, without opening his eyes.

He knew how to talk with simple people.

The manager Ivlyev immediately lost all his Napoleonism and, having sat on the small edge of the trestle bed, began to recount simply:

"Yesterday, I swear on my mother, me and my wife made 500 pelmeni dumplings. I swear on my mother, that we used to make 1000 at a time. And when guests come — he-ere's something to go with vodka. Very convenient."

Trostnikov slept peacefully. And woke up — already at home.

Well, I never... he thought, surprised.

"Here's something else," said the ex-pilot Rusanov. "Once I fell asleep in a tram. And woke up in a sobering-up station."

...A used-up old fogie sat in a local cafeteria. This was the snitch Parfyonov. He had a thinning little beard and reddish little eyes that blink often.

The snitch Parfyonov drank tea. He would take a swallow, pull a caramel from out of his mouth, lay it on its wrapper, spoon some brown pulp out of a jar, quickly chew it with his mouth shut, once more take the caramel from the table, stick it in his mouth, take a swallow, pull the caramel out onto the wrapper, eat a spoonful of pulp...

And so on.

"How are you?" he said, seizing Trostnikov with a tenacious stare.

" Alright," replied Trostnikov.

The snitch Parfyonov jiggled around in the jar with his spoon.

"Why do you answer me like we're in kindergarten? 'Alright.' I need a more specific answer."

"More specifically: I eat, I sleep, I talk."

"Well, now, that's better," said the snitch Parfyonov, sipping his tea. "Now we've got a topic for an interro... for a conversation. What do you eat? With whom are you sleeping? What do you talk about?"

"What's it to you?" asked Trostnikov. "What're you, a KGB snitch?"

The bastard suspects, maliciously thought the snitch Parfyonov, sucking his candy all over.

...There was a light rain. For two weeks, already. Trostnikov woke up again. His body ached sickeningly. His head wasn't working straight.

He looked out the window. Outside it was the same scene as yesterday. Trostnikov opened his notebook.

What the heck could I write? he thought, gnawing his pen in anguish.

There were no ideas of his. Nor other people's.

Trostnikov went down the stairs. On the ground floor, in the doorway, the girl Inna was standing and waiting for True Love.

"Would you like me to open up my rich inner world to you?" she proposed to Trostnikov.

Trostnikov didn't listen to her. He thought, *What a bore everything is.* Near the entrance, the stylish Muse was casually smoking. A big black car rolled up. The stylish Muse, after telling an obscene joke, rolled away in the car.

Professor Elenev kept on shooting the breeze on the National Channel One...

The alkie Grisha was drunk as usual, but wearing a white shirt.
"I got married," he boasted.
"What dump did you find her in?" scoffed Granny Manya.
"They'll give us an apartment soon," said the alkie Grisha, bursting with self-satisfaction. "She's a class-one invalid."
"Why'd you go and marry a cripple?" asked Trostnikov, puzzled.
"You gotta do what you gotta do," answered the alkie Grisha, craftily screwing up his eyes. "Now I'll live in peace. No one'll tempt her."
Granny Manya reasoned about death:
"It's not pleasant if they burn you. And drowning you in water, you don't want that either. A cemetery is in a low place. Water gathers there in the fall... But they say that in the conservatorium the temperature's such to raise the dead..."
"*In the crematorium*, bumpkin," corrected the alkie Grisha.
"It'd be better to die soon," harped on Granny Manya. "Living's become a nightmare. People are lower than dogs... And God still won't let me die. You can't lie down in the coffin still alive..."
It was a humid night. Trostnikov sweated. He couldn't sleep.
"He-e-e-lp!" resounded a high-pitched female voice outside the window.
Trostnikov lay with his eyes open. His head split into two parts.
The night is full of evil, he wrote in his notebook.
The pale dawn emerged. March began. Everything was melting. Including the money in Trostnikov's wallet. In the women's locker room they were singing something Russian in a drawl...
"The women are loaded again," the alkie Grisha commented on their singing. "Every day they drink, the bitches."
Trostnikov was eating a sandwich. The alkie Grisha watched with hungry eyes. He'd spent his last rouble three days ago on beer.
"Ah, the songs we had when I was young," sighed Grisha nostalgically, swallowing spit. "You ain't never heard nothing like them. *A lone slut was working Broadway*, Or this one! *Hey, buddy, don't drink from the john! You'll croak, for it's teeming with germs...!*"
Trostnikov was finishing his sandwich. A little piece of sausage fell onto the dirty floor. The alkie Grisha urgently dived after it and stuffed it into his mouth.
"It doesn't matter. You wouldn't have started eating it up off the floor," he said in justification.

What you gave away is yours, wrote Trostnikov in his notebook. Thursday was beginning. Or, actually, maybe Friday. Trostnikov walked along the street and read all the signs in turn. *Club* for some reason he read as *Bread*. *Cinema* he read as *Meat*. A warm summer rain started. And just as suddenly stopped. A rainbow hung in the sky. The girl Inna skipped along. She held some sandals in her hands.

"I love it so much to run barefoot on the puddles," cheerfully laughed the girl Inna, "when I'm doing it it feels like I'm not really me. It's so wonderful..."

Trostnikov looked at her lively face and thought, *I'll get old soon and die.* Illustrating this thought, a black hearse with a sign, *On his final journey!* drove by.

...At home Trostnikov lay in bed and wrote down in the notebook: *I do not exist. Even though I sit in an armchair under a lampshade.* He put his pen aside and got lost in thought. The sentence seemed rather strange. It was even more strange for the fact that never in his life had Trostnikov had either an armchair or a table lamp with a shade. Trostnikov got up and approached the mirror. In the mirror were reflected the table, the television with Professor Elenev on the screen, an overcoat on the coat rack. Trostnikov himself was not in the mirror, not even a trace of him.

I've philosophized myself out of being! he suddenly thought, frightened, and rushed to the doctor.

An announcement hung on the doors of the hospital: *Needed: general purpose nurse.*

"Follow me," ordered a nurse in a mini skirt, taking him down the corridor.

Trostnikov stared at her long, graceful legs in black stockings, and his imagination flared... flared...

Whoa, hey, hold it! his inner voice severely shouted at him. *You're a philosopher, remember?*

Trostnikov glanced at the legs one last time and then stopped looking.

"Vadim Nikolayevich, another schizo for you," announced the nurse as she opened the doors to the office.

"Bring him in!" echoed a cheerful voice inside.

"You may enter," said the nurse in an official tone.

Trostnikov entered the office. The psychiatrist sat at his desk.

"So, you're crazy, I take it?" he joyfully asked, rubbing his hands. "It happens. But just imagine if the whole world went crazy."

"I can imagine," said Trostnikov.

The psychiatrist placed a blank case history form in front of him.

"Well, what have you got there?" He gave Trostnikov a wink. "You think you're a vampire-horse?"

"I think I just totally don't exist," said Trostnikov.

"Ex-ce-lent! And have you not existed for long?"

"Since Friday."

The psychiatrist thought for a long time. Then he asked:

"And what are we today?"

"Thursday," said Trostnikov.

The psychiatrist again thought long and hard.

"Well then, that's that," he finally said. "You haven't existed for a full week?"

"So it follows."

The psychiatrist would have gone into another long think for a third time, but Trostnikov got to him first.

"Well?" he asked.

"What're you, late for a train?! What're you 'well'-ing me for!" the psychiatrist said, nervously pounding his fist on the table. "If you haven't existed for a week, then you've got nothing to be 'well'-ing about! Got it?"

"I'm sorry," said Trostnikov.

The psychiatrist grabbed a pen and started to write.

"Have you had mumps?... What about syphilis?"

Trostnikov shook his head no. The psychiatrist noted it down.

"Right," he said and slammed shut the case history. "You may go. You're in complete health."

"What do you mean 'in complete health'?" Trostnikov started to protest. "I don't exist!"

"Well, so what?" the psychiatrist said, dismissively. "I don't exist either, maybe. What, is that a reason now for people to go mad? Then someone else has no money... and someone else no wife... and someone else no children..."

Trostnikov walked out into the street. A company of soldiers was marching along. Some prostitutes were smoking in the entranceway to the hotel Oktyabrskaya. Deep below the earth the metro trains rushed on, stuffed to the rafters with the simple Soviet people. The ex-pilot Rusanov was recounting how he'd played chicken head to head with a Nazi ace!

"Ye-ah, that was a time," said the ex-pilot Rusanov, puffing on a cigarette. "It so happened that I was playing chicken head to head with a Nazi ace! I thought, That's it! You're fucked, puppy!... But it never got into my head to turn away first..."

Trostnikov slept peacefully. Beyond the window, snow fell. Beyond the snow, the snitch Parfyonov walked along. Electric barbed wire topped the high wall that surrounded the children's toy factory. Then someone else's thoughts came. Trostnikov, without waking, wrote them down... At the window, the girl Inna sat and waited for True Love.

"I don't need anything," she didn't tire of repeating. "Only love. My soul thirsts for a huge love."

"That's your problem," said Trostnikov to this.

He went to a photo studio to have his picture taken for a "registration card." The police, in addition to passports, had ordered everybody to get "registration cards."

"Why'd you make a sour face like that?" said the photographer to him. "We're not taking your picture for the grave."

Trostnikov examined the finished photographs with disgust. An old, emaciated face...

A strong wind blew. Some light trash was blown off the garbage heap and whirled around in the courtyard. Spring came again. But the birds, for some reason, didn't return. Black crows sat around everywhere and croaked.

Croaked...

Trostnikov lay on his trestle bed. Granny Manya dragged herself along the corridor.

"You're still lying around," she shook her head disapprovingly.

"What do you mean, 'lying around,' grandma?" listlessly answered Trostnikov. "Can't you see? I'm standing."

"There were no people, and these aren't people," Granny Manya continued her conversation with herself. "It's just filth!"

The manager Ivlyev was in anguish from not having anything to do.

"Read a book, maybe?" he thought out loud. "What do you recommend?"

"Dickens," mumbled Trostnikov through his sleep.

"Is that about a war?"

Dirty clouds floated across the sky. Two old women were almost crushed to death in line for sausage. More and more stray dogs and policemen appeared on the streets. A Water Safety Board announcement said: *Ten people drowned in our region over the last month. Of these, three drowned in their bath tubs.*

"How sad our lives are," sighed the girl Inna in a melancholy way. "Near and far..."

Professor Elenev shot the breeze from the TV screen...

"Just how do these people get to be professors?" puzzled Trostnikov.

A street lamp swung in the wind. A cat meowed. A piano was being tortured.

Fallen leaves rustled underfoot. Cold water dripped from above. A black car rolled up. Professor Elenev stepped out of it with an air of importance.

"You're free," he released the driver.

"Hello," Trostnikov greeted him.

The professor, not looking at him, walked by.

At work, Granny Manya died. Trostnikov noted on the bulletin board: dead. And he even talked about her a bit with the ex-pilot Rusanov.

"Once Granny Manya crawled across the front line, dragging the wounded, with bullets whistling: fyoot! fyoot! fyoot! And she would keep on dragging them, not even thinking about how they could kill her."

The ex-pilot Rusanov swore under his breath, out of habit.

"Ah, she spent the whole war deep in the rear, washing foot bindings. And you actually raised your ears: 'bullets whistling, fyoot! fyoot!'"

Trostnikov turned over onto his other side and fell asleep. Working hours went on...

Winter began. The country's immortal leader died. Trostnikov went to the public bath house. Inside the bath house sat an attendant. A fat lady in a kerchief with a bright flower pattern.

"What're you...?!" she stared at him like at a madman.

"What?" Trostnikov didn't understand.

The fat lady was turning purple with rage.

"The country's in mourning, and you go to the bath house!..."

Blah blah blah.

Trostnikov got dressed and went out onto the street. A funereal melody flowed over the city. Red flags with little black ribbons were hanging. Some guy was standing with his sheepskin coat thrown open in a telephone booth, bawling into the receiver:

"When the hell are we going to install the toilet?!"

The leader was buried in the earth... and in a year they buried still another... and in a year another...

Professor Elenev's wife, Muse, was telling a new joke:

"The Prime Minister of England is talking to the president of the United States: 'It's a shame you didn't make it to Moscow for the funeral. The funeral feast was splendid.'

'No problem,' answers the president calmly. 'I'll go next year.'"

Everybody laughed. The snitch Parfyonov scribbled in his notebook: *Wif. Prof. Elen. tol. antisov. jo.*

Winter ended. There was a humid summer. The mosquitoes were biting. The alkie Grisha's mother came. A hunch-backed old woman with a crutch. Crying.

"Was it really so long ago that I was taking him to kindergarten, and now it's been four years since I buried him."

"What do you mean, four years?!" Trostnikov raised himself on his elbow. "... Four years!!!"

But it was as if just now the alkie Grisha had sat here and said, "Ah, to get totally sloshed and puke!"

The country seethed. An excited crowd rushed to the square. A burly lad with a cross around his neck turned a white poster with black letters towards Trostnikov:

Everyone to the Rally!

The Rally is Dedicated to the Memory of Nadia Andreyeva,

Poisoned Exactly a Year Ago by the Mead Company

During a Routine Rat Poisoning!!!

Mead, thought Trostnikov dreamily. He was in the mood for something sweet. There were jars of sea cabbage in the stores. The sun warmed them. Crows jumped about. Down from the poplars was in the air. The girl Inna sat on a bench in a small courtyard and waited for True Love. In her hands she held a small volume of verse.

"Say," the girl Inna drew up her sharp chin towards Trostnikov. "If you like, I'll give you these heavenly poems to read. Would you like to?"

"No." Trostnikov rushed past. "Even without reading it I know it's crap!"

"But why? Why are you so... implacable?" The girl Inna ran after him, clutching the bluish-coloured little book close to her heaving breast.

"Excuse me," Trostnikov put his hand out near the door to his residence. "I've just come off the night shift. I absolutely have to rest."

He went to bed. The girl Inna slowly descended the stairs. She was crying one second, laughing the next. Her lips whispered:

"I thirst for love and warmth."

Wednesday began. Or Tuesday. Trostnikov did two things at once. He slept and at the same time thought. Trostnikov thought more or less the same thing Jesus Christ had thought a thousand years before. Namely:

Lord, why have you forsaken me?

Summer flared up. Stuffy heat hung in the air. His T-shirt sickeningly stuck to his sweaty body. The majority of people busied themselves with things they would rather not be doing. They stopped showing Professor Elenev on television and in addition took away his car along with the driver. He began using the trolleybus. He turned into a democrat.

"It's no-o-othing," said the professor with a crooked grin. "We made it through the war and we'll make it through this. The main thing is to have regular bowel movements."

Now Trostnikov was able to calmly ask what was to him the most interesting question.

"Please tell me, how do you become a professor?" he asked.

"Elementary," answered Professor Elenev, openly and honestly, in the spirit of the time. "You have to screw the wife of an academic."

Muse went up in the world. She was voted chairman of the "Society for the Protection of Animals." She stopped telling obscene jokes and started having discussions only about animals.

"All around us are just beasts!" she constantly grumbled.

The snitch Parfyonov admitted that he was a snitch. Smearing his tears all over his face, he howled hysterically:

"I'm a murderer! A murderer!"

"My God, how could it be?... How could it be?!..." The girl Inna cried together with him. "Why are we all so unhappy?!... Why?..."

"I'm sorry, kind people," the snitch Parfyonov hit himself on the chest with his fist. "I was young! They forced me! I informed on my friends!"

Professor Elenev patted him on the shoulder, trying to cheer him up.

"We're all guilty. Repentance is demanded of all of us. But now, my brother, a new life is beginning!..."

The summer ended. The "new life" began. The ex-pilot Rusanov died. Trostnikov noted down on the bulletin board: dead. And he even spoke about him a little with the manager Ivlyev.

"It so happened that Rusanov was playing chicken head to head with a Nazi ace. And he thought, *Well, that's it. You're fucked, puppy!* But he never got it into his head to turn away first."

The manager Ivlyev swore under his breath, out of habit.

"Ah, all through the war he was at the airfield, pulling blocks from under wheels. And you raised your ears: 'playing chicken head to head with a Nazi ace...'"

Trostnikov slept on his trestle bed. Crows strutted about on a dirty ice floe in the river. Street cleaners scraped the sidewalk. A tram tinkled. Snow melted on the roof. The melted water dripped right from the ceiling to his blanket.

I want to lie down and fall asleep under the trees, Trostnikov wrote in his notebook.

Professor Elenev became an uncompromising democrat. He even dropped by Trostnikov's for a visit. His wife Muse came along with him. The girl Inna and the ex-snitch Parfyonov, too.

Trostnikov treated them with a coffee drink, "Dawn." Muse talked about her new work:

"If a dog attacks you, then you should beat him not on the paws, and not on the head, but exclusively in the balls."

She finished smoking her cigarette and threw the butt into Professor Elenev's cup.

"My dear," the professor's eyebrows shot up in offense, "I hadn't finished my coffee."

"The same thing applies to men," Muse didn't acknowledge him. "If someone bothers you, right away a foot in the balls, and that's it."

"May I read some lovely verse?" the girl Inna timidly asked.

They let her.

> *White roses*
> *faded in glasses.*
> *Patches of moonlight*
> *lie on the table...*

The ex-snitch Parfyonov noted down in a piece of paper just in case: *Rea. vers. of dub. cont.*

"Where is your bathroom?" loudly asked Muse. "I want to wash my hands."

"I only have water in the kitchen," said Trostnikov in an apologetic tone. "And only cold."

They went into the kitchen. Muse turned on the faucet. There was no water. *What could I talk to her about?* thought Trostnikov.

"Is this really your second marriage?" he remembered. "And where's your first husband?"

"They caught him red-handed. Kicked the bucket," Muse carnivorously stared. "And why aren't you married? Some kind of sexual deviation?"

"I'll find a ballerina, and get married."

"What's a ballerina got to do with this?"

"They eat very little. Economical."

Muse laughed sensuously.

"Do you want to have sex?"

These words put Trostnikov on fire.

"I still haven't decided," he muttered in embarrassment.

"Well, then, let's decide," Muse pressed against him with her hard breasts.

"But I'm a philosopher," Trostnikov tried to free himself.

"That's what I want to find out from you, as a philosopher: what does our philosophy think about sex without love?"

145

And Muse painfully nibbled Trostnikov's ear. Trostnikov senselessly fixed his gaze on the badly-scratched surface of the kitchen
table...

"Our intelligentsia is not very intelligent!" Professor Elenev thundered in the next room.

The ex-snitch Parfyonov quietly scribbled in the corner: *Prof.
Elen. sland. the consc. of int.*

"What is it you're always writing there?" the girl Inna was interested, full of good will. "Are you composing poetry?"

The ex-snitch Parfyonov blushed and awkwardly stuffed the note,
covered with writing, in the sleeve of his jacket.

"Aha," he mumbled. "Poetry."

In the door of the room appeared an embarrassed Trostnikov. Behind him, fixing her skirt, entered unsatisfied Muse.

"Would you like to hear a new joke?" she asked from the doorway.
"An intellectual is walking along Nevsky Prospekt and sees a man uri-
nating at the Kazan cathedral. 'Excuse me,' the intellectual says, 'could
you please tell me how to get to the Hermitage?' 'What do you need
the Hermitage for?' answers the man. "You can piss right here.'"

Everybody laughed. The ex-snitch Parfyonov wrote down: *Wif.
Prof. Elen. – ano. antisov. jo.*

Life flowed, like water. On its surface lay the little trash, yellow
leaves, some kind of dark planks, dead fish floated belly-up from the
bottom.

Trostnikov stood on a bridge and watched. A distinct rotting smell
stank in the air.

A boy ran up.

"Hey uncle, have you been standing here long?"

"Yeah," said Trostnikov.

"Has a raft floated through here?"

"No," said Trostnikov, "it hasn't."

The sun set. It was time to go to work. To sleep. Trostnikov set
off. From a taxi stop angry Muse was coming toward him.

"It's easier for us to catch the clap than a taxi," she said with irritation. And added: "Do you want to hear something new?"

"Well?" Trostnikov stared with a frown.

"Someone snitched on the snitch Parfyonov. Tonight some Soldiers of the Invisible Front arrested him."

"Who? Who?"

"KGB, that's who."

Trostnikov walked farther.

"It couldn't have been you who snitched, huh?" she maliciously inquired after him.

"Fuck off!" answered Trostnikov, without turning.

He knew how to talk to the intelligentsia.

...When Trostnikov arrived at work, everybody was lying around dead. The manager Ivlyev in his office. The workers in the locker rooms. Women − in the women's. Men − in the men's.

It turned out that a radioactive leak occurred at the children's toy factory. Trostnikov walked up to the list on the bulletin board and in his careful handwriting put down next to each name: *dead... dead... dead... dead... dead... dead...*

Near his own name his hand hesitated for a second. Then Trostnikov wrote down hard: *long dead.*

When he got home, Trostnikov went to bed. But sleep didn't come. It was as bad as if someone had bored a screwdriver into his stomach.

He thought, *Why am I feeling so bad?*

Before long the girl Inna came and said in her thoughtful voice:

"Well, I don't know... of course... − the winter will end soon... You must try to live through this winter... not work, but try to survive..." Her hands flitted over Trostnikov like two stirred-up butterflies. "...You must read books... naive, good literature... *The Count of Monte Cristo...* As for me, I surround myself with books and think that, reading them, I'll survive... Later summer will come... it can't not come... It'll get warm... Everything will be alright... everything will be alright..."

"But there's something wrong with me," whined Trostnikov. "Something's really wrong."

The girl Inna's hands flitted before Trostnikov's face with renewed vigor.

"Think of Pushkin... of Blok... of Marina Tsvetayeva... Not long ago I discovered... I made a small discovery... They didn't die. They're all THERE," she pointed at the ceiling. "They turned into little stars... And from THERE it's as if they're signaling us..." The girl Inna tried to represent with her fingers how they signal.

Trostnikov attentively studied the dusty lamp hanging from the ceiling. The lamp had a *Pravda* newspaper over it in place of a shade.

"And we won't die," the girl Inna suggested to him. "On our modest little graves we'll grow, as green little grass."

Trostnikov let out a heavy sigh. He didn't want to grow as green little grass...

I don't want to work, he thought at first, then said out loud. "I'm just sick of work."

"Yesterday I was at the philharmonic," the girl Inna wasn't listening to him. "It's so magical... Debussy... Ravel... All around people with human faces... then I was riding on the metro... Everybody so dead... empty..."

"I pretty much in general don't want to do anything," Trostnikov continued his own.

The girl Inna came to. Now she was looking at Trostnikov right in the eyes.

"You must leave," she said. "Leave anywhere."

Trostnikov liked that: "anywhere." It reeked of something philosophical and even cosmic...

... any ... where ...

"I would leave," he said. "I'd leave for Tahiti. I want to lie down next to Gauguin. And what, can't I?... In the distance the ocean would sound... But who will let me go?..."

"Leave..." the girl Inna unplugged again and smoothly rocked back and forth. "Leave... Leave..."

"I'll go!!!" Trostnikov suddenly resolved, firmly.

He got up from his bed and went to the train station. In the courtyard a drunken Professor Elenev barked at a stray dog.

"Woof! Woof! Woof!" loudly woofed the professor.

The stray dog silently watched him with human eyes.

In the train station Trostnikov told the ticket collector:

"Give me one ticket."

"Do you want a ticket for close by or farther away?" asked the cashier.

"Whatever's cheaper," answered Trostnikov.

Translated by Chip Gonzales

Published in Russian in *Znamya* No.2, 1992.

We All Died
a Long Time Ago...

"You're never so completely lonely as when you're in a car at night, and it's raining." Straight away I had to admit that this thought was really too long for me. Mine are usually much shorter and simpler, so this one clearly belonged to someone else – just like the car I was now driving, in fact. Heavy raindrops were battering the windscreen and the wipers couldn't cope any more. I turned in to the side and switched off the engine and headlights. The lights on the dashboard went out as well.

Now I was in pitch darkness, here on this god-forsaken road at dead of night.

Leaning back in my seat, I lit a cigarette. The patter of raindrops on the roof was pleasantly soothing. Soon the rain stopped, and, stuffing my cigarette-end into the ash-tray, I drove on.

I was on my way to see my father, who used to be a sea captain but was now just a crazy old guy who went about all year in an open raincoat and darned striped vest, wearing his sailor's cap at a jaunty angle, and with a huge pipe clenched between his yellow, nicotine-stained teeth – a very expensive pipe it was too, presented to him by an English admiral for some wartime exploits or other.

It was five years or so since I'd last seen him. Then, the week before, quite out of the blue, I'd received a telegram: "Come: there's a little surprise waiting for you."

And then, naturally, it was signed: "Cap'n". That was what he called himself.

So I'd set off, without even knowing why, to be honest. Certainly not because of the "little surprise". I suspected this to be just another example of Dad playing the fool.

Why had I done it, then?.. Why, indeed, had I borrowed a friend's car and driven flat out for two days... instead of simply buying a train ticket and stretching out on a couchette, to wake up at my destination the following morning?

I don't know... I really don't... There are things which one can't explain logically and which you don't even want to explain.

It was nearly morning – about five o'clock, in fact – by the time I reached the town. I decided to book in at a hotel. A young girl with a fringe down to her eyes was sitting behind a glass screen in the empty lobby. Aware that I was looking at her, the girl raised her head from the book she was reading.

"The night train to Germany has already left," she said, smiling.

"Pardon me?" I asked, perplexed.

"That's what it says here, in the novel," the girl explained. "It's a beautiful sentence, don't you think?"

It was just a sentence. Nothing special.

"Sure," I said.

"D'you want to stay at this hotel?"

"Yes," I nodded. "Assuming that you have a room vacant, of course."

"You assume correctly," laughed the girl, holding out a blank form. I quickly filled it out.

There was a pause.

"Is the book interesting?" I asked, to make conversation.

"Well, there's this hero who has breakfast, and then he gets into a lift and goes down..."

"*What* an original plot!"

We laughed.

Sticking out a delightful little pink tongue, the girl flicked it rapidly over her full lips.

"Let's have a kiss, then," I coaxed, laying on the old charm.

"You *are* a fast one, and no mistake," she said. Clenching her fingers against the palms of her hands, she lifted them to shoulder-height, and then stretched herself languorously.

"It's just that I'm in a sexy mood today," I said as if in justification.

"Ri-i-ight." There was an irresistibly playful lilt to her voice. "Well, come on then. But through the glass, mind."

"Kissing through glass," I declared in a dogmatic tone, "is like smelling flowers in a gas mask."

"Well, I suppose that could be quite nice too."

Taking the initiative, the girl held her face to the screen, and we kissed.

"Have you ever kissed a dead person on the lips?" she asked quite unexpectedly.

"I can see you're keen on horror stories," I said, taking my cigarettes out of my pocket.

"Ooh, no," the girl replied with a mock shudder. "I don't like horror stories."

"What about love stories?"

"Ooh, no," she said, continuing the game. "I get all excited."

"What about..."

"Quiet!" snapped the girl, jerking her forefinger in the air. "Can you hear the music?"

I listened, but couldn't hear any music.

After a minute she said, "Have you ever had the feeling that it's all stage scenery? These buildings, cars, people. Our whole life. Sometimes I even get the feeling that *I* simply don't exist, that I'm just a piece of scenery too."

"I don't know," I replied with a slight frown. "I've never thought about it."

Everything had started off so well, yet now here I was bogged down in this stupid conversation that was verging on the mystical.

The girl took a pack of cigarettes from her brown handbag and lit up as well.

"So what brings you here?" she asked.

"I've come to visit my dad," I said. "He used to be a sea captain, you know."

"Oh, I know him!" exclaimed the girl, coming alive. "That strange old bloke who always went around in an open raincoat, summer and winter."

"That's right," I confirmed. "And a striped sailor's vest."

"I think he's dead," said the girl, frowning. "Yes, that's right. He's dead."

Dead?.. Dead?!.. How extraordinary!... Was this perhaps the little surprise I'd been promised in the telegram? Well, it would be quite in character...

"When did he die?" I enquired.

"A long time ago," she replied with a shrug of the shoulders. "It must be about a year ago now."

When? When?

"About a year ago... I know because a girl friend of mine lives in the same building."

Hmm... a year ago. Yet the telegram had been sent about ten days ago.

"Where's his grave, then?" I asked, stupidly.

The girl hooted with laughter.

"Where do you think – in the cemetery, of course. Then there was that odd name he always used," she recalled. "Captain... Captain..."

"Cap'n," I said. "He called himself The Cap'n."

"Yes," the girl nodded. "That's it: The Cap'n. My name's Kira, by the way," she added, and smoothed her hair with her hand.

"Pleased to meet you," I said, taking my key and heading slowly up the stairs.

"Sleep tight," Kira called after me.

2.

I went upstairs to my room, undressed and got into bed. I had a dream that was in the style of a thirties film: brisk, jolly music blaring from loudspeakers in the park; plump girls in snow-white dresses strolling along well-trodden paths; smart soldiers in shining boots, also out for a stroll. As for me, I was sitting in a little boat in the middle of a pond with a panama hat on my head, holding a fishing rod. Not far away a natty little steamer with the name 'DEATH' on it was sailing past.

As this was a dream, both the steamer on the pond and its name seemed quite normal.

When I opened my eyes, for a second or so I thought I was still dreaming. A strange man in black was standing by the door.

Black patent-leather shoes, impeccably pressed black trousers, a black overcoat (unbuttoned), a black jacket (buttoned)... A black hat, black gloves and a black walking-stick completed the overall picture.

"Mr Schulz," said the strange man by way of introduction, "Pyotr Ilyich. I'm an old friend of The Cap'n."

Kira burst into the room all out of breath and launched into an indignant tirade:

"Now listen, just what do you think you're up to? Walking in here as if you owned the place! Didn't you hear me call – are you hard of hearing, or what?!"

"Pyo-tr Il-yich," I repeated, as if savouring the name and patronymic on my tongue. "You don't happen to compose music, do you?"

"Bah! Music!" Kira scoffed contemptuously. "He happens to work at the cemetery, that's what."

"No, I don't compose music," Mr Schulz replied in his somewhat toneless voice, completely ignoring Kira. "Actually, I'm the proprietor of a modest establishment known as Bon Voyage. Wreaths, coffins and ribbons at twenty per cent below state prices."

"I heard that my father has passed away: is that right?" I asked, pulling on my trousers.

"That would be putting it mildly," muttered Mr Schulz in an off-hand manner.

"But hang on – what about the telegram, then?"

"I sent you that."

"I don't get any of this," I said, my head spinning.

"Don't worry, I'll explain," promised Mr Schulz, adding with a sideways glance at Kira: "Only not here."

...Outside in the street a fine drizzle was falling. Mr Schulz strode out at such a brisk pace that I could hardly keep up with him. Soon we arrived at the cemetery.

It was a cemetery like any other. Graves, headstones, a hushed silence... Mr Schulz, excusing himself, popped into a little house to the right of the cemetery gates, soon to re-appear holding a long iron bar.

"Come on," he said.

Following one of the paths, we walked further and further into the cemetery, almost as far as the perimeter fence. Here, next to a luxuriantly growing bird-cherry bush, was my father's grave, with the following inscription emblazoned on its modest headstone:

"Even now I am more alive than the living... The Cap'n."

"He thought that up himself," said Mr Schulz (whether as a disclaimer of responsibility or a simple statement of fact was not quite clear).

Then, handing me the iron bar, he commanded: "Stick it in." I stuck it in. Practically the whole length of the bar disappeared into soft earth.

"So what?" I said, turning to Mr Schulz. And in the same split second realized *what*.

There was no coffin.

Mr Schulz made no response but headed for the way out.

We entered a cafe not far from the cemetery. Here we bought a small coffee each and found somewhere to sit in an out-of-the-way corner.

"When I was about four months old," declared Mr Schulz, taking a sip from his cup, "my father threw me up high in the air..." He bit off a piece of biscuit and chewed thoughtfully. "But he didn't manage to catch me."

"Yes," I said, "accidents can happen."

From an inside pocket of his overcoat he swiftly pulled out a thick wad of photographs held together with a rubber band, and threw them on the table. He looked at me expectantly.

I drew them towards me cautiously, with a vague premonition of something very nasty. I was not mistaken. They were all, without exception, pictures of funerals. Or more exactly, not actual funerals, but the faces of the dead in their coffins. In close-up.

There were all sorts of people – old men, children, young women, young men, teenagers... I slowly examined each picture in turn before laying it aside. I can't say this gave me any great aesthetic pleasure.

"Your father took the pictures," explained Mr Schulz. "There are about a hundred here."

"Actually, I don't quite..." I faltered... and then became completely tongue-tied, as in the cemetery not long before.

Sorting through the photographs, I suddenly saw one of Kira.

It was in colour, and I recognized her light-blue dress, the one she had been wearing at the hotel reception desk. It was Kira, without a shadow of doubt – only not alive, but dead. Her eyes were shut, her hair was neatly coiffured, and her hands lay lifeless on her breast; a thin candle had been inserted between the fingers.

I shot a questioning glance at Mr Schulz.

"Those marked on the back with a small red cross," he declared in a subdued tone, "*have returned.*"

What did he mean by that?.. Hastily I turned over Kira's photo. A thick red cross had been drawn in the bottom right-hand corner...

I recalled what she had said: "Sometimes I get the feeling that I simply don't exist." Now these words took on a completely different meaning.

Outside a car drove past. Somewhere in the distance a dog barked.

There was a roaring sound in my ears. I opened my mouth wide and then closed it again. Sometimes this helps, but it didn't now. A young girl came into the cafe, went to the juke box, inserted a coin and began quietly swaying her head in time to the song that started playing.

"Sometimes I get the feeling that I simply don't exist," I repeated out loud.

"What?" asked Mr Schulz, not catching what I had said.

"Nothing," I replied, and emptied my coffee-cup in one go. "Carry on."

"What more is there to say?" he said, looking at me with a puzzled air.

"The dead return. On that occasion..."

"Just a moment," I interrupted, and went to the counter. "Do you have any vodka?" I asked the tall woman who was serving.

"Vodka?" Her pencilled eyebrows shot up. "This happens to be a children's cafe, in case you didn't know."

But on taking a second look at my face, she disappeared behind a curtain without further comment. A minute later she re-appeared with a cut-glass tumbler. I downed it in one gulp and returned to my seat.

"On that occasion..." I said.

"What?" asked Mr Schulz.

"You said: 'On that occasion'."

"Ah," he remembered. "On that occasion The Cap'n took a few cylinders of compressed air and got into his coffin. Then my assistant and I buried him at the cemetery. Next day the coffin had disappeared. That's all there is to it."

"Could somebody have dug him up without being detected?"

Mr Schulz heaved a noisy sigh.

"No," he said firmly. "We sat next to the grave all night. It poured with rain, too. We got soaked through."

A bevy of schoolgirls crowded into the cafe. Giggling and chattering, they began eating scoops of ice cream of various colours. My head had started to ache – or rather, my temples. Gradually the vodka was having an effect on me; already I was beginning to think that our visit to the cemetery and the conversation we were now having were all a hoax. A common-or-garden hoax.

But Mr Schulz was sombre as he sat there opposite me.
"Why did you send for me?" I asked straight out.
He chewed his lips.
"I thought you'd want to know all this."
"Oh, I do," I said sarcastically, nodding my head. "I do indeed."
"Apart from which," continued Mr Schulz, twisting his empty cup in his hands, "I thought perhaps you'd have a go as well. After all, he *was* your father. That's about the long and the short of it..."
Aha, so that was it...
I used my fingers to massage my temples, which felt as if they were splitting.
"Forget it..."
"Well anyway," he declared emphatically, rising to his feet, "I'll see to the grave, and get your coffin and air cylinders ready. You just think about it. Think about it *very* carefully."
Mr Schulz gave a slight bow and left the cafe, while I remained seated at the table, staring vacantly and fixedly in one direction.
My head felt empty...

3.

The following day I took Kira to the cinema. Gunshots rang out from the screen. We were sitting in the back row, and I was pulling segments off a tangerine and putting them in Kira's mouth; sometimes her lips brushed the tips of my fingers. As the story unfolded, the film stars started making love, and leaning towards me, she whispered in my ear:
"I shall have a baby, too. We need children to justify ourselves."
"Why is that?" I asked, my thoughts on something quite different.
"Because," rejoined Kira and turned her face to the screen.
The film ended. We came out of the cinema and immediately turned off into a side-street to avoid walking with the crowd. Gateways appeared as black chasms. Television screens glimmered in windows. It was very warm, more like a summer than a spring evening.
"Why did you kiss me?" asked Kira.
"When?" I queried, momentarily at a loss.
"In the hotel. Through the glass."
"Ah," I smiled. "Who'd miss out on kissing a pretty face?"

She pouted provocatively.

"I don't like people saying I'm pretty."

"In that case," I suggested, "let me kiss you again."

"I've never yet given anyone a real kiss," Kira declared indignantly. "Believe me, I'm not interested in *that*."

"What are you interested in, then?"

Instead of answering she looked up at the sky.

"You see that red ring round the moon?" she said, pointing. "It's a bad omen. There'll be trouble before the year is through."

I too looked up at the moon, but I couldn't see a ring.

"Trouble before this year is through," I declaimed. "Either I shall die, or you."

"He-ey," she intoned admiringly, "you're a poet!"

"Indeed I am," I conceded.

"Do you know this poem, then?" She stopped and began to recite:

> *Once somebody walked past beneath my window.*
> *I think that it was raining; I think there was thunder, too.*
> *Once somebody said 'farewell' to me.*
> *I think it was on the veranda; I think we were having tea.*
> *Once somebody left me, never to return.*
> *I think it was a Tuesday – or Wednesday, who can say?"*

"No," I said, "I don't know that one. Who's it by?"

"Me," replied Kira.

We turned off into another side-street and then another... Slowly we strolled through unlit, narrow streets. Even the occasional passers-by had disappeared by now.

All at once, without warning, Kira gave voice to a full-throated "A-a-ah!" and smiled with delight. "How lovely! There's nobody here. I like the night-time." She thrust her hands into her trouser pockets and mischievously, urchin-like, kicked an empty cardboard box lying next to a litter bin.

"I like toys, too. Why don't they sell those toy snakes any more – you know the ones..." And taking her hand out of her pocket, she made writhing motions with her wrist. "They used to move like this. Why?" she demanded, almost petulantly. "You must remember them, those lovely green snakes."

"Yes, I remember," I said, although in fact I didn't.

"So why don't they sell them any more?" she asked, pouting her lips like a child.

"Because your childhood is over," I replied brutally.

Immediately Kira seemed to wilt, and she said no more.

The sky was veiled with clouds now. A sharp wind got up and it began to drizzle.

Ahead of us we saw the cemetery.

Mr Schulz was not in the least surprised that we should visit him so late. He and a muscle-bound hulk of a fellow were seated at a table, playing cards.

On the floor, not far from the front door, stood a spacious coffin.

"Pyotr Ilyich," I asked, "can we wait here until the rain stops?"

"You can do what you like here, as long as you pay," joked Mr Schulz. He was in a good mood. "Would you like a game of cards?"

I declined.

"A pity," he commented, and yawned expansively. "This is Alik," he added, with a casual nod in the direction of the hulk. "My assistant. I take it you haven't met?"

"How do you do, Alik," said Kira.

"You're wasting your time," pointed out Mr Schulz. "He's deaf and dumb. Would you like some hot milk?"

"We would," I replied.

Mr Schulz went to the kitchen and returned with a large cup of hot milk.

"There you are, young lady," he said, offering the cup to Kira.

Kira kicked off her boots, curled up in a deep armchair and, cupping the milk with both hands, began to sip at leisure.

"Excuse my asking, Pyotr Ilyich," she said, "but do you happen to know where I might find the grave of a young man who was killed in a motor-cycle accident two years ago?"

"As it happens, I do. But why do you want to know?"

"He was my first love," explained Kira, blushing.

"First love — that's a good one," said Mr Schulz and began shuffling the cards. "You don't even know where his grave is."

"People don't always regret the loss of their loved ones," Kira said quietly.

I left to wander round the house, examining the modest bachelor furnishings and decor as I went. When I returned, I found a lively conversation in progress. Mr Schulz was relating something with great enthusiasm. The morose Alik was frowning with displeasure. Kira was laughing out loud: there was no sign of the melancholy mood she had been in before. Her cheeks were flushed, her eyes sparkled, and she gave the impression of someone drinking spirits rather than milk.

"Why don't you get married, Pyotr Ilyich?" I asked, sitting down on the sofa and lighting a cigarette.

"Because all women are potential whores!" came his answer as quick as a flash.

"Wha-at?!" spluttered Kira in mock indignation. "So according to you, I'm a whore too?!"

"Of course!" declared Mr Schulz confidently.

"And you're a berk!" chortled Kira, leaning back in the motley-patterned armchair.

"Edmund Burke?" asked Mr Schulz in an impish tone, turning his face towards her, at the same time rolling up his eyes to reveal the whites, and sticking his long tongue out to one side.

"What a performer!" cried Kira with delight, clapping her hands.

Alik the deaf-mute impatiently rapped his knuckles on the cards which lay scattered on the table, but Mr Schulz had lost his enthusiasm for the game.

"Indeed I am a performer," he concurred readily. "Before finding my true vocation here at the cemetery, I spent many years working in a circus. As a magician, actually."

"Oh, so you're a magician," said Kira, her eyes narrowing vindictively. "We'll put that to the test straight away. Right, then: tell us what we were talking about just before we got here."

She wiggled her shoulders with excitement.

Mr Schulz's face took on an intense, solemn expression.

"You were reciting poetry," he proclaimed in a sepulchral voice. "Am I right?"

"Got it in one!" shouted Kira, jumping up and down. "Long live Mr Magician!"

"Do you like poetry, Pyotr Ilyich?" I asked.

"I do, rather," he nodded. "Best of all I like that poet... What's his name?.. Anyway, it doesn't matter. There's one poem by him. My all-time favourite... Hang on, how does it go? Ah, yes:

> *Ti − tum − ti − tum*
> *It's night!*
> *Ti − tum − ti − tum*
> *Take flight!*

"What a *splendid* poem!" laughed Kira, tossing her head back and shaking her thick hair. "So, what else did we talk about, Mr Magician?"

"What else?.." Mr Schulz furrowed his brow. "Apart from that, you were talking about people's different aims in life."

"Wrong, you've got it wrong!" shouted Kira. "Nowhere near − nowhere near!"

"Well, all right, you didn't exactly discuss that, but in general... philosophical questions."

"That's true, in principle," I confirmed.

"So what about you, Pyotr Ilyich: what would you like to be?" Kira asked.

"A fly," replied Mr Schulz without pausing for thought.

"How do you mean?" Kira actually straightened up slightly with surprise.

"Just what I said: a fly," declared Mr Schulz, vigorously describing circles in the air with his forefinger. "What's wrong with that? It would be great: flying round the room to your heart's content, and buzzing."

The deaf-mute gathered the cards into a pack and stalked out, the picture of injured pride.

"Bzzzzzz," buzzed Mr Schulz, scampering round the room in a hunched posture.

This time Kira was even more convulsed with laughter.

"If you're a magician," she said when she had recovered, "do some magic."

"No problem," rejoined Mr Schulz. There was a brazen note in his voice. "But you'll have to help me, Kira my sweet."

"All right," agreed Kira eagerly, rising to her feet. "What do I have to do, then?"

Somehow all this was beginning to jar on me... In particular, I didn't like the intense look in Mr Schulz's beady little eyes.

"It's getting late, Kira," I said, grasping her arm. "We have to go."

"No way," she retorted, pulling herself free. "I'm not going now until I've seen some magic."

Mr Schulz whistled: "Fyootee-fyoot", and, flicking his cane up to the ceiling, said, "My cane will turn into a sabre."

And indeed, he now held in his hands a long thin blade.

"Is that all there is to your trick?" Kira asked, disappointed. "Pooh!.. And there was I thinking..."

She had already turned to leave.

"Stop, stop!" called Mr Schulz cheerfully, holding her back.

"The main trick is still to come... So, look into my eyes and pay attention. Now for some hocus-pocus... One! Two!! Three!!! Allez-oop!"

With these words Mr Schulz brandished the sharp blade and... cut off Kira's head!

At first I simply couldn't understand. My conscious mind just refused to accept as real what had taken place before my very eyes. It had been so grotesque... so sudden... and so fast... The blade, entering Kira's neck, had sliced through it easily and without resistance. Her head had fallen to the floor.

"Eh?.. Eh?.." was all I could get out.

"'ay is for 'orses," said Mr Schulz calmly. "Close your mouth, or you'll catch a fly."

The body had not slumped to the floor with a dull thud; no dark blood had come gushing out to spatter all over the furniture and walls... Nothing even remotely like this had happened... The head had rolled under the table, and now lay there. As for Kira's decapitated body, it just carried on standing in the same place as before.

"A graft," said Mr Schulz tersely.

"What?" I asked in a state of shock.

"I call them 'grafts'," he explained. "Those who have returned, that is. Why, didn't you realize from our conversation yesterday that they *aren't human* any more?"

My legs gave way. I sat down.

"No," I mumbled, "to tell the truth..." − but I was too dazed to continue.

161

Mr Schulz evidently sensed the state I was in.

"Go and sleep now," he advised. "Alik has made up a bed for you."

I nodded apathetically, and slowly, on legs that were like jelly, went up to... to Kira and took a look in through her neck.

It was empty and dark in there.

"Great!" I said, gradually beginning to get a grip on myself. "And I was thinking of marrying her."

Mr Schulz made no reply.

4.

When I entered the room next day, having slept until nearly midday, I came across a familiar scene. Mr Schulz and his deaf-and-dumb assistant were playing cards. Kira was sitting in an armchair — although minus her head, of course.

While there on the floor was the spacious coffin.

"You might at least have put her out of the way somewhere," I said with a sidelong glance at the body.

"What for?" asked Mr Schulz, genuinely surprised. "Let her sit there. She doesn't bother us for food or drink. There's even a peculiar kind of aesthetic appeal to it. The aesthetics of putrefaction." He quickly shuffled the cards. "Will you have a game?"

"No," I said.

"A pity," commented Mr Schulz, and yawned expansively. "Then try out your coffin."

He was in no doubt whatsoever as to what my decision would be. He *knew*. Just as he had known that I would be bound to come after I received his telegram.

I got into the coffin, lay down and fixed my eyes on the ceiling. There was a cheap-looking chandelier up there, with some flies buzzing around it.

I began to feel good inside. At peace.

"It's my belief," I said, "that everyone should spend at least an hour a day lying in their coffin, meditating about the point of their existence. It's so spiritually purifying."

Mr Schulz brought two large cylinders from the next room.

"Here you are," he said, placing them next to me. "Compressed air. You can purify yourself to your heart's content."

...Towards midnight we dragged the coffin to the grave, which had been dug earlier. With well-practised movements Alik took a hammer and nails out of his bag.

"Listen!" I protested on seeing the deaf-mute's preparations. "What are you up to – you're not going to nail the lid down, are you?"

"For a start, you can stop yelling and getting worked up about nothing. And anyway, everything's got to be done for real. Otherwise what's the point?"

I heaved a sigh and climbed into the coffin without a word. It felt uncomfortable lying there. The cylinders were sticking into my sides quite painfully... At last I managed to settle myself more or less. Above me hung the black sky. No moon to be seen, no stars. Nothing but darkness...

My heart sank.

"Lord," I thought, "how dismal it is indeed to die in early spring."

"My, you're a poet," sniggered Mr Schulz, and gestured to Alik to nail down the coffin.

"You might as well dispense with the formal goodbyes, Pyotr Ilyich," I said sarcastically.

Mr Schulz rummaged in the pocket of his black overcoat.

"Here, take this," he said, holding out a grimy-looking sweet. "It's chocolate."

...On the stroke of midnight they shovelled earth over me. When I started to have difficulty breathing, I took the rubber tube in my mouth and opened the valve in one of the cylinders.

So there I was, lying in a coffin, in the cemetery, under a thick layer of earth.

Buried...

Soon afterwards I heard a sort of scratching sound from above, as if somebody had scraped the lid of the coffin with something sharp.

I blinked...

It must have been in that instant, while I was blinking, that it all happened.

I was lying in a forest. The coffin had gone. It was a sunny day, and the birds were singing.

163

I stood up, dusted off my trousers and started walking.

I wandered slowly through the green grass, kicking at the yellow heads of flowers that lay in my path... And suddenly I was overcome by a quite unexpected feeling of joy. It just hit me like an avalanche. *I was alive!*

I could have died! I was supposed to die! But I was alive! Here I was, walking through a birch forest, kicking yellow flower-heads, and there was an orange sun in the sky – the rising sun! For already it was dawn, and dawn would soon be followed by day. A new day!

The plethora of emotions surging through me made me want to shout out loud.

And so I did...

"Who are you, some kind of nut?"

Not far off stood a middle-aged man in a jersey. To judge by his appearance, he was a typical holidaymaker staying at some nearby dacha.

"Yes, I'm a nut," I gladly conceded. "But tell me, how can I get into town?"

"That's the railway halt just over there," he said, gesturing with his arm.

There was indeed a platform, and a suburban train was already approaching, sounding its thin, quavering hooter. We broke into a run and just managed to scramble into the last carriage.

I leaned back on the hard seat and looked out of the window. I felt... I felt... No, I didn't feel anything. I just looked out of the window, rejoicing at the sight of everything gliding past the dirty, scratched pane of glass.

Opposite me sat an old man with a bushy beard, reading a newspaper.

"Excuse me," I said, "is it far into town?"

He looked at me over the top of his newspaper, annoyed at being distracted from his reading, but replied nevertheless:

"About twenty minutes."

Before going to Mr Schulz I walked around for a bit. I went into the cinema and had a look at an exhibition of children's drawings... I found everything interesting: it all gave me the most intense pleasure... For a long time I stood in front of the window of a women's clothes shop, examining the dummies. I was immediately reminded of Kira, of us kissing through the glass – and then of Mr Schulz cutting her head off. A light drizzle had started up again and I went into a public toilet. A pigeon was sitting on the window-sill, its feathers ruffled. There was a thousand-rouble note lying in the lavatory pan. I pissed on it and then left. The cafe was already open. Some music was playing: "Take the A Train" by Duke Ellington. I had a coffee, without sugar this time, and set off for the cemetery.

There was an Orthodox cross on my grave, and two wilting carnations lay on the mound of earth.

...Mr Schulz was having breakfast. Kira was still sitting in the armchair as before.

Thinly cut slices of cheese and smoked sausage were laid out on little plates. He had already eaten an egg: the pieces of white shell were arranged in a neat pile on the edge of the table.

"*He*-llo, squire," he called out cheerfully on seeing me. "Welcome back again!"

"Thank you," I replied, and poured myself some coffee from the pot. "Listen, Mr Schulz, who put those stupid flowers on my grave?"

"I did," said Mr Schulz. "In your memory."

"Why, were you so sure I wasn't coming back?"

"Of course. It's been a whole year."

I nearly choked on my coffee...

"How could a whole year have passed?"

"Quite simply," replied Mr Schulz, applying himself to spreading a large piece of butter on a large piece of white bread.

"We-ell..." I said.

What else could I say in the circumstances?

"We-ell..." Mr Schulz repeated after me, and added: "Go on, tell me what happened."

I told him... Although basically there was nothing to tell.

We sat in silence, I rubbing my face with my hands while Mr Schulz picked his teeth.

"We-ell," he drawled again. "So we have an interesting scenario here. Assuming that about fifty million people die every year, and someone is bringing them back to life again, what do we conclude? That we're all dead: that we all died a long time ago? Right?"

"I don't suppose they bring *everybody* back to life," I mused. "All in all we're left with a whole lot of unanswered questions here. Er, for example..." But no single example sprang immediately to mind, since it was *all* just one big unanswered question. "Er, for example..." I repeated, "what about identity papers, or the whole question of residence permits? And then, what if people bump into their former relatives? There could be all sorts of problems. Anyway, what's it all for? What's the point?"

I lit a cigarette and inhaled avidly.

"My dear fellow," replied Mr Schulz in a condescending tone, "when bees have all their honey taken away from them without so much as a by-your-leave, I think they're left with a lot of unanswered questions too. After all, they gathered the honey, intending to feed their little ones. And suddenly: *gone*, the whole lot of it – every last drop! So don't worry your head on that score. I think it all makes sense to *them*. As for our 'unanswered questions', *they* couldn't give a monkey's for them."

"Well... I don't know," I said, spreading my arms in a gesture of confusion.

"There *is* nothing to know," he rejoined, standing up and stretching himself lazily. "'There are more things in heaven and earth, Horatio, than are dreamt of in your philosophy!" And turning his face towards me, enunciating clearly, he said: "Ey-jiz..."

I looked at him perplexed.

"*Ey-jiz*. That's English for 'eternity'."

"What about it?" I asked, not getting his drift.

"Nothing," said Mr Schulz. "It's just that I bumped into The Cap'n in town yesterday."

5.

We didn't have to wait long for Dad to show up: he appeared the following day towards evening. As always, he was wearing his unbuttoned raincoat, striped vest and sailor's cap – and, of course, he had that pipe clenched between his teeth.

"Ahoy, shipmates," said The Captain in a breezy tone, as if he hadn't disappeared for two years but simply gone out for a walk for an hour or so. "How's tricks, sonny boy?" he asked with a wink in my direction.

"All right, Dad," I replied.

"Pah! Dad!" scowled Mr Schulz. "He's no more your father than I'm Tchaikovsky."

The Captain gingerly touched the glistening flank of the teapot.

"Right then, me hearties," he proposed, "shall we knock back some tea?"

"Listen, mate," hissed Mr Schulz, breathing heavily. "Cut out the play-acting."

Dad's bushy eyebrows shot up.

"Pyotr, old ship-mate," he said, "I don't know what you're talking about."

"Ha, just give it a rest," rasped Mr Schulz with even more of a scowl. "You understand everything perfectly!"

"Ve-ery well!" said Dad, striking the table with the palm of his hand to emphasize his words. "Let's put our cards on the table. Secret project 'X'. Re-cycling of waste material. Ultimate goal: the conquest of other planets... After all, what's the point of letting assets rot away in the ground?" he said, breaking into a strident laugh, and I flinched involuntarily. How well I knew that staccato laugh.

"Is it the re-cycling of corpses we're talking about here?" enquired Mr Schulz with feigned innocence. "As cosmonauts, yes?"

"The outer shell," my father corrected him gently. "Just the outer shell. The rest is discarded as surplus to requirements. So..."

"You can stop spinning us a yarn," Mr Schulz interrupted in an icy tone, and then continued, prodding my father with his finger: "He – I don't mean *you*, but the one this body really belonged to – *he* rumbled you straight away. And that's why you killed him. Well, isn't that how it was?"

"No," said my father. "Or rather," he continued after a brief pause, "maybe it was, and maybe..."

"Oh yes, oh yes," Mr Schulz promptly cut in.

"What are you getting at, Mr Schulz, or whatever it is you call yourself?"

A distinct quiver of hatred had entered my father's voice.

"Don't pretend you don't know," retorted Schulz, leaping abruptly from his seat.

"There's something fishy about all this," I thought, looking from my father to Mr Schulz and back again. "Something definitely..."

167

However, I didn't manage to complete my train of thought. Mr Schulz suddenly started waving his arms and gabbling nineteen to the dozen in a shrill-sounding language like the twittering of birds. My father started chirping like a bird as well. Mr Schulz lurched towards the table, where his cane was lying. From his appearance he was clearly in a resolute frame of mind, to say the very least... When he grasped the cane, I realized exactly what was going to happen.

"Hand over that cane!" commanded my father imperiously, holding out his hand. "And don't try any funny stuff, right?"

Mr Schulz froze on the spot. His face was twisted with malice.

"Here!" he shouted in a hoarse voice, and with a flourish threw the cane at my father's feet.

Dad bent down with a triumphant smirk... In that split second Mr Schulz whipped a shiny little box out of his pocket and aimed it at the stooping captain. There was a soft (I would even say *velvety*) buzzing sound.

Dad suddenly *burst* into flame all over, as if he'd been doused with petrol.

He straightened up, engulfed in flame, dropped the cane, took a few steps towards Mr Schulz, tottered... All this took place in absolute silence. I said nothing. Mr Schulz said nothing. My father said nothing... Then he began to collapse in upon himself. First his head sank through his shoulders and disappeared inside his trunk, then his legs disintegrated; and finally his body fell to the floor without a sound and also disintegrated...

All that remained of The Cap'n, my father, was an amorphous pile of ash.

Mr Schulz put the shiny gadget back in his pocket, fetched a dustpan and brush, painstakingly swept everything into a pile and then into the dustpan and, half-opening the window, emptied the ash outside.

"There's our life for you," he proclaimed gloomily, and began to rummage for something in a cupboard. "We are all ash in the wind. Am I right in thinking there's a novel of that title, by a German writer?"

"Yes, there is," I confirmed. "Except it's called 'We Are Not Dust in the Wind'."

"Well, it's not important," said Mr Schulz with a dismissive wave of the hand, and produced Kira's head from the cupboard.

He placed the head on her shoulders and started quickly applying something like cement or plasticine to her neck, rubbing it in. At least, that's what it looked like from where I was standing.

"That's it!" announced Mr Schulz after five minutes.

I had been watching Kira continuously. She opened her eyes and looked around with an air of slight bewilderment.

"Excuse me," she said, "I seem to have dozed off."

"Don't worry about it," rejoined Mr Schulz, giving me a conspiratorial wink.

"Oh!" cried Kira, looking at her watch and jumping up. "I'm on duty at half past seven. Well, I must dash. See you tomorrow, love." And she gave me an uninhibited, noisy kiss on the cheek.

"See you tomorrow, sweetie," I said.

Kira ran off.

"Well now," said Mr Schulz cheerfully, "shall we have some tea? Or would you prefer coffee?"

"So you too," I said slowly. "You too... But I don't understand... why you had to pull the wool over my eyes... why you had to bury me in the cemetery..."

"And I don't understand your passion for logical-empirical systems," declared Mr Schulz as he poured a strong brew of tea into two cups. "If one starts with two and then adds another two, why does one necessarily have to end up with four? Why not twenty-two?" Having finished with the tea, he proceeded to dilute it with hot water. "Eh?"

"... is for 'orses," I said, pulling the sugar basin towards me and putting two spoonfuls of sugar in my cup. "Don't give me all this flannel. I just want a straight answer: are you an alien?!"

"Good Lord!" exclaimed Mr Schulz, holding his head in his hands in mock dismay. "You know, I really think you've flipped. You're quite obsessed with these aliens." He suddenly broke into a loud guffaw. "Just the slightest provocation, and out you come with your flying saucers, cosmic forces, other worlds... I don't understand," he said, shaking his head.

"And there's something else I don't understand..." I tried to say.

"Ah, but I know exactly what you're going to say now," Mr Schulz interrupted me with a sour expression. "Only don't think I'm going to explain anything to you, because I'm not. You wouldn't understand a thing, anyway."

"Perhaps I would," I said, not giving up. "Give me a try."

"Your mother did that when she had you... No, joking apart, there's no point. It would be as if I were to switch into ancient Persian now, in the middle of a sentence. What would you understand then?"

"There's only one thing I do understand," I said stubbornly. "That *they* are extra-terrestrials" (I nodded in the direction of the window to indicate my father's scattered remains), "and that you are too. So tell me, not in ancient Persian but in plain Russian: *why are you here*? What the hell do you want here?.. And why are you re-animating our corpses?.."

"Phe-ew," puffed Mr Schulz. "Quite honestly, your head's filled with a kind of verbal mish-mash, young man. And not just you personally" (shaping a sphere in the air with his hands), "but *all* of you here on the planet Earth. What a load of rubbish you've stuffed your heads with! Extra-terrestrials, outer space... Well, none of this exists, right? There is no outer space. *It doesn't exist.*"

"What do you mean?.." I must admit this was the last thing I'd expected to hear. "But what about the stars?.. And the other planets?.."

"There aren't any other planets," Mr Schulz explained patiently. "There isn't *anything* at all. So there's no need to get in a stew and make life complicated for yourselves. What a way of going on, really! There's a nice proverb you have here, a French one: 'It's not true that life is simple: it is even simpler'."

"I don't understand anything," I mumbled. "I don't understand a damned thing."

"I did warn you that you wouldn't understand," Mr Schulz lectured me. "Console yourself with the thought that you have succeeded in fulfilling your purpose here on earth. That's something not everyone manages, quite frankly."

"Hang on, hang on," I appealed in sudden animation. "So just what is my purpose here on earth?"

"To come here, of course. To have these conversations with me."

"And is that all?" I asked, dumbfounded.

"That's all," nodded Mr Schulz. "Why, did you have visions of something universal again?" And Mr Schulz started whistling a cheery little tune to himself.

I mechanically picked up an apple that was lying on the table and took a bite out of it. A breeze blew in through the half-open window making the blind flap. "What a strange thing life is, though," I thought.

"What a strange thing life is, though!" I said out loud. "There's you and me sitting here, talking. Outside it's spring. Some people are lying buried in the cemetery; others, as yet still alive, are suffering, rejoicing, lamenting, falling in love, sleeping, eating..."

"Get to the point," Mr Schulz interrupted impatiently. "Stop waffling. What is it you want to say?"

"Or take you, for instance," I continued, ignoring his remark. "Who are you? Where are you from? And then, this whole weird business..."

"You talk too much," he remarked again.

"No, you see..." I went on, not listening – but immediately brought myself up short. "The universe doesn't exist... That's beyond belief..."

Mr Schulz sniggered, rubbing his hands with satisfaction.

"You can't believe it? I knew all along that you wouldn't."

"And we don't exist either?" I asked.

"That's right," he confirmed.

"Well, that's it," I thought. "Here we are. End of the line..."

Mr Schulz reached towards the table, seized the apple which I had taken a bite from, and ate it with relish.

"You know what," he said, "why don't you go back again – back where you came from? I did give you a friendly warning that you wouldn't understand anything. Everything has its limitations, particularly the human intellect. So don't attempt to understand – or even less, explain – anything on the basis of your own thoughts and feelings. To put it crudely, quite by chance you've blundered into a maze with no way out again. A maze *designed* with no way out. You can understand that, I hope?"

"Well, more or less," I replied weakly.

Suddenly I felt dead tired and drained of all mental energy.

"So go back again, seeing that you're so tired," Mr Schulz urged me. "After all, you have a female, don't you, or whatever it is you call them here – a girlfriend?"

I remembered Masha, a peroxide blonde in black silk stockings.

"Yes," I nodded, "I have a female."

"Well, off you go, then," he said, giving me a friendly pat on the shoulder.

And I did...

...To be more precise, first of all I put on my raincoat and went out into the street. As I recall, it still hadn't stopped raining. I walked past my grave, where I'd been buried a year before, and leaving the cemetery wandered round my native town, past everything that had once gone to make up my childhood, adolescence and youth. And which, according to Mr Schulz, simply didn't exist.

Then I came to the station, where I purchased a ticket and boarded my train. For some reason the lights in the carriage weren't switched on, and we sped through the endless expanses of Russia in pitch darkness. More than half the seats in the carriage were occupied by deaf-mutes who were inarticulately mumbling among themselves. A musician was telling no-one in particular how he had had his violin and all his money stolen. He was on the top bunk, travelling on a warrant issued by the police. Opposite me sat a stout woman in a woolly hat who spent half the night reminiscing about how as a young girl she'd seen a UFO over the pigsty in her village. There wasn't enough bed linen for everyone. I spread a mattress on one of the middle bunks and, stuffing my rather new shoes under the rather grubby pillow, fell into a deep sleep.

When I woke up, the train had already stopped and there was nobody in the carriage apart from myself. I made for the way out. On the platform I saw the train attendant.

"Goodbye, then," I said to her.

"Blow me!" she chortled. "And I thought you were deaf and dumb too."

Passing through the station building, I came out into the town. In a restaurant I found Masha: it was where I had left her a year before. She was sitting with her legs crossed, sipping a milkshake through a straw.

"Oh, it's you," she said without enthusiasm.

"Yes," I said, "it's me."

Actually, I wasn't completely convinced of this.

There were candlesticks holding lighted candles. Glasses were filled with bubbling champagne. A half-naked woman stood on a small stage, singing a song: 'Take me while I'm young'.

It was all so very familiar.

I took a cigarette from its packet and put it between my lips without lighting it.

"We're all dead," I said, and the cigarette jumped up and down in time with my words. "We all died a long time ago."

"You seem a bit touchy or something today," commented Masha and, leaning slightly towards me over the table, patted me on the cheek like a dog. "What's up, sweetie?" she asked with a faint, languid laugh. "Knotty problems? Well, don't lose any sleep over them. You know what the French say: 'It's not true that life is simple: it is even simpler'."

With these words Masha swiftly pulled a shiny little box out of her handbag and held it right in front of my face.

My heart missed a beat. However, it was only a cigarette lighter.

Translated by John Dewey

Valery Ronshin

Valery Ronshin, in his early thirties, graduated in history from Petrozavodsk University in Karelia and presently lives in St Petersburg. He started writing relatively recently, and immediately became one of the most published authors in both Russian capitals. He says that for his first thirty years he was "just living a life," moving with his family from one provincial town to the next, and then travelling on his own, mainly on foot, the length and breadth of Russia. He tried many menial jobs and taught history for a while before becoming a professional writer. He is very prolific as a children's author, while his stories for grown-ups are reminiscent of Daniil Kharms, the acknowledged master of the absurd, and are in fact what Kharms would probably be writing had he lived today. His first one-man collection of stories (published by IMA-Press in 1993) is actually called **Hello, Mr Kharms!**

Ronshin has also produced a number of screenplays for animated cartoons that won him several prizes in Russia.

He formulates his credo as a writer as follows, "A writer should describe his age and die." He also believes, "Real humour is always black".

FOUNDATION FOR THE SUPPORT OF
NON-PROFIT PUBLISHING PROJECTS

This is a newly founded association of non-commercial publishers dedicated to the preservation and promotion of contemporary Russian literature and scholarship. It is also concerned with reintroducing the formerly forbidden classics of Russian and world literature and philosophy.

The president of the foundation is Ruslan Elinin, poet and publisher, on whose initiative it has been launched.

More than forty publishers around Russia have joined the Foundation up to date. They represent all fields of the humanities as well as literature and poetry.

The aims of the Foundation are the following:
- expert analysis of contemporary works of art and literature;
- search of various means of assistance to non-profit publishing;
- creation of an information bank on literature and arts;
- search for new talent;
- restoration of forgotten names and works;
- support and development of new trends in literature and arts;
- all forms of protection for non-profit publishing projects.

For the last four years, Ruslan Elinin and his colleagues have been collecting manuscripts around Russia which were then carefully selected by a council of experts consisting of topmost writers, poets, critics and scholars. As a result, an impressive collection of unpublished works has been compiled. It is the intention of the Foundation to publish these as a series.

Committee:

Boris Axelrod (poet, head of the St Petersburg branch), Victor Krivulin (poet, publisher), Alexander Eremenko (poet, publisher), Genrikh Sapghir (poet, writer), Konstantin Kedrov (poet), Mikhail Sheinker (critic, editor of *Vestnik Novoi Literatury*), Yuri Maisuradze (publishing expert, representative of Pubwatch)

Address: 141090, Moscow, Bolshevo, P.O.B. 79
tel/fax: (095) 515 2551
190000 St Petersburg, Isakievskaya Sq. 5-15
tel: (812) 314 8923

Solo: New Names

Little
Booker
Prize
1992

ANATOLI GAVRILOV

Very Short Stories

Rose

Marshy woods at the back of beyond, an autumn night, the left wing annexe of the barracks, Rose's room, Rose, the civilian cook from the village of Glybotch.

Bare walls, a high ceiling, a drab, misshapen lampshade.

Window blinds tightly drawn, door under lock and key.

The last flowers of autumn in a mayonnaise jar.

It is cold in the room − the heating is not on yet.

Rose, in an acrylic dress and nylon stockings, covered with a coat, is lying on a bunk.

She is tired after a day in the kitchen, but, for some reason, cannot sleep.

For some reason, she is afraid and so does not put out the light.

She has not been here long − before this she worked on a farm in Glybotch.

At the end of August her one and only friend moved to the town.

Rose also wanted to leave, but somehow could not make up her mind. Maybe, it was because of her looks...

Not long ago, she came to work here, in an army camp.

Maybe, things will turn out well...

Although, of course, there was very, very little hope, almost none.

Rose lies and thinks of Glybotch. It is not far away, only ten kilometres from here. Now, there would be a damp autumn darkness there, only the windows would be gleaming. Now, her drunken father would be lying on the couch in his dirty boots and jersey, her mother would still be busy with her housework...

Here, the battalion was out for its evening stroll: she can hear commands, the tramp of feet, songs:

> *Firmly go!*
> *Listen, foe!*
> *Fear a cruel reply!*

After lights out someone will bang on her door, but Rose will not open it, for tomorrow the whole battalion could find out that she has visitors at night...

She would be summoned before the deputy political commander.

She would be dismissed for immoral behaviour, something she was warned about when given the job...

They will knock on the door, though, they will certainly peep in at the window, same as yesterday and the day before...

No wonder, the battalion was stationed in remote, marshy woods, enclosed by an electrical fence, they were never given leave, and, apart from Rose and an older married woman staff officer, there were no women here...

Here it is – they are knocking already... Rose starts and pulls her coat over her head... Maybe, she ought to ask who is knocking and open the door?

No – no, not now, not today...

There is already a noise under the window: someone is standing there in the dark, burning a hole in the blind with his eyes...

No, she must turn out the light, cover her head and try to go to sleep.

Rose leaps up, runs to the light switch, undresses quickly and dives into a cold bed, under the coat and blanket.

She shivers with cold... Tomorrow, they say, they should turn on the heating... Snow had fallen this afternoon... She ought to go home on her day off to help her mother...

There was a peremptory knock on the door. Rose opened it and saw an unfamiliar officer in full dress uniform.

"Rose Kulbakina? Five minutes to get ready!"

She dressed quickly and went out. A big car was waiting by the barracks.

"Get in," said the officer.

They drove silently through dark endless forests, when suddenly a brilliant light glowed ahead of them, there were doves and balloons flying in the brightly lit sky, garlands of multi-coloured fairy lights, magnificent bouquets of flowers were suspended in the sky, there was a smell of expensive perfume, beautiful music was heard.

"Moscow!" said the officer.

They stopped at a huge marble building, climbed the stairs, went in... On the walls hung portraits of statesmen, amongst whom Rose suddenly saw a portrait of her father.

"But mother and I thought he was a worthless drunkard!" she had time to think, when, to her surprise, the Commander-in-Chief stepped out from the wall, the escorting officer stood to attention and reported:

"Rose Kulbakina delivered according to your orders!"

Frightened, she backed away.

"Don't be afraid, Rose!" said the Commander-in-Chief. "I invited you here to express my gratitude personally for your courage, your steadfastness and your heroism! I know that they keep knocking on your door at night, but you don't open it! You don't seduce anyone and haven't been seduced yourself! It is a pleasure to meet you, and if you have any wishes, tell me, don't be afraid, don't be shy! Why are you silent? Maybe, you need something? Wouldn't you, for example, like to live in Moscow? Here you can have plastic surgery and become a beauty, get married, have a nice life. Maybe, you need some cold cream? Lipstick, mascara, earrings? I can arrange for a special medal to be cast for you "For Steadfastness in the Face of Knocking on the Door by a Rocket Battalion, Stationed in Remote, Marshy Woods..." Well, why are you silent, Rose Kulbakina?"

"Why am I silent?!" Rose thinks with alarm, tears choking her, she sobs − and at that moment her alarm rings: it is time to go to the kitchen.

The Album

When he retired Nikolai Petrovich was presented with an album and an alarm clock.

"That's not much," said his wife.

"Trinkets," smirked his daughter.

Nikolai Petrovich did not reply. He went to his room, a hastily built extension, where he had been living for some time: a table, a couch, an old wireless.

After reading the instructions, he wound up the alarm clock, set it and heard a familiar tinkling melody of a song about a coachman freezing to death in the remote steppe.

The album cover was of green velvet with a golden inscription: "To Dear Ivan Petrovich from the collective of the Mincing-Machine Shop."

Now, he could transfer his own photographs from the family album to his own personal album.

There were about fifteen of these: school, army, wedding, Mayday parade, trip to Gorlovka...

The first thing that struck him was that in all the photographs he looked gloomy, frowning for some reason, and only in that small faded one − was he smiling: a naked chubby child, legs in the air, two front teeth showing, he was lying on a floral rug and smiling...

On the back was written: "Nick one year old."

"Nick one year old," Nikolai Petrovich said out loud.

Through the window twilight was darkening over the village.

It had become completely dark.

The dog began to howl.

On the other side of the wall his daughter had switched on her tape recorder: "Li-ife can-not be tu-urned ba-ack..."

The Hen

It was an overcast day, heavy clouds were gathering, light, bluish snow was falling and melting.

Nikolai Petrovich was mending a hole in the fence with bits of tin-plate, tarred roofing paper and wire.

Hens were roaming about the yard, poking about in the ashes behind the lavatory, and only the hen with the blue markings, one leg drawn up and one eye closed, was standing still in the black, dug over kitchen garden.

Nikolai Petrovich was working slowly, often stopping for a smoke.

The neighbour's sick little boy, tongue sticking out, was looking out of the window.

A coach rumbled by.

Across the road stray dogs were fighting on the waste land.

The local louts walked by with their wheezing tape recorder and one of them asked:

"Is Vera at home?"

"No, she's gone to town," answered Nikolai Petrovich.

His wife, stockings at half mast, threw out the slops from the porch, and all the hens flew at the swill as one, only the hen with the blue markings remained in her place.

A gust of wind ruffled her dirty feathers.

Nikolai Petrovich went to the lavatory, came back and saw a stranger in a dirty coat and shabby fur hat standing at the fence.

"What do you want?" asked Nikolai Petrovich.

The stranger did not reply, just looked with dull eyes at the garden.

"What do you want?" asked Nikolai Petrovich and picked the hammer up from the ground.

"Cluck! Cluck-cluck!" the stranger replied, frightened, a bubble of spit burst on his lips: he recoiled from the fence and plodded off down the street.

A gust of wind nudged him in the back and lifted his coat tails, showing a checked lining.

The boy at the window got anxious, began to pull faces and knock on the window.

"Something the matter with you!" shouted Nikolai Petrovich at the little boy. "And what the hell do you want here!" he shouted at the hen, raising his hammer. "Why are you hanging about? Go away to your own... peck over there... cluck-cluck!"

The hen jumped aside and again stood still.

His work finished, Nikolai Petrovich took the remains of the tin plate, roofing paper and wire to the shed and went into the house.

There the stove was blazing hot, his wife was husking sun-flower seeds at the table, his daughter, humming "A Million Scarlet Roses", was making up her eyes in the hall in front of the cheval mirror.

"What are you getting dressed up for?" asked Nikolai Petrovich.

"Don't nag," his daughter answered.

"I'll nag you, before it's too late!" shouted Nikolai Petrovich.

"Leave her alone," said his wife. "Have you mended the hole?"

"Yes."

"Do you want to eat now?"

"Yes."

She filled a bowl with hot soup a sharp bone sticking out of it. He ate silently and then lay down on the couch.

The daughter, still humming, pulled on her new patent leather boots, put on her coat and hat and went to the door.

"Have you put something warm on?" shouted the wife.

"Yes, I have!" shouted the daughter.

"Where?" shouted the wife, running up to her daughter and lifting up her coat hem.

The daughter pulled herself away, slammed the door and ran off.

Nikolai Petrovich turned his face to the warm wall and closed his eyes.

He pictured his daughter walking down the dirty asphalt road in her new patent leather boots to the local shop, he pictured her drinking wine with the louts, smoking, laughing hoarsely...

So as not to see this picture, he opened his eyes and began thinking that he must get hold of a bag of sawdust from somewhere and cover the water pipes – the forecast was for frost...

He fell asleep. He dreamed he was at a station, the trains were being shunted. Suddenly, one of the carriages uncoupled and sped off down the slope towards the crossing. He had to run and place a chock under the wheels, he had to stop the carriage, but Nikolai Petrovich could not move from his place. The carriage was picking up speed, was speeding towards a passenger train... "That's it, the end, prison!" thought Nikolai Petrovich with a sense of doom... At this point his wife woke him up: the hen with the blue markings had disappeared.

He dressed and went outside.

Dusk was falling over the grey day, the wind was blowing from the north, was thundering and rattling, was tearing at the remaining red leaves of the cherry tree, was chasing the smoke from the distant factory chimneys towards the village.

Nikolai Petrovich counted the hens in the hen coop, looked in every nook and cranny of the yard and garden, glanced down the lavatory hole – the hen with the blue markings was indeed gone.

She was not in the street.

He went to the neighbours.

There they told him that they had no strange hens, no, impossible, and that there was no point in coming here, teasing the dogs.

He went down the street, peering into other people's yards and gardens.

He turned towards the wasteland.

He glimpsed something white, but it was not the hen, just a piece of paper soaring up into the dull sky.

The wind whistled and howled. Tall frozen weeds crackled under foot.

Darkness fell quickly. The humpbacked chain of factory lights was already quivering on the horizon. A coach went by with its headlights on. The village lights shone dimly, as if through a gauze.

There was something black ahead, where they had found the body of a man after the November holiday.

Nikolai Petrovich did not feel quite himself.

He stopped.

At the factory they had begun smelting, and the glow was spreading quickly towards the village, lighting up the wasteland.

Nikolai Petrovich took a few indecisive steps towards the black object and sighed with relief: a charred bus seat lay before him. He bent down to have a look, to see if the seat might be useful for the house, and he saw the hen.

She lay behind the seat, in a shallow gully, in a fresh pool of blood.

He stood for a long time and looked at the hen.

The Apprentice

It is a sultry night. A melancholy purple moon is gazing down on the steel works enveloped in fire and smoke.

In the control room are two people: the foreman and the apprentice. The foreman is dashing from the controls to the telephone, he is worried, he is cursing and eating some sandwich as he goes, whilst the apprentice is sitting timidly in a corner behind an iron table and diligently follows his movements: he will be a foreman one day, have a good salary and retire early on a pension with a good service record...

It is stuffy, hot... there is a smell of blast furnace gas... the underground engines rumble... time is almost standing still...

Suddenly, the foreman leaps up, hangs upside down under the ceiling, and in this position makes notes in a log book...

"Will I have to learn to do that?" thinks the apprentice, frightened.

"No sleeping!" shouts the foreman. "Have a look at the blast furnace gas pressure!"

The apprentice starts, runs to the instrument panel, looks at it for a long time.

"Well, what is it?" shouts the foreman. "Where are you looking? Where's the blast furnace gas?"

The siren is wailing, the foreman runs out of the control room, and the apprentice sits down at the wobbly iron table and opens a grubby safety instructions booklet.

It is stifling hot... there is a smell of blast furnace gas... the underground motors rumble... time is standing still...

Suddenly, the apprentice sees a small village, he is running along a burning path amongst scorching flowers, now he is jumping from the steep bank into cool water, is shivering blissfully and is falling asleep on the other bank to the hum of the summer woods...

"No sleeping," shouts the foreman. "Go and look at the natural gas pressure!"

The apprentice starts, runs to the instrument panel, looks for a long time...

"Well, what is it?!" shouts the foreman. "Where are you looking, stupid? Where is the natural gas? Go outside and get some air!"

The apprentice goes out of the control room.

Din, dust, carbon monoxide.

Up above, squashed by the chimneys, hangs the purple moon.

Figures of workmen flicker in the dim trench.

The safety valve is wailing at his side, the apprentice jumps with fear and everything is shrouded in acrid smoke...

Dacha

Ivan Sergeyevich bought a dacha. Not very expensive, not very far away, a decent little house, apple trees, raspberries, gooseberries... The area is slightly elevated, to the left – a waste heap of a disused mine, to the right – a cemetery, in the gully – an oily cesspool, on the horizon – cylinders, cones and pyramids of a large metallurgical plant...

To the left of the main entrance – a notice board, to the right – a board of rules.

The soil is studded with ferro-concrete scrap.

The water supply is according to plan.

Meetings, payment of dues, sudden inspections.

During funerals he can hear the wailing of the trumpets from the cemetery, and the heavy thumping of the drums.

Easterly wind brings smoke and dust from the nearby chemical plant. Occasionally the dachas are raided by the local thugs.

"How do you like our dacha?" asks Ivan Sergeyevich.

"Well, it's... all right..." answers his wife.

"All right – that means nothing! Do you like it or not?"

"Well, I like it..."

"Oh, please don't do me any favours! I see, you don't like anything here! The air, the water, even... the people! So, what's the matter? You don't like it-get lost! No one's keeping you! Good riddance! But, this is my homeland, I was born here, I grew up here. My career was made here. I don't drink like your relations, I don't get sent to the sobering centre! And I won't allow any scum to insult my homeland!"

"Who's insulting it, Ivan?"

"Don't! I'm not blind! Every wretch is going to start criticising! The water's not right, the air's not right, the people aren't right! And, what's your homeland like, eh?! Over there... they've never had and never will have sausages!"

And, Ivan Sergeyevich, soothed by this outburst, appreciatively thought about sausages.

The Old Woman and the Idiot

A morning in May, a courtyard.
On a bench sits an old woman, a retired teacher; out of the doorway steps Mitya from wretched flat No. 10. Medals jingling on his jacket, his eyes screwed up against the bright sunlight, he looks dreamily towards the bushy maple, smiles enigmatically.

"Time?" he asks.

"First of all, Mitya, you have to say hello," the old lady says, "then, you have to ask the time like this: could you tell me the time, please. Understand?"

"Understand," answers Mitya and shrugs his shoulders, making the medals jingle.

"And now, sit down here next to me, and we'll continue our lesson. Where did we stop yesterday, on what subject?"

Mitya looks intensely at the woman, moves his lips and answers: "On cows!"

"Correct, Mitya, well done!" the old lady is pleased. "You're not a stupid boy at all, only educationally neglected but that is not your fault, it is your parents' fault... By the way, what was that noise in your flat last night, who shouted so loudly and groaned so terribly?"

"Yesterday?"

"Yes, yesterday, after the evening news."

"That's... that's... no, I don't know," answers Mitya, eyes down. "I can't talk about that... or else... or else they'll twist my stupid head off, they'll drown me in the sewers, they'll stuff me down the rubbish chute..."

"Mmn... Well, fine, we'll continue our studies! Today, Mitya, we'll talk about the industrialisation of our country! It's a very serious topic, so pay attention! And so, towards the end of the first five-year plan..."

"Do you think the department store already opened?" Mitya asks anxiously.

"Here you are again with your department store!" the old lady is upset. "Well, what have you lost there, what do you need there?"

Mitya again looks down and is silent.

"I suppose, you can't talk about that either? Tell me, don't be afraid; I shan't reveal your secret to anyone!"

"I've got a girlfriend there," answers Mitya.

"Oh, Mitya, Mitya! What sort of girlfriends can you have there! Those painted fools are laughing at you, are mocking you, and you believe them!"

"No... girlfriend... girlfriend... we'll get married... we'll always be together... we'll always stand together at the window and look at the trees..."

And he quickly goes to the department store, where he has a million girlfriends in unbearably short skirts...

Translated by Vera Liber

Anatoli Gavrilov

Anatoli Gavrilov (b. 1947) lives in the small Russian town of Vladimir where he works in a post office and has little contact with the outside literary world. After first appearing in SOLO, having been recommended by writer Evgeny Popov, his elegant short stories have become very sought after by literary periodicals in Russia and have caught the attention of foreign publishers, with the result that he has now been translated into most European languages. Two collections of his stories have been published by Golden Gate, a publishing house in his native town of Vladimir.

Gavrilov's stories reflect Russian provincial life as perceived by someone who accepts it as it is, and who can find beauty where another person would see ugliness. He writes about the "little man" with a compassion traditional for Russian literature.

ALEXANDER SHARYPOV

The Bedbugs

A bedbug ran across the matress. The matress was grey with green stripes, the bedbug was red with bandy legs, and his name was Prokopych.

The bedbug turned left as usual at the black stamp, climbed up the hummock and was about to climb down when he ran into another bedbug, Sidor Kuzmich:

"That's okay, Prokopych, turn around, the food man ain't deliverin'."

"What?!" said Prokopych, taken aback.

"May I rot in hell!" Kuzmich crossed himself. "The guys are gettin' together over by the fence, let's go see what they gotta say."

With anxiously bowed head, Prokopych began mincing along after Kuzmich. On the way, they met one more bedbug, Vasya Guba.

"What's this about our rations gettin' cut?" he asked.

"The hell with it!" Prokopych muttered gloomily.

"It's like this, Vasya, Belogrudov ain't here, and he ain't sacked out," Kuzmich announced, and the three of them ran on.

Over by the fence there was a hum, smoke, grumbling, countless tracks and cigarette ends everywhere.

"Si'down, have a cigarette, Prokopych," said Misha Chuchin,

putting his hand out. He squatted as if he were celebrating the call of nature, and, arms dangling, smoked.

"What happened, guys?" asked Prokopych, shaking hands all around.

"I'm tellin' ya," the runt Ivan Burakov began, blinking. "Just so happens I was the first one out today. I thinks to myself, he ain't asleep yet, the rat, he'll crush me, but I'll risk it 'cause a guy's gotta eat, yeah and it's real quiet, okay; my-a pad, ya know, it's right by the springs, I listens, they ain't creakin'. Jeez, I thinks, what a lousy life, ya motha's nose nine times, I'll risk it! So I crawls out, I runs my heart's in my mouth, but I can feels they ain't creaking, the rat! Okay, I thinks, poet – I got ya numba, he ain't breathin', ain't breathin', and then he grabs ya with some cotton – and burns ya alive! That's the latest thing with him – grabbin' us with cotton. So, I'm runnin', duckin' into ditches – and suddenly, it's like it hit me: somethin's funny, seems to me there weren't no heel on the seam! That means, I got this superstition, see: there's a seam at the end o' the mattress, sewn with black thread, see, and that's where his heel always is. So I stops, goes back – and right, no heel!"

"Oh, Christ!" Prokopych couldn't contain himself.

"Yeah! It was like it hit me on the noggin! So now I'm runnin' over the top and I ain't duckin, I'm lookin' as hard as I can: ain't no Belogrudov, for the life of me! I'm runnin' every which ways, under the hill, along the longeron – but he ain't there, Dresden drum, what a drag, ya motha's nose nine times! Then I ran into Misha..."

"Hey there, Simon," said Misha Chuchin, putting his hand out to the latest arrival. "Si'down, have a cigarette, put your feet up."

"Na, so whatta we do, whatta we do?" – one young bedbug was getting nervous.

"I tell you he's sittin' under the bed," declared Slava Pen sullenly. He was standing, leaning one shoulder against the fence, twirling a new green hat around and around on his head; first back to front, then front to front.

"He's gotta be sittin' somewhere," said Prokopych, scratching his side "He take his pants off?"

"How the hell should we know, Prokopych?" Ivan Burakov sad blinking. "We know he killed the light, we all saw that, and he locked the door from inside. But the pants, who was lookin'!"

"We shoulda known to watch out," agreed Prokopych.

"He's gotta be sittin' under the bed, there's nowhere else," Slava Pen repeated, turning his hat around.

"Na, so whya we sittin' here, guys, whya we sittin' here fa nothin'?!" – the young one was feeling jittery. "Let's go look fer 'im!"

"Listen, kid, you're the fastest guy we got," Prokopych reasoned. "Run down and take a look, go on, see, straight ahead, over the longeron, and you're there! Go on!"

"So gimme some smokes and I'll go."

They immediately handed him two cigarettes, he stuck one behind his ear, the other in his mouth and was off, only his pants twinkled in the distance.

"Oh, me," sighed Prokopych, taking a seat. "Who's he anyway?"

"He's Pumpkin's son," said Misha Chuchin.

"Dont think I know him."

"Sure you do! Pumpkin's son! His wife was poisoned to death with superphosphates last year."

"Pumpkin's wife?"

"No, not Pumpkin's! Kolya's! Called her Red Wanda! Loud broad! Garibaldi!"

"O-o-oh! Ofonya Pumpkin's Kolya!"

"Yeah!"

"Look what a bruiser he's turned into!"

"Yeah."

"When I lived in Apt. 97...," said Slava Pen.

"That's where there's a family, right?" Prokopych specified.

"Yeah... When I lived there, ya know, so, sometimes they'd crawl under the bed too – and sleep there, as if I wouldn't gonna find 'em... Or else in the closet. Wait a minute," Slava Pen declared importantly and spat, "if he ain't under the bed, that means he's in the closet."

"Hey, closetbugs! Any closetbugs here?" yelled Prokopych, craning his neck.

"Like they're gonna come out, go ahead and wait," said Slava Pen sullenly. "I'm tellin' you he's in the closet."

"There's nowhere else, I guess," said Prokopych, scratching his side, furious at the thought of how far he'd have to run.

"Na, he's a rat, ain't he?" said Ivan Burakov, looking around. "And the world puts up with rats like that! They'll do anything to screw us!"

"Ha!" said Misha Chuchin and touched his palm to his brow. "Whata ya bellyachin' about? Here's a closetbug for ya! Hey there, Kozlovsky! Finally wake up? Si'down, have a cigarette."

Rubbing his eyes with his fists, a dishevelled, unshaven bedbug in a tie wandered over to the fence. He greeted everyone self-consciously, and began grinding the dust with his boot.

"Check it out, he's wearin' a tie!" Misha Chuchin teased. "Like he's an MC o' somethin', you motha! So, Mr. Kozlovsky, what are we celebratin' today? Or did you hit the jackpot?"

"What? No. I thought it'd be... like the usual," Kozlovsky waved his hand, and started pacing quickly and fitfully back and forth, throwing sharp looks at everyone.

"What? Ya mean he's not at ya place?"

"What?..." Kozlovsky turned away.

"That motha," Misha Chuchin was so discombobulated he missed his mouth with his cigarette.

A long pause ensued. In the silence, they could hear Misha Chuchin's cigarette hissing and crackling: as if the tobacco weren't lousy enough as it was, someone had cut it with wood shavings – life's a rip-off!

"Somethin's wrong, guys," Prokopych noted.

"Look it, here comes Kolya!" the rearguard had seen him.

"Guys!" the young Kolya called to them gaily. "Belogrudov ain't under the bed!"

"Ah, shit!" Prokopych slapped his knees and spat on the ground. Again the uncertainty, the anxiety.

"Listen to me, guys," screamed Kolya, thrusting his sweaty, dusty face up out of the crowd. "Will wondas neva cease," he suddenly burst out laughing, hugged himself, and doubled over.

"Whata ya snickerin' about, ya dog?" they threatened him, and he began bawling:

"Na, swear ta God, I'm not lyin': the jerk's sittin' on the ceiling."

The bedbugs began droning. Prokopych finished scratching his side and stood motionless for a time, staring at the speaker, and pondered. Then he blinked hard and bellowed:

"Hey, kid! How can he be sittin' on the ceiling when he'd fall right down from the ceiling?"

The bedbugs were struck dumb.

"Huh?" said Misha Chuchin, shaking his head. "Some people are so smart!" And he threw his cigarette away.

"This is Belogrudov we're talkin' about, not just anybody," Prokopych yelled angrily. "You drink ya fill o' blood and ya legs'll barely keep ya on the ceiling, 'cause there's such a thing as gravity! And this is Belogrudov! He's got so much fat on him, even the bed sags down to the floor!"

"So whatta we do?" screamed Kolya, wide-eyed. "Huh?" He pushed his way to the front of the crowd and jumped up: he'd stepped on a burning cigarette butt. "Huh?" he repeated, holding his heel and hopping up and down on one foot. "If that's the deal, then the whole gang should go take a look!"

"So, let's go," Prokopych declared gravely. He rose, the bedbugs droned, and the whole gang advanced behind the crippled Kolya.

"Thing is, Prokopych, I need a fix real bad," Vasya Guba explained, stamping his big boots "If I don't get it, I can forget goin' home. Ya know how it is, I gotta wife an' five kids besides."

"Yeah, it's tough," Prokopych stayed on his point.

He walked faster and faster, his hands in his pockets. The tramp of hundreds of feet kept up a dull roar and the earth shook. The bedbugs pushed each other, stepped on each other, and in the confusion, as they were clambering over a wire, Misha Chuchin missed something in the darkness, slipped, and fell headlong, cursing, onto the floor.

"There," said Prokopych somberly.

"Swear ta God, I'm not lyin'," Kolya responded hastily, turning angry and scared.

His words were drowned out by the dull roar. The agitated bedbugs hurried along, kicking up dust and thundering like a herd. But when they got there, they all stopped, the roar subsided, and a hush fell over the crowd.

Then Kolya Pumpkin, the bruiser, rolled out in front and began to explain, hobbling and bobbing up and down:

"Here, look it, I mean he, o' course, he ain't exactly sittin' there like a normal guy, actually it's like just the opposite, I mean he's standin' upside down on his head, I mean not upside down, but if you figures the gravity... Wait, hey yeah! His head's down! I mean he tied his head to the ceiling with a rope! "

The bedbugs stood there, open-mouthed, they didn't understand anything.

"Hold it! You're all excited!" Kuzmich said with annoyance. "Now where's this gravity of ours goin'?"

"This gravity's goin' head-down."

"Up yours! Whatta ya mean head-down?"

"Huh? On the ceiling the gravity's head-down."

"Hold it! You're all excited! Now come on, guys! How'd we get here, wait a second."

"Whatta ya mean... Prokopych... How come... The rope... Huh?.. How come this-a rope don't break?"

"The rope," said Prokopych coming to, and solely for the sake of his reputation, since now he understood everything, "it's a British rope and that's why it don't break."

"Oh! That's it... British."

"I got ya numba, poet..."

"Hold it! Guys! Somethin's wrong here. How'd we get here, wait a second."

Pushing each other aside, the bedbugs climbed over the jerk, but Prokopych hung back and let them all go by, then looked round, turned on his heels, and tore home.

"Oh, Christ!" he screamed to himself, panting and turning purple. "Ya work like a dog! What a lunk I am! If I'da sat there any longer –- I'd a never got past those bruisers!"

"Well, woman," he said slamming the door. He walked past his wife, helped himself to a ladle of cold water and started gulping it down, then paused and exhaled: "Get your junk together, we're gettin' out o' here!"

"The eensy, weensy spida went up the wataspout; down came the wain and washed the spida out," a chubby child babbled, dragging a block across the floor.

"What a life," sighed the dour Prokopych.

He swung his arm wide and slung the rest of the water under the table.

The Pants

Icouldn't sleep that night. The window panes were shuddering with the bad weather, a moth was thumping against the ceiling, I was having all sorts of thoughts, they drove me outside: what was it like out? What was going on?

Yellow light bulbs were burning, and I walked down the stairs with one hand in my pocket. In our building they dump all sorts of scrap metal under the stairs, that's just where someone's camp-bed was, bent and rusty, and sitting on that camp-bed, hunched over, was a man. When I saw him, I immediately took my hands out of my pockets and dazedly sat down beside him, and all the thoughts that had been torturing me disappeared.

This man was wearing a dark blue jacket and tie, patent-leather boots, and, I hate to say it, frayed black undershorts.

"So your, what do you call her," I said, turning to him, "wife gave you the old heave-ho, huh?"

He looked at me and sighed heavily.

I put my hand out.

"Greetings, comrade."

He shook my hand, but again said nothing.

"Yeah," I said then. "Some weather."

And I pointed to the door.

He was still silent.

"Ah!" I wasn't giving up. "Ho-o-ow could they? To us? Huh?"

And saluting like a Young Pioneer, I slapped my knee.

"Scum," the man in the patent-leather boots readily agreed.

"No, but how come?" I said, staring at the floor, since I had no idea who the scum were.

"Scum," he repeated. "Just tell me what they want? What do they want from us? Those assholes, are they ever gonna pipe down or what? Huh?"

"Yeah..." I sighed. "So what apartment do you live in?"

"I'm the next street over."

"So that's it. So why'd she give it to you?

"Who?"

"You know, your wife."

"What wife... I don't have any wife."

I began thinking. Here I should mention that even as a child I never liked riddles, they always made me nervous.

"So where are your pants?" I angrily put it to him straight.

"Ha!" he waved his arm and again, hunching over, looked sad.

"What? Did someone steal them?"

"Na."

"Listen, comrade, don't you try to fool me. I'm a sensitive guy, perceptive. Riddles are bad for my health."

"So what is this... I go out for a walk at night... Can't even do that anymore."

"Comrade! On the contrary: everything ought to clear at night because people are sleepy and slower on the uptake."

"Well I'm such an idiot I was born this way, that's all, so there."

"What do you mean?" I was taken aback and suddenly I noticed he was crying. After a pause, I said:

"Now, now, let's go," and I pulled him by the elbow. He grabbed his umbrella lying on the camp-bed and meekly allowed himself to be led. I took him back to my place, to the kitchen, and made him down a glass, after which he casually removed his shoes and remained in a pair of red socks.

"So tell me," I said.

"So I'm telling you... I'm an ass-backward freak. And what of it? If it hadn't been for this, I'd have shown 'em. Ugh!" he waved his arm, poured himself another glass, drank it and wiped his mouth with his palm. I offered him some pickled mushrooms, but he shook his head and said, waving his hand in front of his face as if he were trying to catch an invisible fly, "I'd of whipped'em all! I'd of whipped'em all! I'm strong! I ain't complainin'! And not bad lookin' either! And brainy! I can beat anyone ya want at checkers! So! But God didn't gimme pants. God just didn't gimme any pants." He fell silent and broke off bits of bread with trembling fingers.

I sat there feeling depressed and rubbed my knee.

"I can't get used to it at all," he was saying, breaking off bits of bread. The other day I walked into a store. Broads, they feel sorry for me, o' course, they don't stare, and I can deal with it... They pretend... 'Good morning, Valery Petrovich... Would you like some macaroni, Valery Petrovich?' I was on my way out when some little girl, maybe five years ol', says: 'Mama, why doesn't that man have any pants on?' It felt like she'd burned me with boiling water, ya know, the little button... You can't shut 'em up, kids..."

"I know," I said and began scraping the lemon stenciled on the oil-cloth off with my nail.

"Now, say it's winter. In summer it's okay, but just try in winter, try in winter, that's when the damn truth comes out."

I shook my head.

"Worst of all I'm all alone! The blind guy goes to his meetings for the blind, to his special libraries, because there are so many of 'em, blind guys piled up! But I'm all alone! I'm the only freak like me in the whole wide world! The only one without pants! What fool would marry me? What fool? They feel sorry for me, sure they do, but come home with me, not if you paid her. She'd marry ten blind men, but not me. Asshole!"

We talked until dawn. Or rather, he talked, and I just listened sympathetically. After seeing him to the door, I put my hand in my pocket, leaned my shoulder against the jamb, and fell to thinking. Some bright new feeling was being born in my soul. I wanted to do something for this unfortunate person, ease his suffering. I remembered that I had a yellow musk melon in the fridge, I decided I'd take it over to him the next day, and immediately cursed myself because I'd forgotten to ask him for his address, and then sighed heavily. There are so many of them on this earth, of these miserable and unfortunate people plagued by suffering, and yet we, the ones who have everything, are always dissatisfied with something, always demanding something, banging our fists on the table, grumbling at life, we can't sleep at night – this is not good, my friends, not good at all...

Translated by Joanne Turnbull

Alexander Sharypov

Alexander Sharypov, born 1957 in Veliki Ustyug in the north of Russia, graduated from a polytechnic in Vladimir. He has been working ever since at an ammunition factory and writing stories no publisher wanted to publish. Latterly he sent them to SOLO where they were enthusiastically accepted, and some have subsequently been published in the Moscow-based magazine Yunost. He has also written two novels (both unpublished) **The Murder of Koch** and **Red Underpants**.

IGOR KLEKH

The Foreigner

Jaundice brought him to the sixth floor of the Hospital for Infectious Diseases. A blizzard was swirling, sticking up eyes and clogging ears with snow. Burring crows announced the coming of the patient's first clear morning.

The window panes had crystallized from the night frost. Scattered light streamed through the broad white screen, the projection of a map: Was that Antarctica? Greenland? Or the jagged edges of Scandinavia?

He was a Foreigner. Just in case, he decided not to ask questions. Not asking other people questions had become his living credo the last few years in this country. They took a urine sample, a blood sample, made a hole in his veins for the drip. He meekly endured all this: he had finally stopped feeling nauseated, and only sank down deeper into the hospital sheets, into the bed, the better to observe the life of this strange people.

...in his poetic underground office, Alyosha Parschikov, managing for the moment without a dictaphone, was inventing a fantastically old-fashioned pneumo-hydrometa-cannon for a new poem called "Poltava"...

...in a mossy pit at the foot of a mountain where a central European city lay fossil-like and grey-green as a river mussel... but the city had long ceased to be central European, forty years ago, because geography was the first thing to be abolished in this country...

...frigid women with secondary and higher educations eagerly searched the cities and villages, resorts and boom towns for personal happiness...

...On a snow-bound farm in the mountains, Nikola had made some potato vodka and was waiting for guests from a distant, next to non-existent city, they were supposed to bring him binoculars – for Christmas, for Epiphany... Guests always turned up unexpectedly, suddenly materializing below on the final ascent from the spruce forest, two or three small figures, with skis and rucksacks resembling camp beds, taking a rest in sight of the farm then tumbling slowly, heavily into the hut, filling it with steam, a jumble of smells, bright belongings everywhere, a bottle of vodka first off, a fire in the stove, festivity.

No one came. The radio batteries had long since died. Nikola knocked back one and then another glass of vodka, glancing wistfully through an ice-hole in the window at the snow, at the wooded slope, at the raw, grey photograph of a gloomy day; he gnawed on a hunk of salted beef that someone had already nibbled at one end and washed it down with a mug of ice water. Then he kicked off his boots, remaining in two pairs of equally holely socks, pulled himself up onto the stove-bench, and reached for his *fuyara* – a brass pipe, cut on the diagonal; plugging the bottom of the pipe with one finger, he forced sounds, struck up a stubborn tune: mournful, immortal and festive, like the life that had once been in these mountains, when the children returned with their father from the annual fair spread out along the bank of the rushing mountain stream, and the father, having visited the tavern, kept by a clean-shaven Huzul, whips his horse strapped with a new-smelling harness, while at home Mama scrapes and washes the floors with a yellowish infusion of beech ashes, and will again strip the children of their linen trousers, to be hidden in the chest, and let them run around in just their long shirts until they are grown...

And Nikola is dreaming about his Binoculars – a black, unnaturally, even obscenely huge 16x, if there is such a thing – his cupped hands clench, and yearn, his deft palms, strong as a shovel or an axe, squeezing the slender reed, the icicle, the silly piece of iron, warmed with his breath, his vodka scent, his heat, its hoarse sounds turning increasingly shrill, but with an echo of the hoarseness still, like the receding dream about that which one can never forget, that which only teases, teases, your hands reach out – and there is nothing in them, only a brass pipe, hindering...

Twilight seeps in the window, creeps out of the corners, darkens, casting an optical illusion – a crab – shaggy binoculars over half the hut:

> *– and all this longing is but*
> *a futile languor of the spirit...*

...because fifteen hundred kilometers away, Nikola's friend – the Foreigner – has foul-colored urine, so far the only thing he finds he has in common with the incomprehensible people overcrowding the ward.

The Foreigner has been sleeping for days on end, and even, or so it began to seem to him in his sleep, once again, has begun to gingerly finger the map of his dreams: in the oblivion of the endless strip of dream, locked in its optics, when, even waking, one is still within its confines, in his mind's eye sleepy landscapes overlapped, streets and buildings, visions jostled one another, small groups of somehow familiar but blank-looking people, unobtrusive, but also inescapable, the sorts who have been in our dreams for decades; a country was taking shape, the size of a district, but strange, built of a deceptive semi-transparent substance; Haven for Broken Hearts, homeland to children, somnambulists and adolescents: fantastical Gel-Gew, brutal like all port cities;

...a beetle's journey along the Mobius strip. You could also say: a country the size of binoculars.

His smashed, smarting body had finally found peace, washed up by raging storms along the Midlife Crisis onto a tiny island of a bed in a hospital for infectious diseases on the edge of the Eurasian capital. He lay motionless, his face buried in the pillow, one arm dangling, his waterlogged lungs wheezing, his ears full of sand, seaweed in his matted hair and scraggly beard. The beaten, bile-soaked small of his back ached sweetly.

> *O, eternal Foreigner!*
> *O, bilious vegetarian!*
> *What don't you like about this country?*
> *Where are you off to now?*
> *Take a rest, sleep a while, sleep.*
> *No, there is no Africa, no Patagonia,*
> *there is only Mother Russia.*
> *She is the only magnet,*
> *so long as we are with her,*
> *we won't need any compasses at all;*
> *She is one Big Kursk Magnetic Anomaly,*
> *repelling and attracting our hearts,*
> *magnetized by her nightingales,*
> *her blast-furnaces, her Baikonur, her Bolshoi Ballet,*
> *her Russian literature.*
> *Sleep, my boy; I don't love you, sleep.*

And he slept and slept, as he hadn't slept, hadn't been able to sleep in a long time, without boring a hole in the mattress with his penis, without torturing the pillows and being tortured by them, with all his aching muscles, his urethra, his sphincter relaxed, rising in roomy pajama bottoms and a night-shirt with the hospital stamps (but without the buttons) only to go to the bathroom – to smoke, to urinate – scrawled across the stall was the inscription: "Long live hepatitis!" and aside from somebody's forgotten feces there were no traces of the mind at work.

The Foreigner turned his head in amazement, inhaling almost to the point of dizziness, realizing suddenly that he wasn't bothered anymore by this sort of graffiti; or by the rivulets under the door; or the slightly slimy bucket of cigarette-ends; or the sink with the standing water; or the cracked window covered with a gelatin-like film of nicotine; what trifles compared to the first spasmodic drags, to the warm radiator, to the whiteness of the tiled walls, to his feeling of spontaneous gratitude to one and all. No one talked to him, they sensed he was a Foreigner. He was grateful for that too.

He leaned his forehead against the glass. It was already evening. The street lamp below was bathed in a pool of light, illuminating the station, the stairs, the brick warehouses. The hospital was huge, at least eleven wings, the eleventh was the morgue. The visions would not leave his tired mind in peace. He was drunk from the cigarette, it was beginning to burn his fingers, when below he caught sight of what seemed to him a small figure in checkered tights and a short Renaissance coat, it flitted across the yard, darted about in the light of the street lamp, hugged the platform, dissolved into the shadows, a carnival figure "del arte" in the snowy Moscow suburbs...

Again he sank into a deep sleep, he had only just reached his bed, his head had barely touched the pillow. This time the light of reason and memory was powerless to pierce the thick of the dream; several times the jaws of deep-sea fish swam right up to his face, but a minute or two went by, and – as if an ink tablet had dissolved – pitch darkness enveloped them and they disappeared forever.

When he awoke, he felt as if he had finally made up for the sleep lost over all the past months and even years. He felt fine. It was the third day, the eighth since the onset of his illness. . .

These people around him: they were not simply incomprehensible, they were unfathomable to him.

In his ward, the aesthetically trained Foreigner was immediately struck by a Breughel-like picture of a proletarian from Red Presnya: the slit of a smiling lipless mouth, as if carved out of wood in two swift strokes; with dominoes in cupped palms, he peered merrily and in amazement at the fantastic composition, a black cross growing across the table like a polyp.

This proletarian from Presnya's entire concentration was absorbed by a noiseless visual energy, that hard energy which causes the pips of the ancient game of coal cards to shine like phosphorous in the dark.

The spectacle of whimsical turns and crossings – the flux of hexagrams of fate – gradually began to excite even the Foreigner's imagination. They played for days. The point of this game, the rules were utterly unknown to him, in spite of his already having spent a good many years in this country (he was paid to do so, albeit in rubles). From the very start, from his awakening almost, he had begun to suspect that the point of the game was not that simple, just as the people playing it were not that simple. Or maybe they weren't playing at all: maybe the game was just a semblance, a form?

He should look – but how? – at the proletarian's partners through other eyes:

The brusque, aggressive Stumbler, squinting from the tension of following the game and his partners. This Stumbler suffered from a rare form of asthma: if it were not for several four-letter words, he would have suffocated long ago, unable to finish even a single sentence – he would have started gasping for air, choking – and he would have dropped dead. Thank God, these four-letter words existed! Two or three of them accompanied every neutral word of the Stumbler's, preventively propping it up on all sides. For their faithful service, he cherished these words and in his own way even loved them, caressing their suffixes, rewarding their prefixes, inventing verbs and verbal nouns of extraordinary novelty and daring. Thanks to an unflagging strength of spirit and ruthless exercises, he came out a winner every day in the struggle with the illness stifling him.

"Cossack Squadron" spat every morning in his own policeman's eyes and, scrabbling about under his forelock, polished them with his sleeve until they shone; he massaged his plump shoulders – panting like a weight-lifter – with eau de cologne, it's obvious why; he gave the ward inspired and graphic descriptions of the "swallow" position in handcuffs and the strait "eight" with the help of a tawed strap, his girlfriend had passed her tests, he was in for his, soon he'd be released, and he'd be a "big fish"; he sang two verses from a popular song for days – only two! – which attested to an advanced echolalia system – and loudly cheered himself on, every turn:
"Goo-oo-d move!"

Just try and understand them! The Foreigner thought to himself: "I see them and I don't see them..."

Medium – the fourth partner – always sat with his back to them (and thus a description of him is omitted) – kneading the dominoes with the broad, concentric movements of a virtuoso pianist. He was a military man, a lascivious worm, worn out by the active career of a loser.

Drawn into the game unwittingly, the Foreigner became more and more aware of the outlines of his own cherished "I" crackling and eroding under the blows of the dominoes.

As the game progressed, the players mattered less and less as individuals.

In the abandon with which they gave themselves to the game, in the totality of the game itself, behind the frightening openness, he sensed the presence of something else – diffuse, elusive, and mysterious, like the Slavic Soul, like the Truth that can fit on the tip of your nose – just shift your gaze, touch it!

The ward was a bit like a locker room at a major international tournament. A short nap after lunch – to restore one's physical strength – a luxurious respite before reimmersing oneself in the game. Then all the listlessness evaporated, the blank expressions were dispelled, a slight tremor ran through the ward, refreshed the tired air – the world's body felt suddenly younger.

There was, perhaps, one more thing, besides the foul-colored urine, besides the common passion: they were all Russians, in their eyes one could see a readiness to obey the Motherland's every command. The Foreigner felt ashamed of himself for not liking them. But another, more complex feeling was already stirring in him, forcing its way, pressing in on his diaphragm...

The point of the game was gradually becoming clear to him – as always, persistence and patience paid off; the many days spent observing the game from his bed had not been in vain, the secret jottings, the comparisons, the sullen lying in wait, the diet, the exhausting intuitive efforts – and then something flashed, sparks flew inside his head, something turned over, came together, dawned – and suddenly EVERYTHING fell into place.

You pathetic foreigner, you; why are you a foreigner?
The sooner you get it the better!
You didn't have the luck to be born here, in our country,
where everyone knows from the time he's a child
and anyone can tell you that the point of this game,
the crowning achievement is
when the first player slams down his last domino
and screams "Ryba!" ("Fish!")
And what is Ryba? It is ICHTHYS!
It is Jesus Christ, IHS.

Have you seen the faces of these "incomprehensible" people when one of them, rewarded for his prayers, his fasts, his black masses of "blasphemous" magic charms, when any one of them suddenly has the chance to finish the game with RYBA?!

This is the Game's true consummation – the moment of open contemplation of the truth! What a state of ecstasy the other "players" are in, jealously envying their fellow now ahead of them on the path of spiritual glory!

Even the names of the Game contain clues; on the simplest, most profane level, it is called "slaughter the GOAT" (the goat being an ancient symbol of the Devil).

But was it given to you, shackled with karmic chains, blindly following the trail of the Game, bewitched by its symmetry and asymmetry, by the magic of double sixes, by the mystical perfection of twin blanks, was it given to you with your scattered consciousness, your immigrant's arrogance, was it given to you to understand that this ancient and everlasting all-conquering GAME, that it has a profound God-seeking, God-building meaning, that it is none other than our secret innermost national religion – a synthetic religion embracing and recasting Catholicism, Orthodoxy, astrology, spiritualism, I Ching, certain sectarian dogmas, the Avesta cult, scheming and crystallography, card-reading, Hesse's conjectures, the rules of the road plus hundreds of other components, while resolving all their seeming contradictions on a new level.

This Game emerged from enclosed Arabian courts, from defiles in London pubs and exclusive Dutch clubs, from the filth of Trinity college at Oxford to the spaciousness of Moscow squares where the world center of religious life had long since relocated.

The very etymology of the word: DO-MI-NO, get it? DO-MI-NO Anno Domini", don't you know Latin? You should!

But you saw; you were given to see!

– Benedictine monks, a black cloak with white lining; Monte Cassino? Marco Polo?

"Dixit Dominus Domino meo!.."

The Foreigner made a bitter note that evening: "We are lazy and incurious".

A week later he made his last note and signed his name sideways somewhere in the margins of humanity's book of suicides: in the pre-dawn murk he plunged the electric immersion heater – which he himself had made the night before for the ward with a wire, two razor blades, a pair of matches and black thread – into his mouth, clamping his teeth down firmly on the parallel Schicks.

It was morning, one minute to six. The loud-speaker began coughing, in a minute it would strike up the national anthem.

Translated by Joanne Turnbull

Igor Klekh

Igor Klekh (b.1952) lives in Lvov, a city in the Western Ukraine where Leopold Sacher-Masoch also lived. That, however, is Klekh's only link to the founder of masochism, a concept he emphatically dislikes. A philologist by training, Klekh makes his living restoring stained glass in Lvov. He finds his quiet life in the provinces suffocating, claiming that, "The provinces provide rich material for fiction but none for real life. It is fine to be born there and to come back there to die, but it's no place to actually live." The theme of man's loneliness in the huge wide world dominates Klekh's stories, which are very manly in spirit. He avoids the sarcasm and irony so typical of today's "new" writers, and treats very seriously a variety of existential problems. His short novel Farmstead in the Universe, published in Novy Mir in 1993, has been nominated for the Russian Novel Booker Prize.

SOPHIA KUPRYASHINA

Dreamless

She suddenly somehow began to feel a dull yearning for his body and for his smell, just to touch him. Just to touch him. Just. What was it? Some sort of ordinary desire – at daybreak, towards evening, after forcing herself to finish all her jobs, at her limit, her puffy eyes glued to an object, so senselessly, so doggedly. How slack her stomach felt, and all these old rags with the stretched elastic – as if they too had strained themselves, and – it's almost a habit: stopping up the pain in the joints with brandy, and all these dreams, and conversations with the old mirror are just face exercises, and tomorrow you'll go back to your little cellar and your broom, and they'll ask you to also clean up there and there, and again all this will drag on until it gets dark, and you'll fall asleep, sitting on the window sill.

And again the bucket, the light, the familiar sounds; the carpenter has come. She will stare at him for a long time, trying to find him out. And she will find him out, like everyone and everything, she'll catch this intonation, and that gesture, but he, like so many, will be frightened by the way she looks at him, because there will be something quite inhuman there; passion, perhaps. And he will leave, and again she will crawl about in the half-mad room and feel her throat shrink to a speck; and then suddenly there will be a moment – at night – it's light: little texts are raining down, like sleet, someone is ironing and saying: "Only you shouldn't drink..." But what else can one do? And... an exchange.

This will not be a convalescence, but a sign, on the far side, beyond which is the end; and she will somehow manage to escape the abyss; she'll do a superhuman entrechat, and she'll be left sitting on that same upholstered day bed covered with cigarette burns, surrounded by strange people, who are waiting for her to say something, or to let them undress her – and all this is the same madness, which brings no relief, but infuses the body with a catlike plasticity and a spreading strength for that same bucket and that same brandy...

Huge trash bins with bright pictures stand like landmarks in this courtyard.

All these abstract bits of advice – to go with the beer in the abandoned room where fresh-cut twig brooms and a blanket lie in a huge bathtub.

"...Oh, no, it's all over. The mice ate my brain, love ate my beauty. I'm waiting for the ones who live in Bolshevik Lane, in the abandoned house over the wine store; they asked me to join their commune – I suit them; that which was given to me will be forgotten, and my tense attention will be extracted..."

"What? I don't remember, I remember vaguely -- only I would be ashamed to meet anyone who knows them. And I'll carry on, so as to provoke to knife me fast. Or I'll kill them: that's simpler. I've imagined it for years: he's sleeping, like that time, in his boots and jacket, and calling me by some other name in his sleep, and his friend is sleeping on our bed, crosswise; they've drunk four bottles of wine and will drink more; and I take a long rusty knife, lying on the paper with the herring butter – the main thing is it's long enough to reach the heart, and, out of some childish fear of getting a bad grade, I can't remember, which is right and which is left. He's lying on his stomach – that means his heart is on the right because if you turn him over, it's on the left. Where's the heart – higher up? Lower down? You wouldn't want to hit a rib..."

"Tanya," he growls with a vowelful roar: "Tanya, take my pants off!"

"You'll get your pants! Tanya, what does that mean?" The knife goes in fine and then out again. And again. He gasps softly, both sober and losing consciousness at the same time, and I cover him and the knife with a child's blanket. His son cones in with a friend, a neighbor let them in, he asks for a drink to cure his hangover, and I say: "Quiet, he's sleeping; take what's there, under the table." I slip out quickly, before the blood begins to seep under the door, and – I think – in any case they won't remember him anytime soon.

Again, in order: my overalls, which I haven't the strength to mend, dyed socks, lip pencil, head scarf, someone else's shapeless coat, its creases saturated with dust, someone else's boots, hands in pockets – fingering two tokens, and where to – on the eternal wind – to the buckets? By eleven? What can I lean on – ah, the cold tin statue; but he, smiling tragically, always tragically, will say: "Look at her hands..."

Meanwhile the other cleaning woman was trying to pacify her throbbing brow and reading a copy of calming young Pioneer Pravda, found in the assembly hall. Yesterday she drank different drinks for twelve hours straight: dry wine, brandy, vodka, cheap port, wine again; her brow was throbbing like crazy: the cleaning woman pressed it with her hand.

She picked an orange peel up off the floor, bit off an end and started to chew it. Still, she had shouted yesterday, after the coffin with the torn light blue silk, after a kiss in the frigid cemetery, quiet and sunny; she had even wanted the strapping grave-digger in the green sweater – he was chopping the frozen ground with a crowbar; she thought about how he would go into the little graveyard house and drink with the others... All this was vague, slow-motion. And she had shouted at an awkward moment – in front of the guests – long and overhard. The guests had already started talking about something else and suddenly – they were silent. The night was the same sleepless, senseless pouring on...

Before, she never thought that people could sleep standing but now she was going home and she was asleep – sound asleep, and she was dreaming about a snowy road.

Before long, both cleaning women were sitting together in the attic, in that very same Bolshevik Lane.

It's hard to say when time collapsed; I was lying or sitting, a whirlwind was unwrapping me with its tiny nips, someone else's tears were on me; I was gulping down cold brandy breaths.

My hairpin came out in the darkness, then two buttons came off. She somehow unwound me, relaxed me, and something icy was in my throat. Just don't let me remember what it resembles. But tomorrow − to again curl up, to fuse into a frozen mass, and in the bathroom, before the smooth black-stone mirror, to cauterize my broken lip...

She told me her story. A stolen lipstick, prison at 18, gay girls, the usual business. I simply couldn't understand: how can she still be alive -- here, she looks at me, smiles, sweeps five hours a day, the eternal padded jacket, shoulder muscles (I have them too), a hundred rubles a month, but there isn't one living bit of flesh left in her: what wasn't pounded out was cut out, the rest is history; daily torture; she can't have children; in the time left over after sweeping she numbs the pain − basically by drinking. "Vaska died on the 27th, I caught cold at the funeral." Her face is artificial. Deep, resilient wrinkles, red hands, she's incredibly thin and weather-beaten. Scepticism in every octave; we curse, raising our eyebrows: I my right, she her left (childhood tic). "I'll just get myself some false teeth and go whoring."

I felt ashamed to be sitting next to this clot of pain; I felt like a warm healthy hulk, and − strangely trembling out of a squeamish fear, desire and pity − I kissed her hand, and she stroked my head.

Someone said over me:
"She's so young, and already..."
You wouldn't say I fell with a crash, but... with a gurgling. And then, standing on all fours in the middle of the pavement, I thought for a long time: what did he smell of, cruel man? It seemed to me that if I kept my head down and hunched over, no one would see me, and I'd crawl through the drain grate − a prison-cell window with noisy stormy waters − and would feel as small as a child again − head like a raisin. Shaking loose and changing the spaces − do you see the darkness? − the stripes across the walls: the Black Marias are coming − their latticed windows are rolling across the walls, and that part of you, on which you are lying, trembles for a long time more,

and begins to knock – distinctly, warmly: in your heel and in your heart.
I dreamt about war.

Translated by Joanne Turnbull

The Murderer

A wanted criminal – diffident, curly-headed – lay on the other side of the wall and I dreamt about the prison.
The kids liked to listen to me. Not that my stories were anything special, just that I had a certain bent for mimicry and all kinds of spice, so that they always came out funny. The slammer was death to me: they would have beat my brains out in a hurry if not for the kids who kept running up and touching me to see if I was alright – is there really such a thing as a sweet broad who never once beat anyone up (first)? She either rattles on, or goes and sits cross-legged in a corner, and rocks, her head thrown back, her lips pursed, and then you'd better leave her alone, or else...
Their main conversations: what has begun to hurt, whose, where. Then... sex. Then: what to get high on, where, with whom. Prices and debates. Will he or won't he rat. And a drop of worldly philosophy. Too many senseless actions for anyone to lack for ideas. Too many potions here – all kinds – to recall the past. Too many people.
There are "boys", there are "girls", but I have three roles: Mama, boy and girl. The five-year age difference – between 17 and 22 – lends the effect of motherhood. Sometimes an extraneous (uninhibited) sound, or our raw twilight, or our strange nights – something falls into place, becomes clear, but then they will wake me for a late-night feast – and another solo, and just try and refuse. Analyses which I don't have the strength to listen to. I go back to my lair, I see pictures, feel depressed, someone will creep up under my side: drunken tears and confessions, but tomorrow he'll rat. Sleep, my little one, tomorrow it's off to solitary.
I'm too used to keeping myself together to stop playing this role.

What happened to my poor twin sister – who was forgiven and permitted everything – was beautiful and a textbook case, and could not have happened to anyone else. A confirmed criminal selected her for marriage, threatened her with a gun fitted with a silencer, he took her to a little public park (this occurred in the dead of night), and was on the point of coming up with something horrible, but she brought him to see me, so as to share the murder and rape with me sister-like. It was 3 o'clock in the morning, and it felt so good to sleep after a kind of shame and deception. Her lovers, whom she'd asked for protection, had all kicked her out, for, like the train of a dress that has caught fire, she was trailed by that murderer, to whom, according to him, nothing mattered anymore, but they hadn't found anyone killed by him yet, and still he'd get death.

That's how this refreshing meeting came about.

The poor girl was half-conscious. He blushed when I offered him tea, and hid his feet under the table. I, dreading a senseless conversation, was vicious: another sleepless night had robbed me of all superfluous feeling.

Now, pitiful, shivering and sweating, she lunged around the kitchen like a gigantic blue reptile, but her eyes were sad and almost vacant; the criminal occupied me too – for completely different reasons... Inwardly I even cheered up and wanted to drink, and smash the bottles, and have an orgy all three of us, but she (the most limited of creatures!) kept confusing the dishes and slurring her words, and he with a shy, almost childlike familiarity, tried to keep the conversation going and couldn't take his eyes off her.

The story of the murderer sleeping on the other side of the wall went like this: his father and mother were killed by accomplices right before his eyes when he was six; he ran away and lived in an orphanage until it came time to take up the family trade. The first victims were those two. That throbbing love was still in him, he still smelled of milk and twisted his lips into a smile.

They soon disappeared into the room I showed them. There was no death. I had played my part, though I didn't like it. My own uselessness put me to sleep.

It seemed to me that out the window it was winter, and the usual blizzard, rusty in the artificial light, was swirling, and the sleepless windows opposite were cold. The whole day spelled winter; the choosing of sweaters and socks, the long preparation for the first snow and the time when I would set out, alone and impetuously, along the streets with their yellow lights, choking on the air, giving in to it and seeking out forms hitherto unseen; when I, surrounded by forms, would see faces and carry on an endless conversation in my imagination; I am so absorbed I don't hear real conversations. But the endings of the words, stressed with the timbre of the voice, refuse to lie down on paper, and I quietly turn into my kitchen. I hide the pail in the larder and again I go, delighting in old and new forms, empty forms and forms filled with activity, in windows shining with partititions of anthracite and gold (like the rims of a pince-nez); in forms, slightly dried with snowy sleet, and figures of rubber and copper. The grey caps, lively faces – so many polygons smelling of wine and wind, standing in line – but on the other side, opposite the windowless building, a four-table cafe awaits me, it has a new manager and cream-filled pastries on the menu. I glance inside the coffee well and see: the circle has closed. Next stops: an empty spring, an echoing archway, and an early-morning trolleybus.

In the morning it turned out that she had run away. The murderer stood outside the bathroom door, tapping timidly and trying to persuade her to come out. He didn't know that the bathroom door was sometimes hard to open. His pants seemed somewhat worn in the daylight, but his bare torso was handsome and manly. I gave the door a shove and it flew open: he looked eagerly inside and plodded dejectedly off to the room – to relive his futile monologue.

After a brief investigation in the morning kitchen, we sat there without her, drank narcotic-strength tea and talked, carressing each other with our eyes...

"When I saw her, it was like everything inside me flipped."

"So why'd you scare her with a gun?"

"I don't even know. We'd just come back from a hit."

And now this one had come to me to confess. Well then? Let's assume I can keep myself together; let's assume I'm not all that helpless and lethargic. But why receive confirmation of my virtues when there's nobody to use them on?! And after this outburst of fitness, there will again be months of drowziness, or drunkeness, or nasty, petty, consuming hatred, and, evidently, those superhuman efforts

I employ so as not to throw myself on someone came in handy yesterday – in a much weaker dose. Why all this heroism and all this knowledge of my own worth, if no one wants to buy me, if people are scared to get involved with me, – if I don't want this, and if I ever did, then so much the worse: I will start crawling around offices, on my knees, and yelling: "Don't leave me here, dear man!" – and people don't like that...

"You just tell me what she likes and I'll marry her."

"Everyone likes Pepsi, vodka, pizza."

"Can she have children?"

"She probably can: how can she not at gun-point..."

Senseless, senseless, sainted world. Both eyes – one with an incredibly dilated pupil, the other with almost no pupil at all and seemingly flecked with gold dust – both eyes are dead. After a "hit", he walks along the parapets. A century ago, he would have been a real suitor: he would have showered the matchmakers in their peaked caps with dahlias – to the accompaniment of an accordion.

"What's her mother like?"

The sky above is painted with colored markers, it's becoming stuffy, and the apartment smells are coming back to life, but he is still sitting here.

"When the light fell on her, it's like something in me flipped "

What sort of a mission is this – confessing lovers? What sort of torture is this – to know that no one will ever ask about you that way! Just as the peasant longs to don a lordly pince-nez, so I long to matchmake. But the isolation of the castes still exists, as do the laws of biology. I am equal to him in strength, but not in caste. You can respect me, but never love me, for they love... their own. And however curative the touch of a person of another caste, it is cold.

I remember the accidental fortune-teller in the old cluttered park. He was young, divorced, worked in an office, and had stopped by this ancient garden right after the trial. He took my hand bravely enough, but saw something there that greatly disturbed him.

"Well, what do you see?"

"You must excuse me... I feel very awkward..." (agonizing exhalation). "You will have many men..."

"I know that. I've already, as a matter of..."

"Yes, but they won't love you. Only you will love."

He walked away to a side path; he had suddenly and definitively solved a great many problems (his? mine?). And there was never another day of such blissful clarity — that I can say for sure.

We have been sitting for nearly two hours, and suddenly, after a night terror, I am incredibly tense, and his presence is so painful, so empty: he is a minus-person, he smells like carrion; but he likes it here — he's relaxed and boring. Now, his desert is in me, all his "hits", and that dream was his dream; the neutralization reaction has been completed. My heavy gestures, his current complaisance — it's all repugnant!

"Oh, okay," he is scrupulous in his goodbyes, the way they are in the country, he practically bows and, mentally equipped with accordion, dahlias and Pepsi-Cola, he sets off on a long journey.

I touch the dark last grass on the Gobelin tapestry and feel my temperature rising. In the din of dawn construction and the thawing air I read my old feelings. The autumnal blade of grass pokes out beyond the tapestry's expanse. It is almost dead and cool. Horses graze by a tumbledown manor-house fence; a fallen beam blocks their path to a distant yellow forest; fall is in the air —with a single note, or an entire scale, and the black horse turns to meet my gaze.

Translated by Joanne Turnbull

Sophia Kupryashina

Sophia Kupryashina, in her early twenties, is still a student at the Literary Institute, the class of Andrei Bitov. After her debut in SOLO she has been published in several literary periodicals. Her highly individual style reflects the disturbed moods and confusion typical of the fin-de-siecle younger generation, who are very sure about what they don´t want without quite knowing what they do.

YURI BUYDA

Eve Eve

Evdokia Evgenievna Nebesikhina aroused in everyone the antici-pation and presentiment of unstinting love and never-ending happiness when she arrived in the little Prussian town with one of the first special trains that delivered the Russian settlers to Eastern Prussia after the war.

The settlers listened in timid confusion to the ringing names of the ancient towns – Koenigsberg, Tilsit, Insterburg, Welau – while they took the measure of this foreign land, with its cramped fields and clean-swept forests, narrow, tarmacadam roads and stone houses with tiled roofs which sheltered the heads of people whose children had burned their villages. They stepped in timid confusion over the small blue cobblestones of the railway platforms and stuck close to the officer and soldiers of their own army, which was already comfortably quartered and settled in these "burgs".

Evdokia Evgenievna was the only one who looked around with a simple and natural smile, as though she might have been the legal heir to this seven hundred year-old estate where the cramped fields, polders and white dunes ran right up to the cold waters of the Baltic Sea. The soldiers and officers glanced curiously at this tall golden-eyed beauty carrying a small suitcase who kept herself to herself. "A magnetic woman," a sergeant with a black moustache said loudly, but she simply cast him a slightly mocking glance and set off with an assured stride towards the children's home. Next morning everyone already knew that a new nurse had appeared in the children's home. Evdokia Evgenievna: Eve Eve.

The sergeant with the black moustache was right: Eve Eve proved to be a genuinely magnetic woman. Men fell in love with her at first sight, children came running the moment she called, and even women forgave her for her beauty. The burnt and ruined little town, that had changed hands twice, that was populated by Russian soldiers weary with home-sickness and silent Germans dizzy with hunger, who washed the pavements with ashes instead of soap and sold the virginity of their scentless daughters for a piece of soldier's bread – this long-suffering, flame-scorched little town came to life when Eve Eve appeared. The apple and chestnut trees suddenly blossomed luxuriously, the birds that had been waiting out the war in regions where no newspapers are published suddenly returned, and the dreary black bulls and their East-Friesian brides rediscovered the urging of desire.

Absolutely everyone attempted to pay court to Eve Eve – generals and soldiers, officers and quartermasters, from every branch of the forces based in the little town. Her name alone was often sufficient cause for a quarrel that was decided by the breaking of teeth. Two young pilots who quarrelled over the golden-eyed beauty took their fighter-planes up into the air to resolve the quarrel by playing aerial "chicken". But she just laughed, and the only presents she would accept were flowers, although the coffers of the Eastern Prussian Reparation Fund were wide open to her.

Just imagine our astonishment and indignation, when we learned that Eve Eve was living with dumb Hans! With that lanky oafish youth that even the Germans laughed at. He worked in the children's home as watchman, stoker, gardener and herdsman. He was disciplined and meek: even when he was scolded, he merely nodded in assent, struggling to stretch his lips into a smile – he could never do this, because a fragment of a high-explosive shell had pierced both his cheeks, knocking out half his teeth and ripping out his entire tongue. He was seen one morning coming out of her room. How and when they had come together, how and when they had realized they needed to be with each other, and how they managed everything without words, God alone knew, the God who watches over the dumb and the beautiful. She replied to the question from the head of the children's home, Major Reprintsev with a disarming smile and the words: "l love him. I feel sorry for him." And that was all – from a woman of whom a single glimpse was sufficient to turn the head of any male being from a general to a sparrow.

Her laughter also paralyzed our feeble attempt to ostracize her. The most insistent were treated to the sight of her nickel-plate browning, with an inscription on the handle which showed it was a gift from Marshal Zhukov.

At night the men living on the nearby streets tossed restlessly in their beds, chewing on their cigarettes, listening to her groans of happiness and the provocatively meaningless bellowing of her beloved. Men even came from the air-squadron stationed seven kilometers outside the little town to get a look at him. They were wary of touching him – partly out of a desire not to quarrel with Eve, partly, in all honesty, out of respect for his physical strength: Hans could unscrew the rusted nuts on the hub of a car wheel with just his finger and thumb. When the commandant, Colonel Milovanov, took advantage of some plausible excuse to put Hans away in the lock-up, Eve Eve simply came and took the keys from the desk in the commandant's office, and simply let the dumb youth out, while everybody there, including the sentries and Colonel Milovanov, just gazed at her in rapture without saying a word. Hans carried her home in his arms. "Ich liebe dich," she said to him without the slightest shame in front of everyone. "I want a child. I want a big fat belly." Then, swallowing the first sound of his name, she called to him in a voice that brought even the phallic barrels of the tank canon swinging round towards her: "Anss... Anss..."

Time passed, but Eve did not get pregnant.

With the permission of Major Reprintsev, she adopted a ten year-old little boy with one arm, whom the children had nicknamed Jesus. He was a taciturn lad, and his only entertainment was to fire his catapult at the German inhabitants, who were scared stiff of him – he fired steel ball-bearings that the tank crews had given to the children's home as toys. He regarded his new position in life with total indifference. He wouldn't allow Eve to dress him or undress him, he went to the bath-house with the soldiers, and he took his meals with them as well, he only came home to sleep at night. Eve Eve meekly bore his insults, and waited meekly for him to come home, so that when she was sure he was asleep, she could kiss his closed eyes.

The children in the home did not like him and they were hard on him in all their games. When they began to play at war, he usually ended up with the role of prisoner under interrogation. They beat him with double lengths of telephone cable, burned his belly with a cigarette and stuck needles under his nails. Jesus gritted his teeth and refused to talk, driving his "enemies" into a frenzied rage. "It will end badly," the head of the children's' home warned Eve.

He was proved right. One day when they were playing at war, the lads hung Jesus on a pine tree and organized a competition in markmanship to see who could throw a stone so it hit his cramp-twisted mouth. When one of them did hit it, it opened, and out tumbled an exorbitantly long purple tongue.

Hans carried Eve to the hospital after she fainted. Doctor Sheberstov unbuttoned her overall and whistled when he saw the monstrous scar stretching in a sinuous patch from her left breast to the golden pubic hair.

"Where did you get that," he asked, when Eve Eve came round and he had given her a thorough examination.

"Near Warsaw. I was a medical instructor in the infantry."

Doctor Sheberstov swallowed. "Evdokia Evgenievna, I think I should tell you, that... it is very unlikely that you could ever have a child..."

She lay there on the couch in silence, her eyes closed. Then she sat up and looked up at the doctor, who had hidden his hands behind his back.

"Then what do I need this for," she asked in a quiet voice, touching her breast. "And this?.. And this? So all I'm good for is to be a whore?"

"It's the war." The doctor averted his gaze.

"My God, what for?" She closed the overall with sudden movement. "Why me?"

"The war affects everyone," mumbled Sheberstov, "they're not to blame..."

She didn't leave her room for several days. She lay face down in her bed, sometimes asleep, sometimes awake, listening to the dull roaring of her blood. Someone knocked at the door. She didn't answer.

"Eve," called Nastya, the matron, "Eve, don't take on like this. Let's go, they're probably still at the station."

Evdokia raised her head from the pillow with a struggle.

"Who?"

"Who? The Germans, of course."

"Which Germans?" She didn't understand.

Nastya leaned over her. "What's wrong, girl? Are you really that sick?"

"No." She sat up on the bed. "What's happened?"

"They're deporting them all. All the grown-up Germans, and all the little boy and girl Germans. A stone and a half of gear apiece and *aufwiedersehen*! My landlady unscrewed the brass door-knob for a souvenir."

"Why are they deporting them? I don't understand." She glanced out of the window. "What have they done? Where are they going?"

"To Germany. Those are the orders from Moscow. Don't go dashing off, I'll get my boy-friend and he'll have us there in a jiff in the car."

The sergeant with the black moustache helped the women out of the car and yelled at the sentry: "They're with me!" They were allowed through.

Far ahead of them a steam locomotive panted heavily at long intervals. The doors of the goods wagons rumbled as the soldiers closed them, paying no attention to the Germans standing dead still in the openings; the officers put on the seals.

"Hans!" Eve shouted into the nearest wagon. "Anss, my darling!"

A young officer in a Ministry of State Security uniform turned his back and broke match after match as he tried to light a cigarette.

She dashed along the train, lit by the slanting beams of search-lights. Pudgy Nastya ran after her. "Anss! Where are you? Where are you? I won't let you go!" Eve shouted.

Soldiers ran up out of the darkness, forced her down on to the platform and pressed her against the cobblestones.

The train clanked and began to move.

"Anss!"

Eve broke free and staggered into the waiting-room.

"A telegram!" she yelled in a frightening voice at the young telegraphist behind the window. "To Comrade Stalin. Urgent Express!"

The State Security man she had passed shortly before came up to her from behind and cautiously took hold of her elbow. She pushed him away sharply without even looking at him.

"A telegram!.." The girl behind the window turned away.

"Please," the State Security man said in a loud whisper, although there was no-one in the room but them. " Let's go. It's an order, you understand? An order."

She stared at him for a few moments as though she were blind. He led her away by the arm. In the doorway a panting Nastya took her arm and supported her. "Let's go, my dear... thank you, young man... let's go."

In the car the sergeant with the black moustache dwelt over his cigarette, then, gazing into the darkness, he suddenly said: "Colonel Milovanov shot himself." He breathed out a puff of smoke. "Because of his Elsa. Deportation..."

He pressed on the clutch.

The next day Eve Eve collected the pay due to her and bought a ticket to Moscow. Wearing a fashionable, close-fitting suit and high-heeled shoes, smelling of perfume, she appeared at the station one minute before the express was due to depart.

We never saw her again. We only learned later that she stood in the lobby of the carriage for a long time, smoking a cigarette and refusing to answer the conductor's questions – he suspected something was amiss, alright, when after Vilnius he glanced out into the lobby again and saw the door wide open and a slim woman's handbag dangling on the handrail. Her mutilated body was discovered in the brambles growing alongside the tracks: a bullet-hole in her temple, a nickel-plated revolver clutched convulsively in the hand of her broken arm, her legs smeared with blood and creosote – she was dead, of course she was dead. But this was no longer Eve Eve. No, this was not the golden-eyed Eve Eve who gave everyone that trembling feeling of anticipation just below the heart, that presentiment of unstinting love and never-ending happiness... This was just a dead woman, but the other – she was Eve Eve, and that says it all.

Translated by Andrew Bromfield

Yuri Buyda

Yuri Buyda, born 1954, grew up in Kaliningrad (formerly Koenigsberg, E.T.A. Hoffmann's birthplace in Eastern Prussia). In his formative years he witnessed the suffering of the remaining German population in this formerly German city. Later he became particularly interested in the life of Russian Germans, as well as in other nationalities problems in Russia.

Buyda used to work on various Communist Party periodicals, and in order to retain his sanity started writing stories "full of inventions and exaggerations". His stories were first published in SOLO in 1991 and attracted the attention of publishers. In the past three years he has been extensively published in a variety of literary journals. His latest novel **The Dominoes Player** was nominated for the Booker Prize in 1993.

AN EXPLORER'S GUIDE TO RUSSIA
by Bob Greenall
Zephyr Press, 13 Robinson St. Somerville, MA 02145, USA

Prospective visitors to Russia should look out
for a new travel guide combining much sought-after
practical information
with some unusual facts about places mentioned.
**It goes well beyond the bounds of
Moscow and St Petersburg,**
to places unknown even to many Russians.
Never before has Russia been so open to foreigners,
and never before has such a guide been so vital.

ALEXANDER MIKHAILOV
editor-in-chief

SOLO
a Child of Glasnost

In January 1990 I happened to be at the editorial offices of a small, semi-private paper publishing theatrical news, and also some poetry of the former underground. It was sleeting outside, and I had a head-splitting hangover. In spite of glasnost, things were pretty much the same in the literary world. Socialist realism still reigned supreme, and the public, both at home and in the West, was only interested in authors unmasking the atrocities of communism.

It suddenly occurred to me that perhaps this small paper, supported by a private firm called Ayurveda, might be interested in a literary supplement publishing new authors who had been rejected by official literature for years. I had more than enough of such works, rejected supposedly on aesthetic rather than political grounds, to last me for many issues. They came from all over Russia. To my amazement Ayurveda agreed to help with paper and seed money. Hurray!

In June 1991, glasnost still continuing, the first issue of SOLO was being reviewed on TV. The presenter was clearly amazed by a magazine which would have been impossible under the Soviets. Incidentally, SOLO is a Russian abbreviation for "Union of Solitary Authors". Literature never is created in groups or "writers unions", it is invariably an individual, even an individualistic enterprise.

Later when Andrei Bitov, the venerable founding father of Russian post-modernism, saw SOLO he became so enthusiastic that he offered to supply new names and even to compile a number of issues himself. He also invited another eminent writer of the post-modern trend, Yevgeny Popov, to help with our magazine.

Despite all the help and enthusiasm, we only managed to bring out the second issue of SOLO almost nine months later. We still have the support of Ayurveda, but you never know in this country. Post-perestroika Russians have developed the psychology of a secret lover: take your chance today, you may not have it tomorrow. Or to put things more crudely but more accurately: grab what you can today, because tomorrow there may be nothing to grab.

In July 1991 I went to Munich to sign a contract with Piper Publishers for a collection of stories based on SOLO. They chose to call it "Peasant Underground", which sounded pretty banal to me, like "Russian Beauty" or "Siberian Babushka", but never mind, let them have it their way. The main thing was to break on to the international literary scene. In Russia today, if you're not published abroad you are considered second-rate.

Radio Liberty made a program about SOLO — our international fame grew. Critics at home began to sit up and take notice of us as well. Manuscripts kept coming in from all over Russia, and fan mail too.

In January 1992 prices were deregulated, and promptly rocketed. We were in a state of panic. Our sponsor, Ayurveda, was coming apart at the seams. Money was the main problem now. Curse capitalism! The "period of stagnation" seemed so cosy in retrospect. In May 1992 Ayurveda announced that they wouldn't be able to sponsor us for the next few months until their own situation improved. They were no longer able to keep ahead of inflation and rising taxes. But we already had three more issues of excellent material ready for the presses! What was going to become of all these future classics?

During 1992 things went from bad to worse — there was no money, not just for SOLO but for ordinary, everyday necessities. My wife could not understand why I should be so doggedly soldiering on with my hopeless project when it brought in no money whatsoever. Family life grew very tense, to the point of complete collapse.

But in December 1992 — what joy! — SOLO received the LITTLE BOOKER PRIZE! True, the prize of 2,500 pounds sterling was shared between SOLO and *Vestnik Novoi Literatury*, but still, it was an enormous moral and financial boost which came, like a deus ex machina, just when everything seemed hopeless. So capitalism is not so bad after all, especially British capitalism. Long live Booker PLC!

Alexander Mikhailov

Alexander Mikhailov, born 1951, is a Muscovite who graduated from the Department of Journalism at Moscow University. He later obtained a PhD in literary criticism at the Moscow Literary Institute. From 1981 to 1989 he was deputy editor-in-chief of the literary monthly October, and in 1990 launched SOLO, a magazine specialising in new names.

Mikhailov is a noted and prolific critic specialising in contemporary authors.

The Time: Night
by Ludmila Petrushevskaya
Virago Press, 1994, 155 pages

Shortlisted for the Russian Novel Booker Prize in 1992, this novel is about three women: a poet struggling to make ends meet, her wayward daughter and her senile mother.

"Petrushevskaya takes the reader on an unforgettable journey into the domestic hell where there is too little of everything: too little food, too little space, too little love...

"Available now in Sally Laird's eminently readable translation, *The Time: Night* provides a memorable glimpse into the dark side of life. Written in a stark, naturalistic style, the book brings the reader face to face with the harsh reality of life in Russia. It is not often a pleasant sight, but it is one well worth the trouble."

Jean MacKenzy, *The Moscow Times*

VYACHESLAV IVANOV

Chairman of the Jury
of the Russian Novel Booker Prize 1993

The Russian Novel
in 1992/3

In writing this article I am aiming to kill two birds with one stone. My first purpose is to set out my own views on the novel and how it relates to the past and future of Russian literature generally. More immediately, having been nominated Chairman of the second year's Booker Jury to award a prize for the best Russian novel of 1992/3, I am taking this opportunity of expressing my reflections on the works I have read. While gratefully taking full account of the thoughts and suggestions of my colleagues and companions on the Jury, sometimes agreeing with them and developing their observations, on other occasions disputing them, I do reserve the right to display a fair degree of subjectivity. If a novel is mentioned only in passing this does not mean that it is no good. More detailed consideration is given to what is controversial.

We may justifiably hope that the award of an annual prize for a Russian novel will lead to increased interest in new Russian writing generally. Picking one winner out of several strong candidates is inevitably arbitrary to some extent, with a cumulation of personal preferences tipping the scales; and in any case, new Russian writing deserves more than the recognition of one solitary work once a year.

A restriction of genre results from the practicalities of awarding the Booker prize . We shall be talking in the main about novels, although the exact demarcation line between a novel and a novella (and even, occasionally, a collection of short stories) can really be quite difficult to draw at times. Moreover, the nature of the discussion will oblige us to talk about prose fiction in general.

Russian writers have always demanded a flexible approach to genre. Tolstoy made this point a propos of *War and Peace*, and gave as supporting examples every major Russian prose work from

224

Gogol's *Dead Souls* to Dostoyevsky's *Notes from the House of the Dead*. We could indeed also instance Pushkin's "novel in verse", *Eugene Onegin*; yet however broadly we define the novel, there are going to be works which strain that definition, even where the author himself favours inclusion under that heading. Fazil Iskander's recent fine book, *Man and his Environs* (*Chelovek i ego okrestnosti*), may serve as an example.

The novel itself seeks constantly to break through the boundaries of a neatly delineated genre, but more than this, it changes together with the society it is describing, and together with the philosophy it is expressing. In "The End of the Novel", a memorable article written as long ago as the 1920s, Osip Mandelstam formulated reasons why, as he surmised, after Romain Rolland's *Jean-Christophe*, the novel could no longer be the history of the self-creating biography of a single person. The novel in Balzac's or Stendhal's sense ceases to exist when society usurps the autonomy of the individual. The centripetal quality of the classical novel, centred on one or several destinies of people making their way in life in accordance with the dictates of their free will, is replaced by the centrifugal quality of the modern novel with its patterns of many characters in which the hero becomes a passive personage. Here we may instance works of Russian literature written since the Second World War as diverse as Boris Pasternak's *Doctor Zhivago* and Vasily Grossman's *Life and Destiny* (*Zhizn' i sud'ba*), both of which only recently became available to a mass readership in Russia. Yury Zhivago does not choose to join the partisans: the responsible decisions are taken for him by other people.

Present-day society (and not only totalitarian society) takes away from the hero the autonomy he needs to be able to construct his own biography, and it takes away from the novelist any possibility of a succinct plot centered on one individual. A mass of people become the "hero", as in Mario Vargas Llosa's *War of the End of the World*, perhaps the most symptomatic book of recent decades in all of world literature. Among books published in the past year, we find the same phenomenon in Victor Astafiev's novel *The Cursed and the Slain* (*Prokliaty i ubity*), and Yevgeny Fyodorov's *Roast Cockerel* (*Zharenyi petukh*). The latter had its book publication in 1992 but, having previously been published in a journal, was ineligible for consideration by the Booker Committee, although most of us rated it very highly. In the best tradition of writings about the Soviet labour camps, the ordeals which the hero, Krasnov, endures in captivity are described in a very broad perspective, which extends to the other characters associated with him. These characters are described in greater detail in a notable but as yet unpublished work by Fyodorov which I was fortunate enough to read in manuscript long ago. One of the main difficulties in awarding the Booker Prize stems directly from the worsening state of book publishing in Russia, with a number of interesting books by Fyodorov, Dmitry Galkovsky, and Alexey Tsvetkov as yet known to readers only fragmentarily.

Let us, however, return to *Roast Cockerel.* An unruly mob is one of the main protagonists in Fyodorov's book, a mob consisting in the main of people broken or degraded by their unhappy situation. The scene of collective rape in this novel derives its power precisely from the manner in which the reality of the camps is shown to outweigh all Krasnov's intellectual searchings, philosophical insights and exaltations. A comparable episode in Isaac Babel's *Red Cavalry* (*Konarmiia*), published in 1926, is written if anything even more brutally, yet lacks Fyodorov's intense existential despair, a despair born in the novel of a collision between grim reality and the utopian notions which Krasnov, under the pressure of the daily horrors of the camps, is ultimately forced to abandon. Fyodorov's novel is a practical anti-utopia in which the hero's aspirations and philosophy are wrecked upon the malign reality of the camp.

Pushkin himself insisted that "thought and more thought" is essential if prose is to be successful. Precisely this was the root of the catastrophe which befell prose of the Soviet period. The state took away the writer's intellectual independence, while the censorship hindered the expression of thoughts. Without these no revival of Russian prose writing is possible, and this is why the philosophical novel is so crucial.

Of philosophical novels recently published in Russia, I believe Alexander Pyatigorsky's *Philosophy of a Certain Sidestreet* (*Filosofiia odnogo pereulka*) to be possibly the most successful. (It was published in the West several years ago.) This is not only because Pyatigorsky has an original and brilliant mind which combines a knowledge of the wisdom of Buddhism with the highest achievements of modern European thought, although of this we can judge from such scholarly works as his course on the phenomenology of myth recently published in English. In the novel, however, Pyatigorsky speaks less about these abstractions than about the renowned smoking room of Moscow's Lenin Library in the 1950s. His novel brings to life the setting and trappings of an intellectual growth and ferment of the post-war years without which there would have been none of the later dramatic advances in the humanities in Russia, among them Pyatigorsky's own sophisticated Indological philosophical constructs. His talent as a writer is evident precisely in his limitation of specifically philosophical material in the novel. In this respect it is the exact opposite of Dmitry Galkovsky's novel *Endless Dead-End* (*Beskonechnyi tupik*) which, to judge by the parts of it which have been published, is over-burdened with philosophical and quasi-philosophical speculation borrowed, in part at least, from treatises dating back to the early years of the century.

There is no guarantee that even an outstanding philosopher will be able to merge his conclusions with the literary concerns proper to a writer of fiction, but in this Pyatigorsky is resoundingly successful, in marked contrast to A.F. Losev, whose fictional writing has again only very recently become available to the Russian reading public. A collection of his literary efforts, *Dialectic of Myth* (partially published also in *Novyi zhurnal* in Sept-Dec 1990) was brought out to mark the centenary of his birth.

Losev's undoubted philosophical and musicological erudition do not automatically make for interesting prose. Indeed his almost caricatured heroine is a philosophizing lady musician who testifies less to Losev's artistic endowment than to the continuing psychological difficulties of his relationship with Maria Yudina, a great Russian pianist. Losev turned to fiction at a time of great difficulty in his personal life, finding himself unable to continue in his previous profession on his release from imprisonment. Being unable to continue a career as a philosopher is not, of course, a very good reason for becoming a novelist. Neither was Losev the only person to take up writing fiction at a time when being a philosopher was becoming ever more dangerous. Yakov Golosovker's novel originated in the same way. It has finally found its way to the reader through Nina Braginskaya's publication in the journal *Druzhba Narodov*. The novel deserves attention both as an unexpected parallel to Bulgakov's *The*

Master and Margarita and as part of an iceberg, not exclusively lite-rary, of which we are just beginning to see the top. These are books written "for the desk drawer" in the darkest years when there was no prospect of their publication. The more we discover of this lit-erature, the more marginal the official literary canon seems, and the more evident does it become that the entire history of Russian lit-erature in the twentieth century is going to have to be rewritten.

It is certainly true that in the Soviet period public recognition was accorded to literature that was quite devoid of intellectual merit, in-cluding not only the worthless official writings penned by Stalin Prize winners but also the late, phoney, "avant-garde" style and thorough-going mendacity of Valentin Kataev, which was not by any means confined to the systematic lying in his memoirs. Oddly enough, Kataev briefly became virtually a paragon for talented young writers during the Khrushchev Thaw. The root of the problem goes deeper than this, however, and the erosion of the sheer philosophical power which brings the novels of Tolstoy and Dostoyevsky to life may already have set in in the novels of symbolism and post-sym-bolism. In Russia the divorce between philosophy (particularly religious philosophy) and literature (particularly the novel) dates back to the turn of the century. Attempting to re-unite them by piec-ing together a literary text from philosophical axioms, as Galkovsky does, only confirms a continuing rift between thought, literary image, and plot.

When Milan Kundera insists in his absorbing essay *The Art of the Novel* on the uniqueness of the Central-European philosophical novel of Kafka, Musil, and Broch he is right in one respect. If the genre of the novel was being used for reflection on serious matters well be-fore these authors came on the scene, we can nevertheless agree that their (sometimes highly irrational) images are organically linked with their general outlook on the world. Kafka rightly favours the genre of the parable since he communicates his philosophy by al-legory (which at first glance can appear thoroughly obscure). Let us not forget either that this group of authors writing in German in Prague at the beginning of the century included Gustav Meyrink whose *Golem* (recently republished in Russia) was the guiding star of Daniel Kharms, a writer far removed from discursiveness. Of re-cent Russian writing such of Friedrich Gorenstein's novels as *Psalm* merit a place in this category, but as I have already written at some length about *Psalm* in the Introduction to its journal publication in *October*, No. 10, 1991, I will not repeat myself here.

Russian literature, like the rest of Russia, has paused for a moment to take stock. Not everything, perhaps, has yet been fully thought through and found expression, but our new writing is not by any means intellectually barren (which is arguably its main difference from the output of the young writers of the Thaw period). The abundance of playful and jocular works does not contradict this. Kharms himself was often ironical.

A number of the present-day novels stand out for their intellectual seriousness, and prominent among these is Semyon Lipkin's *A Resident Remembers (Zapiski zhil' tsa)*. His work amply conveys to us the history of Odessa from the first decades of the century. We are presented with a whole array of characters of different social backgrounds and diverse ethnic origins, religious beliefs, and political persuasions. Lipkin does not leave us without guidance among all the events but provides background information and shares his own hard-won insights with us.

Mikhail Bakhtin was one of the first to recognize the novel as the foremost genre of modern literature. His powerful concept of the chronotope, a novel's time-space continuum, has gained wide acceptance. He borrowed the term from the contemporary natural sciences, where the world is always conceptualized within a defined temporal and spatial framework. The same is true of the novel. Especially after the narrative has ceased to revolve exclusively around a single hero, the limits an author imposes on the chronological and geographical boundlessness of his material become particularly important. Lipkin relates the history of Odessa, but only to the extent necessary for us to be able to peep into the small fragment of the Odessa chronotope he is showing us. His novel has no epic pretensions to encompass everything that has taken place in the course of half a century. We see only one house, and the shop, warehouse, staircase, and courtyard which adjoin it. We follow the lives of only a few families, but the close-up we are shown of this small corner of Odessa, at first with a bustling business life but later suffering the rigours of the years of revolution, reflects all the history of Russia. The unassuming style of Lipkin's prose and the absence of the grand sweep only serve to emphasize his achievement. One might niggle over whether the concluding episode in Germany is really essential, but even its being relatively less successful only goes to show how completely unfettered and confident Lipkin is within his own, familiar chronotope. We find just the same kind of limitation, in their different ways, in Fazil Iskander and Ivan Oganov with regard to their Trans-Caucasian chronotopes, and in Mikhail Kuraev and Pyotr Aleshkovsky in respect of their provincial urban or rural settings.

Semyon Lipkin unobtrusively communicates his philosophy of history in his Odessa chapters. We learn his views on many matters which even now continue to tax us. With its clever intertwining of reality and fiction Lipkin's novel will stand the test of time. If some are initially deterred by the unhurried traditionalism of his style, for others it may be just this absence of modishness which appeals.

Ludmilla Ulitskaya's *Sonechka* also follows the tried and tested path of classical prose, but in the genre of a family narrative. Her novella is well written, eschewing fancy effects and centring on the destiny of a single heroine which, of course, immediately marks it out as belonging to the earlier tradition. It has the further merit of helping us to appreciate the possibilities of calm, restrained narrative, as does Veronica Platova's recently published collection of short stories, *Roald and Flora*.

A special place among the books of the year belongs to Vladimir Makanin's novella *Baize-Covered Table with Decanter* (*Stol, pokrytyi suknom i s grafinom poseredine*), which differs in style from his previous works. It focusses wholly on characterizing the hero's inner state as he anticipates his confrontation with an official tribunal, and strikes one as a variation of the socio-psychological drama depicted in Kafka's *The Trial*. If Russians tend to read it as an account of social reality, the whole situation can, as with Kafka, be read as a philosophical metaphor. Makanin's chosen manner of abstract exposition might seem to favour the latter interpretation. He does not elaborate on the precise accusations against the main character, who is troubled simply by the ordeal he is facing, but Makanin brings home to us his sense of trouble ahead. This sense of impending catastrophe is something everybody who has lived under a totalitarian regime is very well familiar with. For many this may have been the real terror, something which drained their strength and left them disarmed, their opposition deprived of meaning by a battle already lost, a city surrendered without a fight. Like all real literature, however, *Baize-Covered Table* may also sustain a less political reading.

A critic less encumbered by day to day experience of the institutions of the former Soviet way of life might incline to see Makanin's novella as simply an outstanding depiction of the psychology of a man in trouble, but why then does he highlight the attributes of bureaucratic investigation in the very title, attributes which obsess a hero tormented by the nightmarish humiliation he anticipates. We shall yet live to see a literature which, like some future, free, Utopian life, will be able to put behind it the detail of how people are hounded and judged. For the meanwhile, however, may Makanin continue a tradition begun by Russia's eighteenth-century satirists and continued by Gogol and Sukhovo-Kobylin. This tradition, describing the tribulations of the persecuted "little man", runs through our literature like the tracks of that monstrous state machine alongside which and despite which our literary tradition has developed. These two forces are pitted against each other in an unequal struggle, which works to the advantage of the literary characters, but which can be hard, and indeed dangerous, for their creators. All the more cause, then, for us to appreciate Makanin's courage in not flinching, and for facing up to difficulties, literary and extra-literary, which may ensue. His novella looks both to the hallowed Russian tradition of depicting the misfortunes of the man who is "little" only because he has been crushed by a gigantic state, and to the European literary tradition where what is conveyed is not action itself but a taut psychological account of feeling.

Oleg Yermakov's novel *The Sign of the Beast* (*Znak zveria*) is something out of the ordinary on several counts, and the interest it has aroused among the critics is fully justified. In the first place, with this novel a younger generation of prose writers makes its debut, bringing with it not only its unique personal experience (in Yermakov's case, his experience of the war in Afghanistan), but also the very individual way in which it experiences the world. In the second place, the events with which the novel deals are a scar in our memory and on our conscience which shows no sign of healing. We cannot afford to repress such traumas, whether that colonial war of the recent past or the confrontation between President and Parliament in

October 1993 which brought us to the brink of civil war. If we do, we only risk creating complexes in the subconscious of Russian society which have a potential for future eruption. Quite apart from its artistic worth, a work like *The Sign of the Beast* has a further, therapeutic value both social and psychological.

The theme of East meets West, the theme of Eurasia, is very central to the novel. In a novel written a few years earlier by the young American writer Jay McInerney the hero and his friends come into partial contact with the ramifications of the Afghan war on the border with Pakistan. Yermakov's interest too focusses on how his young characters relate psychologically to Far Eastern culture: where McInerney's hero leaves for Japan, Yermakov's thinks in the imagery of oriental poetry. An enthusiasm for Taoism and the Zen Buddhist trend in classical Chinese and Japanese literature is not, of course, by any means something confined to young Russians: one could even trace a continuity here from J.D. Salinger, who exercised no small influence on our young writers in the 1960s. More salient, however, is the upsurge of interest in Buddhism which began with the translation into Russian of (*Sayings of the Buddha*) *Dhammapada*, published more than thirty years ago, which remains strong and vibrant in Russia to this day. In the nineteenth century Christian thinkers such as Aleksey Khomyakov and Nikolai Fyodorov busied themselves primarily with contrasting the negative and passive apprehension of reality in Buddhism with the ideals and outlook of Russian Orthodoxy. In our times we have begun to gain a fuller understanding of the basic concepts of Buddhism thanks to the work of Rozenberg, Shcherbatsky and other Russian Buddhologists. More than that, Buddhism is seen by our contemporaries as an indispensible source of a serious study of life. While the Russian Orthodox Church continues to mull over the merits of ecumenism, and the state is reluctant to accept it, Russian culture and literature, an integral part of Orthodoxy, are moving unremittingly towards a far broader religious and philosophical synthesis. Yermakov's novel seems to me a landmark of no small importance on a road which may be fraught with difficulties but which must nonetheless be travelled if Russia, and indeed the rest of the world, are to move forward.

Yermakov's title has been taken from the Revelation of St John the Divine, but the apocalyptic spirit informs not only the symbol of the Beast, about whose present-day political relevance Father Sergius Bulgakov wrote so appositely in his *Apocalypse of St John* published in Paris in 1948. The best passages in Yermakov's novel, his Central-Asian landscapes where the sun and the earth are inextricably part of the earthly cataclysms, testify to his profundity. *Sign of the Beast* includes not only scenes of the Afghan war (sometimes rather sketchily linked by the plot). They are presented against a backdrop of the natural world of Asia, suffocating in the heat or itself incinerating, and in the context of the hero's poetical insights. This makes Yermakov's jarring descriptions of the *dedovshchina*, the older soldiers' despotic rule in the barracks, all the more harrowing. He tells us the whole truth about this, and in terms of social criticism the novel is more hard-hitting when dealing with this than in what it reveals about the conduct of the Afghan war. Of even greater significance, however, is the part this despotism plays in the hero's destiny. He tries to stand up to it, coordinating resistance with several other soldiers in his regiment, but is deserted at the last minute and left to face the majority who support the *dedovshchina* on his own. Not only is he physically defeated, he is reduced morally to a passivity which leads him shortly afterwards to kill blindly. He shoots at a deserter, unable in the dark to see who he is aiming at, to find that he has killed the best friend with whom he had had long philosophical conversations in Soviet Central Asia before they found themselves in the theatre of military operations. The role of this random event in the novel's structure might seem to confirm Mandelstam's views on the end of the traditional novel since, even though Yermakov chooses to write in the genre, his hero is unable to impose his own purposeful, ascendant path in life. He is thrown from one random event to another, from shooting his own friend to witnessing a settling of scores with another deserter at an Afghan village which is wiped from the face of the earth. While these events have a logic of their own, the logic of life and war, the hero's actions are not contingent upon his will: they are imposed on him by the course of the war and of the particular military operation. In these chapters the element of chance is structurally justified, but other episodes in the novel seem overly random. This is certainly true of the relatively less successful scenes of "peace" when, for example, the officer from the army's internal security section responsible for destroying the village is punished by his conscience by being unable to have a satisfactory relationship with a lady librarian. These scenes lack the rigour and authoritativeness of the chapters on "war", perhaps as a result of Yermakov's lack of knowledge on what he is describing. In one of the war chapters the security section officer is killed off, and one is left wondering whether this was because Yermakov could not think what else to do with him. The structure seems to be skidding helplessly, and this killing in time of war, unmotivated at a deeper narrative level, fails to rescue the plot. The oriental "visions" are weaker still. They are separated out in special chapters preceding the novel's finale, the long return home (itself only sketchily related to the main plot). Here too Pyatigorsky compares favourably. If *The Philosophy of a Certain Sidestreet* and *Sign of the Beast* are not particularly close as novels, then the overall Far Eastern orientation of Pyatigorsky certainly has much in common with that of Yermakov. Precisely, however, because Pyatigorsky is sure of his philosophical credo, he does not use up his energies expounding it separately. Yermakov's Far Eastern appendage to the novel really does not seem altogether necessary.

There are two good reasons for dwelling at such length on these structural faults in an otherwise fine book. The first is that Yermakov is a promising young writer with a future who has, however, yet to come to full maturity. It will be well worth his time to reflect on ways of fusing together thought and plot, and one episode with another. The second reason is that similar, or indeed greater, structural defects are evident in many another modern Russian novel. If there are a few which are positively well constructed, like Mikhail Bulgakov's *The Master and Margarita* and Andrey Platonov's *Dzhan*, the rest, for all their undoubted merits, suffer to a greater or lesser degree from loose structure. This is a defect which hinders the reader's appreciation of some of the "knots" of Alexander Solzhenitsyn's *The Red Wheel*, but it was already noticeable in his first longer works which, for just this reason, yield pride of place to his less extended writings.

The temptation to create a novel from a chaining of separate narratives not very firmly welded to each other seems to be particularly great in the genre of historical narrative, associated with what Bakhtin called the "monologic" tradition employed by Tolstoy. A writer can be tempted to try to use the periodization of historical events as the framework of his novel. Such is the role of the retreat to Stalingrad in the best chapters of Vasily Grossman's *Our Cause is Just* (*Za pravoe delo*), and of the Battle of Stalingrad itself in the sequel, his splendid *Life and Destiny*. Unfortunately, the lives and destinies of Grossman's characters only partially mesh with the historical framework imposed on them.

Victor Astafiev's *The Cursed and the Slain* derives from the same Tolstoyan tradition of the realist historical novel with a large cast of characters. This is the free-standing first part of a narrative set in the Second World War, and shows us the characters even before their departure for the front. The hardships they endure immediately after being conscripted are detailed in fine language, with all the sophisticated techniques of naturalistic description at Astafiev's disposal. In all that has been written about the Second World War in Russia and elsewhere in the past half century there is nothing of any significance on this particular topic. In terms of its subject matter and historical value, then, Astafiev's novel is deserving of a great deal of praise. At the time, Russian literature was unable to deal with the rigours of life at the front. It was forced to stay silent. Victor Nekrasov's *Front-Line Stalingrad* was pilloried precisely for the vividness with which it describes the misfortunes which befall its officer hero and his comrades. Gradually, however, the voice of the war writers grew stronger, and indeed it was only in this area that literature published in Russia was allowed to be relatively truthful when dealing with the 1940s. With Astafiev's novel we can now see that even this was only half the truth. He opens up a whole realm where there were no limits to the inhumanity and offences against the private soldier's human dignity. Astafiev commands our confidence. Despite occasional *longueurs*, his novel grips us as historical testimony. We make no apology for turning our attention to the work's extra-literary merits, but this obliges us to consider a number of other matters. We learn details of how the soldiers were treated which compare with practices in Stalin's forced labour camps which began before the action of the novel and continued after it. This was the period when people began to perish in German concentration camps (from which the novel's heroes are to save the population of Russia when they reach the front); people were swelling with hunger and dying in the

Siege of Leningrad (Somebody from the Siberian barracks Astafiev describes will later be sent to the Leningrad front); and indeed in other parts of the country. We have no right to forget any one of these circles of hell, but are we within our rights in separating them from each other? After all, these are not memoirs, which might legitimately relate what was experienced at a particular moment in time by a young soldier to whom his own humiliation and pain might have been more real than anything else in the world, and who in any case might have been ignorant of much that was happening. This is a novel written by a mature writer who knows very well what a sea of trouble and degradation was running high in Russia and the rest of the world beyond the walls of those barracks. Can one confine oneself to coming to terms exclusively with one's own unassuaged pain and hurt, or should it not in some measure reflect the suffering of other people, including those for whom many of the characters will subsequently give their lives? Perhaps some of these questions will prove wide of the mark when the remaining parts of the novel are published.

The Cursed and the Slain concentrates mainly on the bad things taking place in Russia, the Russian army, and Russian barracks in the first years of the war. To this extent it belongs with European and world pacifist and anti-heroic literature of the inter-war period (like Remarque or Barbusse) and of the post-Second World War years (of which we should mention at least Heinrich Boll's writings). There is a lot in those works written along the same lines. The reality of life in the barracks which Astafiev is describing is, however, distorted by our appalled awareness of the Soviet labour camps. I find this unexpected epilogue to the literature of the post-war years historically understandable, and it is instructive to compare the novels of Yermakov and Astafiev, writers of different generations writing about different epochs. For all the similarities between Yermakov's treatment of the older soldiers' despotism and Astafiev's description of the rigours of the soldiers' life in barracks, of the two works Yermakov's seems to me broader and more readily comprehensible in purely human terms. He is not so pre-occupied with sub-dividing people into ethnic or social groups, a habit Astafiev seems constitutionally incapable of breaking with. In Yermakov we find a seeking for equilibrium between the powers of evil, so unrelievedly present in Astafiev, and the element of good which opposes them. If there is an inference to be drawn from this about how the generations differ, then it is an encouraging one.

The younger generation of writers has recently delighted us with works which are unreservedly cheerful, and of interest primarily for the exuberant experimentalism of their style. Representative of these is Valeria Narbikova's *Round and Round* (*Okolo ekolo...*), a feverishly happy book with quick fire literary images impetuously following on and flowing into one another. In the novel's second episode the reader has no trouble in identifying a political subtext linking the love story with the contemporary history of Russia. This quirk of the narrative, linking the hero and lover with a prominent contemporary public figure, is not, however, of major importance for the book: it is just part of a high-spirited literary text which knows neither constraints nor restraint. This is a thoroughly untraditional novel, but through its restless literary successes, and occasional excesses, there shines a future Russian literature, emancipated at last, truly daring and fearless.

Russian literature has problems all its own in respect of things official, formal, and solemn. These come in a variety of forms, of which the simplest is servility, the obsequiousness of courtiers like those who so zealously gave themselves awards during the Stalin period and its immediate aftermath. Something altogether more complex than this traditional penning of odes, however, is the way in which Russian novelists have come to take for granted that they have a role as prophet and guru. This applies not only to those writers whom Bakhtin would characterize as monologic: even the dialogically multi-voiced Dostoyevsky hands down moral instruction. Even authors like Vasily Rozanov, whom we see as verging on iconoclasm, seem ready at any moment to burst into homilies.

Alongside official and didactic literature, however, there was literature which ridiculed all things official: in the Soviet period, Bulgakov's *The Crimson Island*, Nikolai Erdman's *Seminar on Laughter*, and the prose and plays of Kharms and the other Oberiuts. Andrey Sinyavsky, whose own articles and literary works make a great contribution to our understanding of unofficial Russian literature, has pointed out that it has an important strand close to the popular anecdote.

As the non-official literature of laughter (in a broadly Bakhtinian sense) has grown stronger in the last few years it has taken on, wittingly or unwittingly, the attributes of anecdote. In a "Soviet joke" (of the kind for which you could be sent to prison under Stalin) or in non-official literature an anti-world is constructed which is the polar opposite of the Soviet world.

The works of one of the most notable young authors of the grotesque tendency, Victor Pelevin, are constructed along just these lines. His novel *Omon Ra* is dedicated "to the heroes of the Cosmos", but his are in fact anti-heroes. The young people he describes are initially full of cosmic aspirations. They want to be astronauts and go to the moon, and they join an aviation college. Up to this point *Omon Ra* seems to be conforming to the canons of the Soviet official genre, but this now begins to be turned upside down. The aviation college bears the name of Aleksey Meresiev, the legendary hero of Boris Polevoy's *Story about a Real Man*. Polevoy's novel, like Nikolai Ostrovsky's *How the Steel Was Tempered*, was built on the contrasting of the hero's physical ills and disabilities on the one hand with his unbending will and faith in the Communist Party and sense of his Soviet duty on the other. Do we see here a modern variation on the traditional dualism of the spirit which is willing and the flesh which is weak, which had been radically reinterpreted in the nineteenth century by Chernyshevsky and the revolutionaries of the People's Will (and later by a great diversity of other revolutionaries), and had affected the way the intelligentsia in general thought of themselves? Be that as it may, the almost ascetic opposition of the frailty of the flesh to the strength of will of the Party man or Soviet military hero became one of the great themes of Soviet prose. Polevoy's hero lost his legs in the war but remained a combatant. In the college bearing his name all the young people matriculating are without warning and without their consent subjected to amputation of their nether appendages. There is a good technical reason for this mutilation, since with stumps instead of legs the prospective astronaut is better fit for the rocket designed to take him to the moon. This entire aspect of the plot can be regarded as an extended sick joke. Similarly disconcerting jokes were common among urban intellectuals twenty years or so ago. There are unexpected parallels in the plots of Pelevin's novella and Yermakov's *Sign of the Beast*. Both of them start off with two young heroes, one of whom is subsequently killed. In Yermakov the hero's friend is shot as a deserter, while in Pelevin the friend is taken out by the security services who have discovered that he is unreliable. The structure of *Omon Ra* reinforces Pelevin's untraditional approach to plot. The reader has no time to catch up with one turn of the narrative before the next twist in the plot hits him. The moon buggy which has supposedly transported the hero over the lunar surface proves in reality to be in a secret military installation: the young astronaut hasn't been in space at all. Pelevin's over-fertile imagination can prove too much of a good thing. There are just too many unexpected twists for one relatively short novel, even if they are partly explicable in terms of that atmosphere of all-enveloping secrecy which Pelevin is to be congratulated on conveying so successfully. In this respect his anti-utopia is wholly realistic.

The sheer inventiveness of Pelevin's mind, piling up revelations each one more mind-boggling than the last, is virtually the dominant characteristic of *The Blue Lantern*, a collection of his short stories. The heroine of one of the principal stories, "Middle Game"[*], appears at first sight to be a woman and indeed a prostitute, but subsequently turns out to be a man who has undergone a sex change operation and who, moreover, had in the recent past been a member of the Party hierarchy. Pelevin's writings truly resemble a matryoshka doll, with revelations nested one inside the other.

Vladimir Sorokin is acknowledged as one of the leading representatives of the "new wave" in Russian prose, perhaps since Boris Groys's much discussed *The Total Art of Stalinism* (Princeton University Press, 1992). The slim collection of Sorokin's short stories which appeared in 1992[**] is the first belated breaking into print of a writer whose word-of-mouth reputation had hitherto been based purely on the circulation of works in manuscript. The underlying pattern of these stories is much what we find in some of his novels (which still await publication in Russia). First comes a text virtually indistinguishable from classical or well written Soviet prose. A sudden twist introduces a deliberately shocking plot, bringing in such taboo matters as mention of the sexual organs and excrement,

[*] See *Glas* No.4. for its English translation
[**] See also *Glas* No.2 for a sample of Vladimir Sorokin's writing.

or cannibalism, murder with dismemberment, etc. There follows a transrational or continuous text bereft of punctuation or with repetition of the same words and word combinations. It has to be said that Sorokin's limitations are very evident. His short stories feature only these three stylistic elements in various combinations, and he avails himself of only a very restricted range of taboo topics. Set against the rest of our effervescent young literature, his virtuosity seems less than versatile.

Breaking taboos and emphasizing the physical functioning of the body was typical of unofficial literature before it could get into print. Defying all prohibitions seems, quite understandably, a splendid way of demonstrating how liberated one is; but given that the number of taboo words and topics is strictly limited, a superficially anarchic writer runs a considerable risk of repeating himself. In Victor Yerofeev's *The Russian Beauty* the expression of faeces is compared to the creation of a poem. The poetics of faeces does, however, seem to belong to a phase in the development of Russian writing which has already passed, a short period of spurious anarchy (which extended also to language). Like Yury Olesha's hero in *Envy*, Russian literature has given up singing in the lavatory. Boris Groys suggests that Sorokin has none of what Bakhtin calls the grotesque body and carnival, and this may well be so. A prerequisite of carnival is total lack of restraint and real merriment. A genuine sense of ancient carnival is only to be found in Konstantin Vaginov's *Goat Song* (1928).

Nikolai Berdyaev said that what the avant-garde imagines today real life will practise tomorrow. The violence so widespread in contemporary art (as in the contemporary world) does not, however, of itself make a work interesting. There is too much blood in the world, in the cinema and in writing for the cinema-goer or the reader to react to it any longer in a normal and spontaneous manner. Anatoly Kim's *The Centaurs* (*Poselok kentavrov*) falls rather flat for just this reason. This archetypal theme for the conveying of violence needs to be imbued with new meaning if it is to speak to today's reader.

Apart from breaking verbal and other taboos and offending against all the rules of normal behaviour, literature which wishes consciously to distance itself from official formality has in its arsenal the powerful weapons of grotesque and parody. Prose writers have not, on the whole, availed themselves of these, unlike the poets. In

Dmitry Prigov and the poets associated with him we see a canonization of devices arrived at over a lengthy period of time in the genres of parody and grotesque, from Ivan Myatlev and Kozma Prutkov to the Oberiuts and Nikolai Glazkov (and later the "barrack hut" poets). For all that, there are wholly parodic contemporary novels, like Yevgeny Popov's *On the Eve, on the Eve* (*Nakanune, nakanune*). The technique of exploiting literary cliche is the same for all the poets and prose writers of this tendency, and while one may debate the relative merits of individual works, the main problem for these authors is the sheer volume of output. When there are so many parodies, and with literature itself consciously bordering on parody, to show real originality is no simple matter. For just this reason, however, this trend has the important function of clearing the way for the literature of the future which will, in all probability, follow quite a different path.

An interesting experiment, also related to the Latin American magic realism of Vargas Llosa, is the re-imagining of history in recent novels by Vyacheslav Pietsukh and Yevgeny Popov. One of the first attempts of this kind was Vasily Aksyonov's *The Island of the Crimea*, reminiscent of Vargas Llosa's historico-fantastic novel written at about the same time. Science speaks to us of several possible worlds, and writers and scholars have started to think along the lines of what might have been in history. Many years ago Alexander Isachenko wrote on how Russian history might have turned out had Moscow not overpowered the free city-republic of Novgorod (see his article in *Wiener Slavistisches Jahrbuch*, 18 (1973), pp.48-55). The genre is gaining favour at a moment in time when history itself seems constantly to be trying out different possible versions of the future.

One of the more singular features of the history of Russian literature (and more generally of Russian culture) is the nature of its links with the outside world. There are times, the very beginning of the twentieth century for example, when the doors are thrown wide open. Translation from a whole range of languages reaches record levels, and the Russian reader is enriched not only by access to current and classical foreign writing, but also by the works of Russian authors drawing inspiration from newly available paradigms. Such, in the age of Pushkin, was the very direct influence on Russian letters of French literature and the English novel. These periods of openness are, however, followed by times of sudden change, followed by cultural isolation. This peaked most recently in the last years of Stalin, but continued long after, when virtually every translation of a significant West European or American novel had to be fought for. We have only to remember the saga over Hemingway's *For Whom the Bell Tolls*. People were talking about publishing it during the Second World War, but more than fifteen years were to pass before, by a miracle, it finally appeared. The dyke shutting out the European novel (and the novels of the best Russian writers in emigration) from Russian literature did spring the occasional leak: one or two works by Kafka got translated; a second translation of Proust by the outstandingly gifted Nikolai Lyubimov began to be published. Lyubimov's Proust is consciously approximated to the late style of Ivan Bunin in his *Aspects (Liki)*. Russian prose writing nevertheless drew its sustenance mainly from its past, a situation which began to change radically only very recently.

Political and economic reform brought with them the opportunity of having Russian translations of the works which were previously known only from hearsay or from relatively brief excerpts. The first full, accomplished translation of James Joyce's *Ulysses* was published only a few years ago, along with Vladimir Nabokov, and Hermann Broch. Joyce's influence made itself felt on our young writers immediately. Reading Vladimir Zuev's *Black Box (Chernyi iashchik)*, with successive chapters written in different linguistic and stylistic (often semi-parodic) registers, one could not but wonder whether the author had read his Joyce and adopted this device from him. This is confirmed by Zuev himself, who acknowledges that his experimental repetitions were prompted by Molly Bloom's monologue in the final chapter of *Ulysses*. The deploying of different styles in successive chapters is not the exclusive property of Joyce, of course. It is a feature of a whole period in Russian letters, and is most strikingly seen perhaps in Velemir Khlebnikov's *Zangezi*. Khlebnikov coined a special term for the genre: the "hypernovella". Each section of a hypernovella is a separate novella with its own language and "Rules", as Khlebnikov puts it. I see Khlebnikov's formulation as a key not only to *Zangezi* but also to the major novels of Joyce. In each section of *Finnegans Wake* we encounter words in one of the European languages, including some, like Finnish, Basque, and Russian, little known to the majority of his readers. There is even, reproduced by ear, part of a line from Mayakovsky: "Grib, grab, grob". Following in Khlebnikov's footsteps we could dub this a "hypernovel".

I see a difference between this line of development and the avant-garde role of an author such as Victor Sosnora. In each chapter of Sosnora's newly published *The Tower* (*Bashnia*) the same structural and stylistic devices are repeated. The entire text is full of palindromes, phrases which read the same from right to left and from left to right. This makes for a uniformity of structure, however, and gradually the sense of improvization, all-important for lyrical prose of this kind, is lost. For all these necessary caveats, the appearance of Sosnora's novel strikes me as highly symptomatic. Here is a major poet introducing into prose devices not previously associated with it. The novel is a genre open to cross-fertilization with other genres, not only of prose but also poetic.

The formal transfiguration of Russian prose writing is still only in its early stages. Its progress towards becoming that truly original, "not officially approved" literature of which Mandelstam writes in his *Fourth Prose*, is still wholly in the future. One can readily understand our Russian writers' search for guidance in a literary heritage with which they are only now coming to grips.

Among the major poets of the 1920s and 1930s Boris Poplavsky is an outstanding figure. The full corpus of his prose writing has only become accessible to readers in Russia and the rest of the world in the past year. The acknowledged leader of the young poets of the Paris emigration, he has finally gained recognition, many years after his untimely death, with his novel *Apollo Bezobrazov*. Significantly, the epigraphs are taken from Rimbaud and other French poets, and their undoubted influence can be felt in the atmosphere of the novel. The literary tastes of a period which saw the birth of surrealist prose are evident in the whimsical behaviour of the hero and other characters, but Poplavsky describes the Parisian milieu rigorously and exactly. His chapter describing the "ball" or party belongs firmly in the tradition of Russian realism and the European naturalist novel. Each chapter of the novel (which again is close to Khlebnikov's hypernovella) is written in a different style. There is a mannered literariness to the episode where a priest seduces a novice, as also in the final scene of the murder which the hero commits in the mountains. There is an awkwardness about the novel's structure and an oddity about its heroes and propositions which place *Apollo Bezobrazov* in the same category as *Doctor Zhivago*. The Russian and European traditions of the novel are not so much continued as distorted, and this underlies its formal originality.

Speculating on possible future paths for the development of Russian prose, primarily the novel, one's thoughts turn to the so far quite unheeded experience of the best writers of the 1920s whose plotless, "not officially approved" prose writing has only just been re-published; and first and foremost to such prose of Osip Mandelstam as his *Egyptian Stamp* and *Fourth Prose*. Vasily Rozanov, recently reprinted in Russia for the first time since his death, is one of those highly original writers of the early twentieth century who inspired Mandelstam. He is of the greatest significance for the future of Russian prose. Venedikt Yerofeev, whose *Moscow to the End of the Line* ranks with the first works of Sasha Sokolov as the peak of "unofficial" prose of times past, wrote appreciatively about Rozanov in 1973 in his *Rozanov through the Eyes of an Eccentric (Vasilii Rozanov glazami ekstsentrika)*. Andrey Sinyavsky too wrote specially about him in *Rozanov's Fallen Leaves (Opavshie list'ia V.V. Rozanova*, 1982). A number of previously unpublished parts of Rozanov's fragmentary prose writings have now finally appeared in the United States, Russia, and France, although they do not add substantially to what readers of *Fallen Leaves* and *Solitaria* already knew. An early article about Rozanov by Victor Shklovsky has also just been republished, where he characterizes the disjointedness of a style based on the montage of fragments grouped around several main thematic lines. Shklovsky contrasts this with the disconnectedness of Boris Pilnyak's prose. Like several others who have written about Rozanov, Shklovsky is impressed by his extreme anti-monologic approach, his indifference to the awarding of judgemental pluses, which can so easily change into minuses. Rozanov, as later Shklovsky, thought it a matter of indifference for art what colour the flag was which flew above the fortress. This thorough-going aestheticism with regard to prose was a departure from the previous mainstream tradition, but may well prove to be in harmony with developments in the recent output of young Russian writers. The fragmentariness which Shklovsky took from Rozanov was developed by Mandelstam in the

Egyptian Stamp and *Fourth Prose.* Venedikt Yerofeev and Andrey Sinyavsky both developed this device in their own way. For all that, this tendency is fairly isolated in Russian prose, for the time being at least. Even if we ignore attempts to exploit established genres of popular literature, like the detective story in Leonid Girshovich's *Swapped Heads* (*Obmenennye golovy*), or the thriller in Pyotr Aleshkovsky's *Seagulls*, contemporary prose tends to straightforward narrative. Not every novelist is fully up even to Pushkin's digressions (which, with a reference to *Eugene Onegin*, Louis Aragon imitated in *La Mise a mort*); while a direct departure from the plot in the manner of Stern or Rozanov, an evident possibility in the work of the writers we have mentioned, has not by any means become a common practice.

The Soviet period, with its weakening of the attention paid to the philosophical dimension of prose, was notable for a preoccupation with language. This showed itself in the 1920s as skaz (use of a linguistically interesting, and usually unreliable, narrator) which we see reappearing in a new form in such authors as Yevgeny Fyodorov, and the replication of the speech patterns of the semi-educated towndweller. Nowadays the short prose pieces of Ludmilla Petrushevskaya run the 1920s masterpieces of Mikhail Zoshchenko close. Russian prose writers have not lost interest in the texture of language, and writers of whom this is particularly true, like Victor Astafiev and Boris Mozhaev, and other masters of prose like Mikhail Kuraev and Tatyana Tolstaya, are invariably and deservedly popular with readers. The relative importance of linguistic virtuosity varies, however, depending on what other possibilities are open to prose writers. One can only marvel that that great master of highly original idiomatic writing, Andrey Platonov, should have succeeded in demonstrating his genius as a writer at all, and not only in terms of stylistic virtuosity. After all, Stalin himself, as if parodically realizing Mayakovsky's aspiration that "Stalin should read reports in the Politburo on the productivity of poetry", swore coarsely about Platonov in that very forum. As Russian writing shakes off the shackles of censorship and other constraints, however, it becomes ever more evident that it needs language as a handmaiden and not as an end in itself, something which even Solzhenitsyn can sometimes seem to be in danger of forgetting.

Russian literature has a long, rich history of stylistic development to draw on. That continuity was never broken and, with all the historical experience of Russia herself, it has all it needs to create truly original, "not officially approved" new writing. The first signs of this are to be seen in the works we have briefly surveyed.

Translated by Arch Tait

BIBLIOGRAPHY

Pyotr Aleshkovsky, "Chaiki", *Druzhba narodov*, No.4, 1992
Viktor Astafyev, "Prokliaty i ubity", *Novy mir*, Nos.10-12, 1992
Dmitry Galkovsky, "Beskonechnyi tupik", *Novy mir*, Nos.9-11, 1992
Leonid Girshovich, "Obmenennye golovy", *Bibliopolis*, 1992
Oleg Ermakov, "Znak zveria", *Znamia*, Nos.6-7, 1992
Vladimir Zuev, "Chernyi iashchik", *Znamia*, Nos.3-4, 1992
Fazil Iskander, "Chelovek i ego okrestnosti", *Znamia*, Nos.2,6,11, 1992
Anatoly Kim, "Poselok kentavrov", *Novy mir*, No.7, 1992
Mikhail Kuraev, "Druzhby nezhnoe volnen'e", *Novyi mir*, No.8, 1992
Semyon Lipkin, "Zapiski zhil'tsa", *Novyi mir*, Nos.9-10, 1992
Vladimir Makanin, "Stol, pokrytyi suknom i s grafinom poseredine", *Znamia*, No.1, 1993
Boris Mozhaev, "Izgoi", *Nash sovremennik*, Nos.2-3, 1993
Valeriia Narbikova, *Okolo ekolo...*, *Ex Libris*, 1992
Ivan Oganov, "Opustel nash sad", *Novyi mir*, No.5, 1992
Viktor Pelevin, "Omon Ra", *Znamia*, No.5, 1992, and Tekst, 1992
Evgeny Popov, *Nakanune, nakanune*, Tekst, 1993
Viktor Sosnora, "Bashnia", *Soglasie*, Nos.1-3, 1993
Abram Terts, *Spokoinoi nochi*, SP "Start", 1992
Ludmilla Ulitskaya, "Sonechka", *Novy mir*, No.7, 1992
Evgeny Fedorov, *Zharenyi petukh*, Carte Blanche, 1992
Aleksei Tsvetkov, "Prosto golos", *Znamia*, No.8, 1992

Vyacheslav Ivanov

Director General of the Library of Foreign Literature in Moscow, a director of the Institute of World Culture at Moscow University, and professor at the Slavic Department, University of California, Los Angeles. Vyacheslav Ivanov is also a member of Signals International Trust for the preservation and promotion of Russian literature.

Born in 1929, Ivanov is the son of the well-known Russian writer Vsevolod Ivanov. He graduated from, and later lectured at, the University of Moscow until his dismissal in 1958 as a friend of Boris Pasternak. Forbidden to travel to the West, he worked at the Institute of Slavic and Balkan Studies and was one of the founders of the Moscow-Tartu school of semiotics. In 1989 he was invited to chair a new department of history and world culture at Moscow University.